A
Risky
Way
to Kill

A
RISKY
WAY
TO KILL

An Inspector Heimrich Mystery

RICHARD LOCKRIDGE

J. B. LIPPINCOTT COMPANY
Philadelphia and New York

for Hildy

1

One of the men in pink coats said he was worried about Grandpa. He said that things wouldn't be the same without the old boy. "Not around all summer," the man in the pink coat said, and shook his head and waggled his highball glass at a man in a tweed jacket with suede patches on the elbows.

"Well," the man in the tweed jacket said, "he was getting along, you know. And then there's this mange going around. They're all getting it. Reds and grays both."

"Could be," Pink Coat said. "I'd have figured the old boy was immune to anything, but maybe it was the mange. Remember how he used to show up on that rock of his and you could swear he was laughing at us? Like he'd won another game?"

"Well," Tweed Jacket said, "he always did. Drove hounds nuts, Grandpa did. Enjoyed every minute of it, it always seemed to me. Won't be the same without the old boy."

"One way to look at it," Pink Coat said, "it's getting built up around here. Could be he felt sort of fenced in. Could be he's gone over toward Brewster for his fun and games. Morning, Miss Mercer. Talking about Grandpa, Harry and I were. Didn't show up this morning. Hasn't shown up for three, four months. Harry thinks it could be the mange. . . ."

Lyle Mercer was not in riding clothes. She was in a light brown dress—a dress lighter in tone than her dark brown eyes and deep brown hair. She said, "Grandpa, Mr. James?" and

7

then, "Oh, of course. Father's told me about him. The one all of you chase every Saturday."

"Pretty much," Marvin James said. "Until four months ago. Not hide or hair of him since. Measly little red today. After him, not a damn thing."

"You killed?"

"No. Not that we wanted to much. Except the hounds, of course. Start to kill, way things are, what with the mange and everything, what we'd end up by killing would be the hunt itself. This one went to earth. Old Grandpa was above that sort of thing."

"Father's talked about him," Lyle said. "He must be—have been—quite a fox."

"Made the hunt, that's what Grandpa did," James told the pretty girl in the light brown dress. "Your father and mother here, Lyle?"

"Golfing," Lyle Mercer said. "And Mother's trying to get Father to use a cart. Poor old Timothy can't get used to it. Hangs his head over the rail and looks wistful when they go off in the car."

"Good hunter, Timothy," James said. "Your father want to sell him?"

"No," Lyle said. "At least he hasn't mentioned it. Wants to keep him to remember the Van Brunt Hunt by, I suppose."

She looked around the crowded taproom of the Old Stone Inn, given over, that October noon, to the breakfast of the Van Brunt Hunt.

She knew many of the men and women who drank their way from group to group and talked of horses and of foxes and—which came to her in bits and pieces, in word snatches—of poor Roger Spence, who had, once more, fallen off his horse. The fall had not damaged Spence perceptibly. He was swaying a little as he drank in a laughing group. He laughed with the others. But he often swayed a little at hunt breakfasts, which were not conducive to the maintenance of equilibrium. Roger Spence looked over people between himself and Lyle. He was tall enough to look over most.

"If you're going to put it in that paper of yours," he said, from halfway down the long taproom, "I didn't fall off the horse. The horse fell under me. Whatever these jokers tell you."

"The horse fell," Lyle called back to him. "I'll get it straight, Mr. Spence."

And, with finger above palm of hand, she made the gesture of writing a note about the falling of a horse from under Roger Spence, from under whom horses so frequently fell. Not that Roger Spence's misadventure would be mentioned in the few sticks she would write of the hunt-club breakfast for the Van Brunt *Citizen*. It was not news when Spence fell off a horse. Further, this was not to be, in any real sense, a news story.

"Just get the names, baby," Bob Wallis had told her the afternoon before. "People like to see their names. Oh, if somebody rides his horse into the taproom, you might interview the horse."

She had learned, in the nearly four months she had been working on the *Citizen*—one has to start some place—that people like to see their names in newspapers. She had also learned the special meaning, in a parlance she must learn, of the word "stick." A couple of inches of type, a stick was. "The annual breakfast of the Van Brunt Hunt was held Saturday at the Old Stone Inn. Among—"

Thirty men and women in the long, low room. Perhaps forty. Harold, tending the bar which stretched across the far end, had two men helping him and needed them. Spares clutched out of the city by Mrs. Oliphant, on this busiest of autumn weekends—clutched, Lyle suspected, with considerable desperation. Saturday, October twelfth, Columbus Day, on top of everything. On top, most of all, of the pre-emption of the taproom from noon until two by the hunt club. When the roads were filled with thirsty leaf-lookers. But locals, not transient leaf-lookers, are the hard core for a country inn. Particularly, of course, locals who own—or sometimes rent—hunters so that they can ride across fields and jump stone fences in pursuit of foxes.

Lyle, stowing names in her mind as she moved, person by person, toward the bar—as she smiled and greeted men and women she had, for the most part, known since she was a small girl—stowed also certain phrases. (Which, she realized, she

9

probably would not use when she sat in front of a typewriter in the *Citizen* office.) "To a degree, the breakfast was a wake for a gray fox everyone calls 'Grandpa,' who for years has enjoyed being fruitlessly pursued by the Van Brunt Hunt Club." No, she wouldn't use that. Names. And the kinds of food on the long trestle table along one side of the taproom. And that many of the hunt had brought along their weekend guests. And, perhaps, that tweed jackets outnumbered pink coats on the men. But not, certainly, that too many of the women were wearing riding breeches they too completely filled.

There were girls of her own age, and boys too, in the crowded room. But most there were older and, appreciably, thicker. People tend to thicken in proper relation to age and bank accounts. Good, or even passable, hunters cost money. A mature group, the hunt was becoming. For the most part, contemporaries, Lyle realized, of her parents, who in recent years had turned to the quieter exercise of golf. Poor, gray Timothy, turned out to pasture when he wanted to meet other horses and jump familiar fences.

"Lovely party, isn't it?" she said to Mrs. Arnold Bracken, who had gray hair cut short and who was reported often to ride off at angles and jump fences not in the hounds' line of pursuit, presumably because the fences were there.

"Where are those parents of yours, girl?" Mrs. Bracken asked her, rather sternly. On being told where Lytton and Grace Mercer probably were, which probably was on the ninth green, working their way toward lunch on the country-club terrace, Mrs. Bracken said, "The poor dears. Such a pity," and then, "They tell me you're working on the *Citizen*." She said this with the inflection of one who rather hopes to be contradicted.

"A cub," Lyle said. "The smallest, newest of cubs. Is Mr. Bracken here?"

"Was," Ruth Bracken said. "Haven't looked under the tables recently. Where's your drink, girl?"

"On my way for it," Lyle said and started on her way. (Among those at the breakfast, Mr. and Mrs. Arnold Bracken, Mr. and Mrs. Marvin James and their daughter Estelle; the Leslie Sondermans. Dr. and Mrs. Frederic—always remember without the "k"—Sinclair. Charles—)

10

She reached the bar, and Harold, who looked harried, said, "Yes, Miss Mercer?" to which she said, "Gin and tonic, Harold."

"Sure you're eighteen?" Harold asked her.

Harold had been tending bar at the Old Stone Inn since the days Lyle had been limited to Shirley Temples. Serving them, he had said, "Don't let them catch up with you, young lady. Pretty powerful, way I make them."

"I'm quite sure," Lyle said to him now. "But plenty of tonic, please."

"And a twist?"

"Please," Lyle said, and carried her drink away from the bar, which was more than a good many were doing. (Mr. and Mrs. Philip Curtis, Mrs. Helen Shephard. Remember "a," not "e." Miss Helen Finley. Inspector and Mrs. M. L. Heimrich. Not, she thought, members of the hunt. Guests? The Armstrongs. Mr. and Mrs. John Alden. Of course, the Inspector was Marian Alden's uncle. Mr. and Mrs.—)

"Know our host, don't you, Lyle?" somebody said behind her, and she turned and looked up at Sam Jackson. She had a long way up to look. Sam Jackson was a long man. He was also one of her father's close friends, in spite of being a Democrat. Lytton Mercer was a tolerant man, granting friends their foibles.

Lyle said, "Hello, Sam. Host?"

The man who stood beside Sam Jackson was almost of Jackson's height. He was almost as slim; he wore riding breeches, which Jackson did not. He wore a brown tweed jacket.

"Paul Wainright," Jackson said and moved a thumb to indicate the man beside him. "His party. Very generous man, Wainright is."

It was somewhat puzzling. The hunt breakfasts had always been a communal charge on members of the hunt. A fixed price, all-inclusive, was set by Mrs. Oliphant; hunt members contributed pro-rata, ginger-ale drinkers as much as sturdier types, nibblers of watercress no less than consumers of rare roast beef. Writing a check for his share, Lyle's father frequently said, "Ouch!"

"Your party?" Lyle asked the tall man who was named Wainright and who had a long brown face and blue eyes and crisp gray hair. He was one of those in the room Lyle had never seen before. She groped in her memory. People named Wainright had—a year or so ago?—bought the old Kynes place on Long Hill Road.

"By way," Wainright said to her, "of being an initiation fee. Not asked for, you know. Token of appreciation, you might call it. Everybody's been most cordial, Miss—" he paused for a name.

"Lyle Mercer," Jackson said. "Reporter for our new newspaper. Also a member of the hunt. Anyway, her father is. Lytton Mercer. Doesn't ride much any more. Golf type, Lyt's turned out to be."

Somewhat unexpectedly, Wainright extended a square brown hand toward Lyle. She took it and he said, "Miss Mercer," which was accurate and, on the whole, friendly. He then said, "Going to write us up?"

"Local events," Lyle said. "One of the things a weekly is for, the editor thinks. Paul Wainright and—is Mrs. Wainright here?"

"Names in the paper," Wainright said. "No, as a matter of fact. One of her headaches, I'm afraid. Been looking forward to it all week, too. This piece of yours, Miss Mercer. Don't need to say I'm—call it 'throwing' the party, is there?"

"If you'd rather I didn't—"

"Nonsense," Sam Jackson said. "Everybody knows it anyway. *And* appreciates it."

"All the same," Wainright said, "Wouldn't want it to look as if my wife and I were trying to buy—"

"Don't," Sam Jackson said, "be a horse's ass."

Paul Wainright shrugged square shoulders to that and smiled at both of them. He had, Lyle thought, a pleasant smile.

"Mention it if you want to," Wainright said. "All for freedom of the press." He looked away from Lyle and from Jackson, closing a subject. He said, "Roast beef looks good," opening a new one.

It did, Lyle thought. So did the turkey, and shiny pans over gently burning alcohol probably held bubbling kidneys in sauce and the curried shrimp for which the Old Stone Inn was, locally, famous. And, as usual, chicken à la king. And people were beginning to drift toward the trestle table and the man in a chef's hat behind it. Another weekend import from the city, Lyle thought of the chef.

"Get you something?" Wainright said, returning to her. She shook her head; lifted slightly her still almost-full glass. "Circulate," Lyle said. "Make a little list." She tapped her forehead, indicating where she kept her little list.

Wainright nodded and looked at Sam Jackson, who shook his head.

"Can't let it go to waste," Wainright said, and went off among people toward the buffet.

"Bought the Kynes place last spring," Jackson said. "Seems an all-right sort. Rides well. So does his wife, come to that. Hiya, Marv."

Marvin James carried a glass. He waggled it at Sam Jackson.

"Been talking about old Grandpa," James said. "Miss the old boy. Harry Peterson thinks could be the mange got him."

"It's got a lot of them, they say," Jackson said. "Infectious as hell, apparently. And—"

Lyle carried her drink away and smiled and nodded and made friendly sounds and added to her list of those among the present. She explained that her mother and father were playing golf. She said, "It's been so long I'd probably fall off at the first fence." She said, "I promise, Mr. Spence. I already promised." She said, "Yes, a little rice with it, please," to the man who wore the chef's cap. She said, "Everything's delicious, Mrs. Oliphant," when the proprietor of the Old Stone Inn popped in briefly from the main dining room, looking harried. "Off the road in droves," Mrs. Oliphant said. "Already we're out of roast beef."

Lyle said, "Hi, Susan," to Susan Heimrich and, "I didn't know you two hunted."

"Just hangers-on," Susan said. "With the Aldens. And Merton's making gestures. Inspector gestures. Meaning he wants to go home."

At a little before two, Lyle put her empty glass down on a table by the side exit of the taproom and went out into the parking lot. Somebody had put a Lincoln with New York City plates at an angle between the lines so that it almost imprisoned her Volks. She wriggled the Volks out and edged into traffic on Van Brunt Avenue, which is also NY-11 F, and waited in a line of cars for the light to change at The Corners. Finally, it did, and the line crept. It changed again, against her, when she was two cars from it. She waited again. She crossed Elm Street, which is also NY-109, and signaled and pulled off to the right and parked behind the low white building which housed the Van Brunt *Citizen*. It was a new building. The *Citizen* was a new newspaper. Until two years before, the residents of Van Brunt had made do with the Cold Harbor *News* and, of course the New York *Times*.

There was nobody in the *Citizen's* editorial room, which did not surprise Lyle Mercer. There would be nobody in the business office, either. The composing room and the press room would be similarly empty. Over weekends, the *Citizen* hibernated. But the door of Robert Wallis's office was open and Wallis was at his desk. Spread on the desk was a copy of last week's *Citizen*. As she passed his open door, Wallis did not look up from the newspaper. What he did do was, abruptly, raise both hands above his head, fists clenched. He said, "God damn it to hell." He spoke loudly into empty space.

He had found another, Lyle thought, and went past the open door to a typewriter desk in a corner. She was seldom in the office on Saturdays, but she knew Robert Wallis, editor and publisher, always was. Everybody knew he always was. Others might golf or play tennis on Saturdays and Sundays; they might jump horses over stone fences. Robert Wallis hunted typos. He crouched over his desk and read line by line through the newspaper which had gone to the Van Brunt News Store, and to shops in Cold Harbor and Yorktown Heights and into the mail the Thursday before. He found typos and shook fists and gritted teeth at them. On Saturdays, Robert Wallis did penance for irretrievable errors.

2

Lyle rolled copy paper into her typewriter and lifted her hands to the keys and then put them down again because she was, instead of thinking about the hunt breakfast, wondering about Robert Wallis. He was, she thought, an odd man. It was a sunny October day and the leaves were turning in the bright air. The maples were yellow and red and blazed in the sun. All the hills around the hamlet of Van Brunt, above the Hudson in Putnam County, leaped with color. And the editor-publisher of the Van Brunt *Citizen* crouched over a desk and scraped last week's edition for errors which could never be corrected.

She knew very little about him. Two years ago he had appeared, more or less out of nowhere, and bought the low white building which James Purvis, who owned the garage across the street, had put up on the site of the former fire station—the fire station which had burned down several years before and could not sound its own siren for help. Purvis had built the two-story white building and put up a sign which read: "Stores and Offices for Rent." And a man named Wallis had bought the building before any of the stores and offices were rented and had had partitions taken out and a newspaper moved in.

"Probably paid through the nose for it, if I know Purvis," Lyle's father had said, and added that he did know Purvis. "Can't say I see Van Brunt's need for a weekly newspaper." But six months later he was saying, with indignation, that the post office had fallen flat on its face again, with no *Citizen* in the mailbox on Friday, and was driving to the Center to pick up a copy at the Van Brunt News Store. "No use waiting until Saturday to see what young Wallis has got to say for himself and about the town."

Bob Wallis was not, from where Lyle Mercer sat—at the moment before an unresponsive typewriter—particularly young. In the middle thirties, at a guess, and not looking less. A man with short black hair which grew to a point on his forehead and a habit of walking with his head thrust forward; a spare man of six feet or so, who looked as if he might play tennis. But who didn't play tennis, although he had joined the country club. Now and then he did swim in the club pool, but there was always something impatient about his swimming.

A few facts she did know about the man from outside who had started a weekly newspaper in the town of Van Brunt and made a go of it. He had worked on an afternoon newspaper in New York and had been city editor when the paper, which had been moldering for some years, collapsed under him and the rest of the staff. He had been married and his wife had died—died a year or so before he started his paper in Van Brunt. He had said that to somebody who had been curious. He had joined the Lions Club, but when they had speakers at their lunches he usually sent somebody else to cover them. He hated typographical errors.

It was not much to know about a man for whom one had worked from late June until this Columbus Day Saturday in October.

The idea of working on the *Citizen* had come to her suddenly, about a week after she had been graduated from Radcliffe. She had not planned to look for a job; she had planned a summer of tennis and golf and swimming at the club; had planned a summer of playing. And after a week she had decided that that was not going to be enough.

She had told her mother and father so one warm evening as the three of them sat on a shady terrace outside the big house and sipped long drinks and listented to music, with grave intervals of news, which trickled through an open doorway. It was WQXR music, which the elder Mercers preferred.

"I," Lyle said, "am going to try to get a job on the *Citizen*."

"What do you think, Lytton?" Grace said. There was doubt in her voice.

"That it's for the girl to decide," Lytton Mercer said. "Also, that it's better if she works here instead of in the city. If she's going to work somewhere. Air's bad in the city. City's full of muggers."

Lytton Mercer was senior vice president of a bank in the city, and in the summer months he went in three days a week. In the winter, he went to the city from Monday through Thursday. He had no desire to be president of the bank. A Mercer, it went without saying—certainly without saying by Lytton Mercer—had no need to be.

It had been on a Saturday that Lyle had, so suddenly, made up her mind to try to get a job on the Van Brunt *Citizen*. The following Monday she had driven the several miles from the big white house on High Road, where High Road ended in a turnaround circle above the Hudson River, to The Corners, where a newspaper had replaced a fire station. The *Citizen* had two front doors, one to the editorial rooms and the other to the business office, where job printing could be arranged and advertisements placed and subscriptions accepted.

Lyle had opened, first, the wrong door, which was that to the business office. She had been asked, by a friendly middle-aged woman behind a counter, if she could be helped.

"I'm looking for a job," Lyle said, keeping it simple. The woman behind the counter said, "A job?" in a tone which implied she had never before heard of such a thing. "What kind of a job, dear?"

"As a reporter," Lyle said. "At college I was on the college paper. Actually, I was assistant editor."

"Well," the friendly woman said, "I don't know, dear. You'd have to ask Mr. Wallis about that. And he's likely to be busy."

"I could come back when he isn't," Lyle said. "If you could tell me when."

"Well," the woman said, "he's always busy. But—all right, I'll ask him."

There was a telephone on the counter, but she did not use the telephone. She went from behind the counter and through a door and was gone for a minute or two and came back and said, "He says you can ask him. Through that way." She pointed at the door. Lyle went that way and walked into an open room with several typewriter desks scattered through it. A large blond boy was in front of one of the typewriters, anxiously hunting and pecking on it. He looked up. He said, "Hi, Lyle," and she said, "Hi, Reggie," to Reginald Peterson. She had gone to the Van Brunt High School with Reggie. "Where is Mr. Wallis?"

Reggie pointed toward a door. She went to the door and knocked on it, a man with a grating voice said from behind the door, "All right. It isn't locked." She went into a small room occupied by a large desk and a man with black hair. The man stood up behind the desk, but kept both hands hard down on it, as if he were preparing to vault over it. He said, "What do you want a job for?"

"To work at," Lyle said.

"Or," he said, "to get into what half-wits call the newspaper game? Or are you one of those who want to be writers? Think working on a newspaper is, for God's sake, a stepping stone?"

"I just finished college," Lyle said. "I just want a job, Mr. Wallis."

"What's your name?"

She told him.

"You're Lytton Mercer's daughter."

"Yes."

"Then you don't need a job," Wallis said and sat back in his chair, as if that ended matters. But then he pointed at a wooden chair and said, "Sit down, for God's sake."

She sat down. He said, "Do you?"

"If you mean need a job," she said, "not in the way you mean it. No, Mr. Wallis."

"Something to play at," Wallis said, and leaned forward, his head jutting toward her.

At first sight he doesn't like me, Lyle thought. She started to get up from the chair.

"Can you type, by any chance?" Wallis said, his inflection implying the high improbability that she had ever seen a typewriter.

18

"Yes," Lyle said. "I learned in high school. Almost everybody takes typing at Van Brunt High School, Mr. Wallis."

"Harry Peterson's kid sure as hell didn't," Wallis said. "He's an all-right kid, for one named Reginald. But he can't type."

His voice grated. Abruptly, he ran his right hand over the stiffness of his black hair.

"Typing wasn't required," Lyle said. "It was elective."

She felt, obscurely, that she was defending Reggie Peterson —even more obscurely all the Mercers and Jacksons and Petersons in the town of Van Brunt, and further, Van Brunt High School. She decided that she did not want to work for Robert Wallis, who obviously disliked her; who acted as if he disliked almost everybody.

"Your people have lived around here for a long time," he told her, leaning forward toward her. It had, somehow, the sound of an accusation. "You grew up here." He looked at her from hard eyes and then, quite suddenly, there were crinkles at the corners of the eyes and he smiled at her. He had a wide, thin-lipped mouth, but there was nothing thin about the smile. "Have started to, anyway. You're sure you can type, child?"

"Quite sure," she said.

"All right," Wallis said. "You can have a try at it. We'll pay you, whether you need it or not. Sixty a week. Go out there" —he pointed toward the door which she had closed behind her—"and call up the undertakers here—two of them, if you didn't know—and the ones in Cold Harbor and Yorktown. Get the names of their new customers. Call up their families and find out about them. There's a *Who's Who* out there somewhere. Check it. You never know. And check the names in the telephone book to see how they're spelled. Even if it sounds like 'Jones,' check it out."

"Now?" Lyle said.

"Of course now," Wallis said. "You came here for a job, didn't you? All right. You've got a job. Get on with it."

She got up and started toward the door.

"By the way," Wallis said, his voice still a grating voice, "do you know anything about taking photographs? Paper like this, reporters double."

"Yes," she said. "I'm not very good but I've taken pictures."

"You've got a camera?"

"Yes."

"Bring it along tomorrow morning. Eight o'clock till God knows when. This isn't a Guild shop."

She did not ask him what he meant by that. She went out into the wide room, where Reggie Peterson still hunted and pecked and where now a balding man in his fifties was attacking a typewriter with what appeared to be anger. She called up undertakers and wrote down names—not very many names; the area seemed momentarily healthy—and checked them. She found a rack of copies of the *Citizen* and looked until she found "Obituaries" and read them, to see how they should be written. She telephoned the survivors of the newly dead and, in a voice which shook a little that first day, asked questions.

After a week of that, during which her voice quit shaking, the balding man, who had turned out to be named Oliver Fermer and to be the man who covered town meetings and other matters of importance, came out of Wallis's office and to her desk.

"Man named Brownley's rented the Atcheson place," he said. "Pretty well known as a painter, Brownley is. Bob wants you to go out and interview him. Know where the Atcheson place is?"

She did know.

"Take your camera."

She interviewed Max Brownley and took pictures of him, one in front of a landscape he was working on, and wrote about him, and at the top of her story that Thursday—a story considerably shorter than the one she had written—there was a line which read: "By Lyle Mercer."

There had not been many of those in her nearly four months. There had been, still, the telephoning to undertakers and to the families of their "customers." There had been a House Tour in July—no by-line on that—and a Book and Author Luncheon for the benefit of the Visiting Nurse Association. No "By Lyle Mercer" on that, either, although she had rather hoped there might be.

She expected no by-line on the few sticks the breakfast of the Van Brunt Hunt would get in the Van Brunt *Citizen* of October 17. Her fingers went up to the keys. "More than forty members and their guests attended the annual breakfast of the Van Brunt Hunt, held Saturday at the Old Stone Inn. The breakfast this year was—"

Robert Wallis, his head jutting forward, came out of his office and walked rapidly, his heels snapping on the wooden floor, across the big room and through the door to the business office. He did not seem to see Lyle Mercer, nor to hear the clicking of her typewriter. She clicked on at it. Her account of the hunt breakfast ran nearer to four sticks than to three; it included a complimentary reference to the cuisine of the Old Stone Inn; it did not include a reference to Roger Spence's to-be-expected misadventure. She was checking names, most of them names she had known all her life, in the Westchester-Putnam County telephone directory when Wallis jutted his way out of the business office.

He saw her, this time. He came over to her desk. He said, "Anybody ride a horse to the breakfast?"

"No," she said. "A good many of them talked about a fox they call 'Grandpa' who failed to show up. They're afraid he's dead of the mange."

"A wake for a fox," Wallis said. "You play it that way?"

"No," she said. "Should I have?"

"Probably not," Wallis said. "They might think we were kidding them. Take themselves seriously, most of them. Themselves and their horses and their foxes. No other highlights?"

"Roger Spence fell off his horse again," Lyle said.

"No highlight," Robert Wallis said and shook his head. There was abruptness in the movement. "When you get the spellings checked come into the office. Something I want to show you."

She finished checking the spelling of some twenty names. In spite of cautioning herself, she had used an "e" instead of an "a" in Shephard. She corrected that. She went into Wallis's office and, as he had months before, he stood up behind his desk with his hands on it. He said, "Sit down, child," and she sat on the unreceptive chair. "See this?" he asked her, and pushed toward her a fragment of newsprint, torn roughly from a page of last week's *Citizen*. "Where I've marked," he said. "Read them."

What he had torn out of the paper was a part of the want-ad section. He had checked two ads, in the "For Sale, Misc." column. The first read:

"For Sale: Bay stallion. Trained hunter. Reasonable. Also .25-caliber Winchester rifle. Telescopic sight. Box No. 375."

She looked up and shook her head. "Read the other one," Wallis told her and she went down the column to another check mark.

"For Sale: Wedding dress. Size 10. Never used. Box No. 376."

She read that twice. When she looked up again at Robert Wallis she did not shake her head. She said, "Oh."

"Yes," he said. "Does stop you, doesn't it?"

"You tell yourself a story about it," Lyle said. "And it makes you want to cry."

"Yes," he said. "End of love's young dream and that sort of thing."

"It's the size ten part mostly," Lyle said. "A little girl. Not tiny, but a little girl. You—you think of someone very young. Someone who—who isn't hoping any more."

"All right," Wallis said in his grating voice. "You're making me cry, baby." He showed no signs of crying.

"You'd think," Lyle said, "that she wouldn't try to sell it, wouldn't you? That she'd put it away some place. Or, maybe, give it to the thrift shop."

"Yes," Wallis said. "One would think that. You know people named Wainright, child? Mr. and Mrs. Paul Wainright."

"I met Mr. Wainright at the breakfast. As a matter of fact, he paid for the breakfast. They've bought the old Kynes place on Long Hill Road. Why, Mr. Wallis?"

"I know that," Wallis said. "We had a piece about it— 'Distinguished Architect and City Planner Is New Resident.' Wouldn't think they'd want to sell a wedding dress, would you? Size ten wedding dress, never used."

She shook her head.

"I didn't see it," Wallis said. "Not until about half an hour ago. Probably I'd have checked it out if I had. On the chance —oh, on the chance we'd been had. No reason, I guess, for Mrs. Allsmith to send up a rocket about it. It was this way, as she remembers it."

Two plain white envelopes, addressed to "Advertising Department, Van Brunt Citizen," had been in the mail early in the week—the day before want ads were closed for the Thursday edition. There was no return address on either envelope. There was no letterhead on the plain 8½-by-11 sheets they contained. There were dollar bills in each envelope, payments adequate—a little more than adequate—to cover the cost of the advertisements. The texts of two advertisements were typed. One offered the wedding dress for sale; the other the horse and the rifle. Instructions also were typed. As Mrs. Allsmith remembered, the instruction for both ads read: "For the issue of October 10 only. Please assign box number."

And under that was typed, "Paul Wainright, Rte. 1, Van Brunt, New York."

"The Kynes place is a big place," Lyle said, as much to herself as to Wallis. "Fifty acres. Maybe more than that. And a big house. It must—"

"Yes," Wallis said. "It must have cost Wainright quite a lot. And throwing this party today. Mrs. Oliphant doesn't give things away."

"A thousand dollars," Lyle said. "At least a thousand dollars. Perhaps more."

"And they want to sell an unused wedding dress," Wallis said. "For—what do wedding dresses cost, child?"

"I've never had one," Lyle Mercer said. "I suppose some of them cost a lot. But a girl I knew at school got hers at Klein's."

"A lot or a little, it doesn't jibe, does it?" Wallis said.

She shook her head.

"Know where the Kynes place is?"

"Of course."

"Then," Wallis said, "suppose you drive there this afternoon and ask the Wainrights why they want to sell an unused wedding dress. Tell them—oh, that we feel we should have verified the ad before we printed it."

"Probably," Lyle said, and stood up, "they'll say it isn't any of our business."

"What's printed in the *Citizen* is my business," Wallis said. "If we've been had—if the Wainrights had been had—it's our business. Because, Lyle, there's a funny smell about it."

3

Autumn had painted all the hills above the Hudson—
painted them yellow and red and accented the blaze with
green. It was as if the still, warm day held its breath lest it
smear the green. When Lyle turned into it from the valley
through which NY-11F ran, Long Hill Road climbed steeply
into a world of almost overwhelming color. Just before it was
time to turn into the drive which led up to a white house at
the top of the tallest hill, Lyle pulled the Volks off the road
and sat for almost five minutes and merely looked—looked
down at color falling away from her as the land fell; looked
down at the Hudson River. There was an island in the wide
river there and the island was gold in the sunlight. The river
sparkled in the sunlight.

It was worth looking at; worth spending time on. People
had driven many miles that Columbus Day weekend to look at
painted hills not by half so beautiful. But it was more than the
beauty around her which had made Lyle Mercer stop her little
car beside the road. I'm stalling, Lyle thought. I'm only pretending to look at autumn leaves. What will I say to them? Ask
them if they have a daughter, size ten, who thought she was
going to be married and was—what? Jilted when everything
was ready and the date set and the wedding dress fitted? Or
was it she who had changed her mind?

Well, she thought, you wanted to work on a newspaper. You
knew, must have known, that part of that kind of work would
be to ask people private questions. But then, she thought, they

24

put the advertisements in the newspaper. It was they who opened the door, and it was a strange thing to do.

She started the car and drove on Long Hill Road for another hundred yards or so and turned at a mailbox marked "Paul Wainright" and drove up a curving drive with maples bright on either side of it. She stopped the Volks in a graveled turn-around and got out of it and walked to the door of the big white house. She pushed a button and heard chimes inside the house.

After a time, the door opened and a pretty Negro girl in a blue uniform said, "Yes'm?" She looked at Lyle Mercer and particularly at her hands. Lyle understood her caution. People showed up for donations to worthy charities. They also showed up bearing tracts and wishing to speak of God.

"I'd like to see Mrs. Wainright," Lyle said. "Or Mr. Wainright, if he's home. I'm from the *Citizen.*"

"The newspaper?"

"Yes."

"Mr. Wainright isn't home," the girl in the blue uniform said. "I don't know whether Mrs. Wainright wants to see people."

"I won't—"

Lyle was interrupted. A blonde woman—a somewhat plump-ish blonde woman—came through a doorway and into the en-trance hall behind the maid. She wore a summer robe which was yellow and black and floating. She walked carefully on the waxed oak floor of the entrance hall. She said, "Lucy. You mustn't send people away. It isn't hospitable."

Then, to Lyle, she said, "Do come in, dear."

There was South in the blonde woman's voice. There was also, Lyle realized, a considerable blur in it. The blonde woman swayed, very slightly, and put a hand on top of the high back of a hall chair.

Lyle said, "Mrs. Wainright?" and Mrs. Wainright said, "Of course, dear. Did you say you were from this newspaper? But I'm sure we already subscribe, dear. Don't we take the news-paper, Lucy?"

Lucy said, "Yes'm. We take the newspaper."

25

"I'm so sorry, dear," Mrs. Wainright said and took her hand from the back of the chair and swayed slightly and put the hand back on it. "We already take the newspaper."

"Mrs. Wainright," Lucy said, "you oughtn't to be up with that headache of yours. You ought to be sitting down, anyway."

"Headache?" Mrs. Wainright said. "I haven't got a headache, Lucy. And this pretty young lady's come all the way up here to get a subscription to the newspaper and it's a warm day and I'm sure she'd like something cool to drink." The "something" was almost "someshing." Mrs. Paul Wainright then said, "Juleps," on a note of triumphant recognition and went back through the doorway she had come out of. But then she reappeared, partially, in the doorway and said, "Do come in, dear. I haven't seen anybody all day. Plenty of ice, Lucy." She then receded into the room.

Lyle looked at the pretty girl in the blue uniform and Lucy shrugged her shoulders slightly. Then she said, "She wants you to, miss. She gets sort of upset when Mr. Wainright's away."

Lyle Mercer was somewhat upset herself, but did not say so. She went into the room Mrs. Wainright had vanished into.

It was a big room. Decorator-furnished, Lyle thought. With no regard for its cost. There were French doors along one side of the room, and sunlight slanted through them and lay warm on a yellow carpet. Through the French doors she could see a maple tree, resplendent with autumn.

Mrs. Wainright was sitting in a deep chair with her back to the sunlight. There was a tall, half-empty glass on a mirror-topped small table by the chair.

"It isn't about a subscription, Mrs. Wainright," Lyle said, and realized that she had followed the blonde woman into the room to clear that up. "It's about an advertisement your husband put in the *Citizen*. We—that is, the publisher, Mr. Wallis —is a little worried about it."

"Worried?" Mrs. Wainright said. "About what, dear? You said, 'advertisement?' "

"A want ad," Lyle said. "About having a wedding dress to sell."

Mrs. Wainright looked at Lyle with widening blue eyes. She picked up the glass beside her and drank from it and put it down again. Then she said, "Wedding dress?"

"Size ten," Lyle said. "Never used. That's what the ad said."

"But how touching," Mrs. Wainright said. "To think of some poor child—" She did not finish. She shook her head and put her hand on the glass again, but did not lift it to her lips. She had small, plump fingers and reddened nails. She shook her head again and said, "Somebody put an advertisement like that in your newspaper? But what a tacky thing to do, dear."

The word "tacky" rattled briefly in Lyle's mind. "Tacky" meant sticky; paint not entirely dry is "tacky." But apparently the word meant something else to Mrs. Wainright. "Mean?" Was that what the word meant to this soft woman; this almost pretty woman? In, Lyle thought, her late forties.

Lyle had brought the tear sheet with her. She went over to Mrs. Wainright and held the sheet out to her, and Mrs. Wainright took it and held it very close to her eyes. She looked up and shook her head, and Lyle leaned down and pointed to the ad about the wedding dress.

"That's what it says," Mrs. Wainright said, after she had peered at it. She spoke as if Lyle had come for confirmation to a person more experienced in reading.

"Mrs. Wainright," Lyle said, and spoke slowly. "The advertisement was sent in to the paper by your husband. It was signed by him. That is, there was a typed signature but it was your husband's name. And there was money in the envelope to pay for the insertion. There was another envelope with the text of another ad typed in it and also signed 'Paul Wainright.' It's the other one Mr. Wallis checked. There."

She pointed again, this time to the advertisement which offered a horse and a rifle for sale.

"Alex was a bay," Mrs. Wainright said. "But he's been dead ever since—"

She began to cry. She groped for her glass and touched it so that it swayed. But then she closed her plump fingers on the glass and held it fast and after a second lifted it and drank from it. She put it down again, gropingly, and went on crying. Lyle waited, wishing she were somewhere else.

Mrs. Wainright looked up at her. "There wasn't any wedding dress," she said. "It wasn't time yet for that."

She put her head in her hands, covering her eyes.

There were footfalls behind Lyle. They were rather heavy as they crossed the strip of polished wood between door and yellow carpet; softer on the carpet. Lyle turned and looked up at a tall lean man in riding clothes. The slanting sun shown on his brilliantly polished boots.

"Florence dear," Paul Wainright said, "you promised —promised to stay in bed with the shades drawn. And to take aspirin. Not to—" He did not finish that. He said, "You're Miss Mercer, aren't you?" to Lyle. "I'm sorry, but my wife really ought to be in bed."

He turned, then, back to the door and said, "Lucy," raising his voice.

Lucy had evidently followed him from the entrance hall. She was in the doorway. She said, "Yes, Mr. Wainright?"

"Mrs. Wainright should be in bed," Wainright told the pretty girl in the blue uniform. "Taking aspirin. She forgets to."

Lucy said, "Yes, sir. I told her that. Her headaches are bad things."

She came into the room and went to the crying woman. She said, "Now you come on and lie down, ma'am. Like Mr. Wainright says."

"She came about that ad in the paper," Florence Wainright said, in a choked voice. "That awful tacky advertisement. She says—"

"Never mind, dear," Paul Wainright told his wife. "I'll talk to Miss Mercer."

"I'm sorry," Lyle said. "I—I came at a bad time."

"She gets these headaches," Wainright said. "She won't take care of herself. She forgets to take her medicine."

He went over to his wife's chair and stood behind it and lifted his wife up. When she was on her feet she swayed a little, and he steadied her. He said, "There, Flo. There, honey," in a soothing voice and moved his head sharply as a signal to the maid.

Lucy put an arm around Florence Wainright and said, "Now you just come along with me, ma'am. Get you all tucked in."

Florence Wainright groped down and picked up her glass. Then, with Lucy's arm around her, she went across the room and through the doorway. She walked steadily enough. She held the still half-full glass carefully so that its contents would not spill.

Paul Wainright watched his wife and Lucy until they had gone through the doorway and out of sight.

"Very bad things, these headaches of hers," he said then. "A kind of migraine. Make her rather dizzy sometimes. What did she mean about a tacky advertisement, Miss Mercer? In the *Citizen?*"

"Yes," Lyle said. "Mr. Wallis thought we ought to ask about it. I'm afraid I came at a bad time."

"You had no way of knowing," Wainright said. "An advertisement, I gather, that has something to do with us? But sit down, Miss Mercer. Can't I get you something?"

"Nothing, thanks," Lyle said. "The advertisement—there were two of them, really—was inserted in your name, Mr. Wainright. Mr. Wallis didn't see them until today. We would have verified them if—well, if anybody had noticed. They were printed last Thursday. Here."

She held the tear sheet out to the tall man, who took it and motioned her toward a chair. She sat down and looked up at him. She said, "The ones checked, Mr. Wainright."

He read. She watched his eyes move as he read each of the check-marked advertisements a second time. Then he looked at her and shook his head.

"The one about the wedding dress is odd," he said. "The other—somebody just wants to sell a bay hunter and a rifle. I'm sorry, Miss Mercer. But I don't see how we—well, how we come into it."

She told him how the Wainrights came into it. He said, "God damn it to hell. Some God-damn—" and stopped and read the advertisements again. He looked at her again and said, "Whoever sent these in stipulated the date of insertion? You said that, didn't you?"

"Yes."

"The issue of October tenth," he said. "It—somebody is being very cruel, Miss Mercer. Viciously cruel. Had my wife seen these before—before you showed them to her?"

"I'm sure she hadn't," Lyle said. "You—you didn't send them in, Mr. Wainright. Somebody used your name. Just—just to hurt you?"

"Some very cruel person," Wainright said. "Some—unspeakable person. Who knew a date."

Lyle looked up at him and slightly shook her head and waited.

"A year ago Thursday," Wainright said, "our daughter was killed. In a hunting accident. We—we saw her thrown. She was riding a bay. He broke his leg when he fell with her and he had to be shot. With a hunting rifle. A twenty-five Winchester. This was when we were still living near Brewster. Riding with the Brewster Hunt."

"Your daughter," Lyle said. "Was she engaged to be married?"

"Yes," Wainright said. "I say 'our' daughter. Virginia was Florence's daughter, really. Virginia Gant, her name was. But we both always—always thought of her as our daughter. I think she had come to think of herself in the same way—as our daughter, I mean. I don't mean she ever forgot her own father. She was sixteen when he died. He'd—oh, taught her to ride and everything. She—"

He stopped and shook his head. He said, "I need a drink, Miss Mercer. You're sure I can't—?"

"Really not, Mr. Wainright," Lyle said. "I'm sorry I—"

She stopped speaking because he was walking across the big room. He walked toward a bar at the end of it. She watched him pour Scotch into a glass and add a little water. He brought it back and sat in the chair his wife had been sitting in. He raised his glass toward Lyle and drank from it.

"I'm sorry," he said. "I'm going over and over it. The way some bastard planned I would—planned both Flo and I would. It's nothing to harrow you with, Miss Mercer. And—nothing to be printed."

"I'll have to tell Mr. Wallis," Lyle said. "I'm sure he won't print anything about it. But—"

She broke off. He took another swallow from his glass, and, when she did not go on, said, "But what, Miss Mercer? Writing about it would only make things worse for us. Be another cruelty. A meaningless cruelty."

She had not, she told him, been thinking of that. She had been thinking that something should be done to find out who was responsible for so cruel an action. "Because," she said, "whoever wants to hurt you and Mrs. Wainright will—well, he might think of some other way to hurt again. You've no idea who might have done this, Mr. Wainright?"

"None. No, none at all. Just somebody who wants to hurt us. I've no idea why."

"Perhaps," she said, "if you went to the police they could do something."

"I don't know what," Wainright said. "Or that putting an advertisement in a newspaper and signing somebody else's name to it is a legal offense. Something the police would feel they had to do anything about. And what could they do? Have you still got these envelopes the ads came in? Or the paper they were written on? For—oh, I suppose, fingerprints and that sort of thing?"

"No, I don't think so. Mr. Wallis would have told me if we had. But—it was a dreadful thing to do. As you said, a vicious thing. Somebody ought—" she paused and shook her head. "Somebody ought to do something," Lyle Mercer said. "It's like—oh, anonymous letters. Obscene telephone calls. Things that ought to be stopped."

He shook his head slowly.

"There isn't anything anybody can do," he said. "Nothing the police or anybody could do. Somebody wanted to hurt us. I don't know who or why. Well, he has. Probably that will be the end of it, Miss Mercer. We'll get a few answers to these ads, probably. Not many, I shouldn't think. I can just tear them up. Not show them to Florence. Not upset her any more. Hope that —that this will fade out of her mind the way things do. If there's anything else—" He shook his head again. "But probably there won't be," he said. "We've been reminded of a tragic thing—reminded to be hurt. I can't imagine why. Can't imagine who would want to do such a thing."

"We've been made a party to it," Lyle said. "I mean the *Citizen* has."

"Innocently," Paul Wainright told her.

"Carelessly, Mr. Wallis will think," Lyle said. "He's very proud of the paper. And he's a very curious man, Mr. Wainright. Hates to have things hanging in midair. Things unresolved."

"You mean," Wainright said, "that he'll think there's a story in it."

"Partly that. Mostly that the *Citizen* has been used. Look, there's a State Police inspector who lives in Van Brunt. He's very good, everybody says. A man named Heimrich. I know him. Know his wife better. If you told him about this he might be able to do something."

Wainright shook his head again. Then he said, "It's not a crime, Miss Mercer. It's a—a private thing. Not a thing for the police. Something Florence and I will just have to take. Take sitting down. You can't fight shadows, Miss Mercer." Then, in a dim way, he smiled at her. "Oh," he said, "I realize you're of an age not to accept that. An age to fight shadows. This editor of yours. I suppose he's older. Has learned to accept things."

"I suppose," Lyle said, and thought of the black-haired man who spent his Saturdays not accepting things which had crept into the *Citizen*. "No," she said, "he isn't, really. Oh, he's older than I am. But he still fights shadows. And he'll feel that the *Citizen* is part of—part of this ugly thing."

"And try to do something about it?"

"I don't know. I'll have to tell him about it."

"You said," Wainright told her, "that you thought he wouldn't print anything about it. Be party to dragging it up again. She was a gay, live thing, our daughter. And—snuffed out because her horse refused a jump. Can't it rest there, Miss Mercer?"

"Somebody doesn't want it to," she said.

"Some psychopath. Some sadist."

"People like that can be dangerous, Mr. Wainright," Lyle said. "You ought to go to the police."

"There'd be no point to it," Wainright said and then, rather abruptly, finished his drink and stood up. He said, "I'm going up and see if my wife is all right, Miss Mercer. Tell your editor what you've found out. Tell him I hope he doesn't print anything about it. Will you do that?"

She said she would do that, and he walked with her to the door. They looked out at the blazing hills and down toward the sparkle of the Hudson.

"It's such a pretty day, isn't it?" Paul Wainright said. "There was fog this morning, but it's all burned off."

He watched the little black Volks go down the drive before he went back into the house.

4

The afternoon sun slanted on the terrace and they lay side by side in chaises, facing the sun. From where they lay they could look down a wooded slope, bright with color, and see the Hudson glittering far below. It was, Susan Heimrich said, almost like summer except that in summer, real summer, the sun would be at this hour way up there. She pointed way up there. "Summer slips through our fingers," Susan said to the big man beside her. "I want to clutch it."

"A habit it has," Merton Heimrich said. "Did Joe Clifford say he'd bring the wood?"

"Tuesday or Wednesday," Susan said. "Which probably means Friday or Saturday. And could we take a cord and a half while he's got it? I said we could."

To which Inspector M. L. Heimrich, New York State Police, said "hmmm." Then he said, "They're very horsy, aren't they?"

"Very," Susan said. "And did they keep telling you about this fox they call 'Grandpa?' The one who's quit showing up?"

"Yes," Heimrich said. "They seem quite worried about Grandpa. Talked a lot about mange. Perhaps he just got bored with them. Same people, same hounds. Perhaps he just got old."

He held a hand out to her—to a wife who seemed to him so much younger, so inappropriately married to an aging hippopotamus. She took the large, square hand which belonged to her large solid man. Neither of them said anything about it. For some time neither of them said anything, but sat quietly in the slanting sun.

34

"Colonel's more than usually depressed today," Susan said, after a time. "Mite's very disappointed in him. He won't play."

"Colonel's getting along too," Heimrich said. "He is putting away childish things."

Colonel, who is out-sized even for a Great Dane, was lying in the shade of an ash tree, just beyond the terrace, on the grass. He had his great head down on his paws. Hearing his name, he slightly moved his tail, which was inadequate for a dog his size. He made a sound which was like a minor moan.

The all-black cat, whose name had once been a good deal more appropriate than it was that afternoon, jumped at the moving tail. Colonel sighed deeply and quit moving it.

"Mite," Susan told the lithe big tom who had grown out of his name, "he doesn't want to play. He thinks it's hot and that the boy went off without him and that you're rambunctious."

Mite turned and looked at her intently. Then he leaped away with violence and went halfway up the ash tree. He turned and looked at them.

"No," Susan said, "I'm not going to chase you. And Colonel isn't going to chase you. Find yourself a mouse."

Mite backed down the tree until he was some ten feet from the ground. He twisted himself and looked down at the ground for some seconds. Then he leaped from the tree trunk and landed and immediately bounded off toward the deeper grass which lay beyond a dry stone wall. He went over the wall.

"He thinks that was an order," Heimrich said. "Did you specially want a mouse?"

"Actually," Susan said, "I'd rather have a gin and tonic."

Heimrich put a leg over the side of the chaise and a foot on the ground.

"No," Susan said, "I'll get them," and she went to her feet as if she were on springs.

He turned to watch her as she went toward the low white house which, long before he knew it, or had met a woman named Susan Faye, had been a barn. He always turned to watch her move. He sighed slightly, thinking that she did not deserve to be married to a hippopotamus.

Colonel sat up, which seemed a somewhat laborious process.

He looked around, turning so he could look toward the stone fence and the field beyond it.

"Don't worry about him," Heimrich told the big dog. "He'll be back."

Colonel lay down again. He got up in sections but he always lay down in one piece, with a considerable thump. He lay, this time, with his head toward the wall the cat had gone over. Colonel did not, although Mite was grown now and extremely agile, trust the black cat out of his sight. After all, Mite was his cat. He had brought Mite home in his mouth when Mite was a very small black kitten and, when Colonel put him gently down on the terrace, a very wet one.

"He's grown up, Colonel," Heimrich told their dog. "People will start calling you overprotective. And—"

He stopped talking to the dog because he could hear the telephone ringing in the house. When the telephone rings in the low white house, particularly on days off, it too often means that somebody has killed somebody. Which means the end of a day off for an inspector, Bureau of Criminal Investigation, New York State Police. Poor Susan, Heimrich thought. She thought my being made an inspector would mean predictable office hours.

He looked at the door in which a long-legged slender woman in blue slacks and yellow shirt would soon appear to tell him the barracks was calling. She did not. Of course, all telephone calls did not mean that somebody had killed somebody. Quite possibly somebody wanted them for cocktails. Or young Michael, who had been playing tennis at the club, hadn't been lucky about a ride home and was asking, in his slow grave way, to be fetched. Or—

Susan came out carrying a tray with two tall glasses on it. She carried the tray slowly across the flagstones, being careful not to slosh. She put the tray down on a small round table between the two chaises. She sat on hers and lifted her glass and they clicked glasses.

"Bob Wallis wants to see you about something," Susan said. "He sounded angry about it. I told him to come along over."

"Wallis always sounds angry," Heimrich told her. "It's the way his voice is made."

36

"Also," Susan said, "he always walks as if he were walking through something. Fighting through something. Where did Colonel go?"

"To find his cat," Heimrich told her. "His very special cat. Who can't be trusted out of sight."

"Everybody is always leaving him," Susan said. "Michael goes off to play tennis. Mite goes off to catch a mouse."

They were halfway down their tall drinks when a station wagon came up the drive and turned to face out, as if it were about to go away again. Lyle Mercer got out on the near side and, unexpectedly, Michael Faye followed her. He wore white shorts and tennis shirt and a sweater draped over his shoulders. He carried a tennis racket.

Lyle waved a hand at them, and Michael, who looked wet, whose shirt clung damply to his lean body, waved his tennis racket. Robert Wallis jutted his way around the wagon and walked toward the terrace, his head thrust forward. He always, Susan thought, looks like a battering ram about to batter.

Susan turned on her chaise and said, "Hi, dear," to Lyle Mercer. Heimrich stood up. Susan's son said, "Thank you, sir," to the back of Robert Wallis and, "Thank you, Miss Mercer," to Lyle, who was following Wallis toward the terrace. She stopped and smiled back at him. Wallis didn't stop or, until he was on the terrace, say anything. The tall, slim boy said, "Mother. Dad," and went into the house.

Wallis thrust a hand toward Heimrich, who took it and found it a lean, hard hand. Wallis said, "Mrs. Heimrich," a little absently and then, not at all absently, "Sorry to barge in, Inspector. Want to ask you something. Also, tell you something."

"All right," Heimrich said. He reached a long arm out and pulled a director's chair up and said, "Miss Mercer." Lyle sat in the chair and Robert Wallis looked around, a little angrily, and then jerked a chair up beside Lyle Mercer's. "I'll get you drinks," Susan said and started to get up from the chaise. But Lyle shook her head and Wallis did not appear to hear her. Wallis sat leaning forward in the chair.

"Is there," Wallis said, his voice grating, "a law against putting lying advertisements in newspapers?"

"Probably," Heimrich said. "There are a lot of laws. And regulations. Federal Trade Commission, probably. Better business bureaus. Fraudulent claims and—"

"Not what I mean," Wallis said. "Look."

He took a roughly torn sheet of newsprint out of a side pocket of his summer jacket. He thrust it toward Heimrich. He said, "From the *Citizen*. The ones I've checked."

Heimrich read the want ads with checks beside them. He shook his head and handed the paper down to Susan. Then he sat on his chaise. He said, "The wedding dress ad is unusual, naturally. There's nothing illegal about wanting to sell a horse and a gun. Should be, I think, as far as the gun's concerned, but there isn't." He shook his head again. "That what's bothering you, Mr. Wallis?"

"What's bothering me," Wallis said, "is that my newspaper's been used by somebody to play a nasty trick. These ads came in in plain envelopes, typed on plain paper. And the signatures typed. And it turns out the signatures were forgeries."

"You can't forge a signature on a typewriter," Heimrich told him. "Whose signatures? Or was it the same on both?"

"On both," Wallis said. "Paul Wainright on both. But Wainright says he didn't send them in. And—you tell him, Lyle. The whole thing."

Lyle told them the whole thing. When she had finished, Susan Heimrich said, "What an awful thing to do. What a—a low, vicious thing to do."

"Mrs. Wainright called it 'tacky,'" Lyle said. "I don't know precisely what she meant."

"Shabby, I think," Susan said. "Something like that. I think of—oh, dirty ruffles on a dress."

Heimrich had closed his eyes. It was some seconds before he spoke. Then he said, "You suggested Mr. Wainright tell the police about this, Miss Mercer? And he thought it wouldn't be any use?"

"Yes."

"And you decided the police should be told?"

"I decided that," Wallis said. "Somebody's played a dirty, nasty trick. Made the *Citizen* party to it. The girl here found me at the club. Swimming." He ran a hand through stiff, still somewhat damp, black hair. "So, Inspector, what can you do about it? Must be a law against that sort of thing."

"There are a good many vicious things that aren't illegal," Heimrich said. "Oh, if it went on. Harassment if it went on. Wainright could get a court order to stop it. If he could find out who was doing it."

"There ought to be some way to find out," Wallis said. "Some way the police could find out."

"These envelopes the ads came in," Heimrich said. "No return address, of course. Anybody happen to notice the postmarks?"

"No."

"Plain typewriter paper. No address—return address—on that, of course?"

"No."

"And envelopes and paper burned after the ads were set. Thrown away, anyhow."

"The refuse people pick up on Friday," Wallis said.

"You see," Heimrich said, "come down to it, Mr. Wainright is pretty much right. Nothing to put a finger on. A crackpot. A sadistic one, with a grudge against the Wainrights. But—a shadow."

"That's what Mr. Wainright said," Lyle said. "You can't fight shadows."

"Or put handcuffs on them," Heimrich said. "Or charge them with anything. Malice—a desire to hurt—those things aren't crimes, Mr. Wallis. Actually, using somebody else's name isn't. Unless it's done for profit, naturally. Wainright told you he had no idea who might have wanted to rake the girl's death up again, Miss Mercer?"

"He said he didn't."

"And that it was a year ago last Thursday his stepdaughter was killed? To the day?"

"Yes."

"And whoever sent these advertisements in stipulated that they be printed in the *Citizen's* issue of October tenth?"

Wallis answered that. He said, "That's what Mrs. Allsmith says. She handled the ads. Handles a lot of things at the *Citizen,* Gertrude Allsmith does."

"Have any answers come in, do you know, Mr. Wallis?"

"Early for that," Wallis said. "Paper comes out, goes into the mails, Thursday. People get it Friday."

"We don't," Susan Heimrich said. "Saturday, sometimes. Sometimes not until Monday. And the carrier gets here, usually, late in the afternoon."

"You get your mail from a carrier, Mr. Wallis? I mean mail for the newspaper?"

"P. O. box," Wallis said. "Boy picks it up. Only the post office closes at noon on Saturdays. But if there are answers, all we can do is send them along. Anyway, I guess it is. Tampering with the United States mail, or something like that, if we didn't."

Merton Heimrich had closed his eyes again. He said, "hmmm." He reached out, without opening his eyes, and picked up his glass and drank from it.

"Really," Susan said, "I wish you two would let me get you something to drink. Something long and cold."

This time Robert Wallis did hear her. He said, "Well." He looked at Lyle. He said, "You, child? You are over eighteen." He looked at her again. "Barely," he said.

"All right," Lyle said. "Something with gin in it. Not much gin."

"With tonic?" Susan said, and started to get up.

"We just barged in," Wallis said. "Hate being barged in on myself. Probably—"

"With tonic?" Susan repeated, and was more firm about it. She also stood up.

Wallis said, "A light one." Lyle said, "Very light for me, please, Susan."

Susan started across the terrace, but Merton Heimrich said, "I'll get them," and was off the chaise in a smooth, swinging movement. He picked up the tray and looked down at Susan's glass, which was still three-quarters full. Susan said, "No, dear," and Heimrich put his own almost empty glass on the tray and went off toward the house. For so big a man, he moves so well, Susan Heimrich thought. Particularly for a man who thinks he's a hippopotamus.

Heimrich was gone some time. Lyle said, "It's beautiful here, Susan," and Wallis turned his aluminum-and-nylon chair and jutted his head toward the Hudson. He did not, for some seconds, say anything. Then he said, "Well, I'll be damned." With that, he pointed.

A very large Great Dane was walking, slowly, with evident care, across the lawn from the direction of a stone wall. He seemed to be measuring his pace. And a very black cat, moving somewhat more rapidly, was timing his movements to the big dog's pace. The cat was weaving in and out under the tall dog, between the dog's long legs.

"Oh," Susan said, "they do that all the time. It's something they made up together. Although I suspect Mite was the one who had the idea first. He has so many ideas."

"Mite?" Wallis said, with some incredulity in his voice.

"The cat's called Mite," Susan Heimrich explained. "It was a very appropriate name when Colonel first brought him home." She looked at her animals. "He has rather outgrown it," Susan said. "But it's his, now, and you can't change names in mid-cat."

Colonel walked to the shade of the ash tree and collapsed in it. His front paws stuck out into the sun. Mite looked the situation over and curled up between the dog's big paws, where the sun was warm on his shining black coat.

The screen door squealed slightly as it closed itself. Heimrich carried a tray with three tall glasses on it across the terrace. Susan said, "Channel Thirteen?" and Heimrich said, "What else? A dance festival somewhere."

"Sometimes we worry a little about the boy," Susan said. "On the other hand, he plays rather good tennis."

"And baseball," Heimrich said, and put the tray down and handed glasses to Lyle Mercer and Robert Wallis.

"Kept you waiting, I'm afraid," Heimrich said. "Got curious. Got them working on the files." He did not amplify. He said, "I see Colonel found his cat. No mouse?"

"He didn't bring one home," Susan said. "Of course, sometimes he just has a picnic."

Heimrich said, "Drinks all right?" and was told the drinks were fine. He said, "I like your newspaper, Mr. Wallis. It's an

41

honest newspaper. You'd published other small-town newspapers before you started the *Citizen?*"

"No," Wallis said and turned his chair from the Hudson so that he jutted his head toward Heimrich. "Worked on city papers. With the idea of a country weekly in the back of my mind. A kind of itch, and God knows why." He drank, rather deeply, from his glass. "My wife and I were going to run it together," he said. "My wife died." He drank again. Then, to nobody in particular, he said, "The damnedest things happen in the country."

"Yes," Merton Heimrich said. "Like everywhere else, Mr. Wallis. You'd thought they didn't?"

"I suppose so," Wallis said. Then, abruptly, he laughed. His laughter, unexpectedly, did not grate at all. "I hadn't," he said, "counted on pit-barbecued children."

They all laughed at that, the most famous of the *Citizen's* typos. "The annual food fair for the benefit of the Visiting Nurse Association will be held Saturday on the grounds of the Memorial Methodist Church. Cakes and pies donated by members of the Van Brunt Garden Club will be on sale, as will pit-barbecued—"

"Reggie Peterson is certain he wrote, 'chickens,'" Robert Wallis said. "And the linotype man is just as sure he followed copy. And the proofreader simply missed it."

"And you," Lyle Mercer said, "went through the ceiling."

"Right," Wallis said. "We've framed the hole."

He finished his drink and looked at Lyle's, which was not much more than begun. "Any time," Lyle said, and sipped and put her glass down on a flagstone. Then the telephone rang in the house. Susan started up but Heimrich said, "Can be they've checked it out," and swung off the chaise and went across the terrace.

Heimrich was, this time, gone almost five minutes. When he had sat down again and sipped for a moment from his glass, he nodded his head.

"All violent deaths in country areas we check out," he said. "Accidental or otherwise. Go into the records. It happened the way Wainright told you it happened, Miss Mercer. And when it happened—a year ago last Thursday. The girl, Wainright's stepdaughter, was Virginia Gant. Her horse threw her. Threw her headfirst into a stone wall."

Virginia Gant had been twenty, he told them. She was the daughter of Robert Lee and Florence Gant. She had been born in Virginia, where her father bred horses. Hunters, for the most part. His father had before him. Robert Lee Gant had been more than a breeder of horses. He had been—

"Wait a minute," Wallis said. "He was head of some damn big corporation or other. Merged with something else, the corporation did. A hell of a big merger. Engineered by Gant —and then he retired sitting pretty."

"Apparently the same Gant," Heimrich said. "About the accident. It was early in the morning. A rather misty morning. Bad footing for the horses. A good many had dropped out of the hunt. The Wainrights hadn't."

Paul Wainright and his stepdaughter had, according to the report of the trooper who had checked the accident out, been riding side by side. Florence Wainright was ahead of them; had already jumped a low stone fence into the next field. Virginia Gant was riding a bay stallion. "Her special horse, apparently." A little inclined to be nervy, according to what Wainright had told the trooper. Some people wouldn't have ridden him. Wainright had, he said, warned Virginia about him. And been laughed at. He had been laughed at not only by his stepdaughter but by his wife.

Virginia had ridden since she was a child. She had never before been thrown. The stone wall was not a high one, according to Wainright. It was an entirely routine jump. He had been riding nearly abreast of his stepdaughter, but a little ahead of her. His horse had taken the jump. Virginia's stallion had refused it.

"Just dug his forefeet in," Wainright had told the trooper.

"I've known it to happen," Lyle Mercer said. "They—sometimes they seem to get notions. But a good rider—" She let it hang.

"Perhaps the girl was too confident," Heimrich said. "Too sure. Anyway—"

Anyway, the girl had been thrown over her horse's head and, headfirst, into the wall. She had died almost at once. The horse

43

had stumbled and fallen against the wall and had broken his right foreleg.

Wainright had jumped his horse back over the wall and had run to his stepdaughter, calling to her. Florence Wainright had heard his shouts and had ridden back. They were leaning over the girl together when others came up, one of them a local doctor. But there was nothing he or anyone could do for Virginia Gant, who was twenty. And who was to have been married the following June.

"To," Heimrich said, "a man named Pointer. Andrew Pointer."

Pointer, who was a script writer for television, had been a house guest of the Wainrights. He was in his middle twenties; he had not ridden with the hunt that morning, or any morning.

After they had got a Jeep into the field and taken Virginia's body to the Wainright house in it, Wainright had got his rifle and ridden back and killed the stallion.

"A bay stallion," Wallis said. Heimrich closed his eyes. He said, "Yes. A bay."

"The girl," Susan said. "Was there a physical description of her?"

"Blonde," Heimrich said, without opening his eyes. "Five feet five or thereabouts. Blue eyes. Weight about a hundred and four." He opened his eyes and looked at Susan.

"Yes," Susan said, "a size ten, at a guess. Perhaps even an eight."

"Only," Lyle Mercer said, "there wasn't any wedding dress."

"Did anybody besides Wainright see the horse refuse? And throw the girl?" Robert Wallis asked Heimrich. He leaned forward toward Heimrich, so that the light chair tilted under him.

"The girl's mother, apparently," Heimrich said. "She had slowed in the next field to wait for the others to catch up. She looked back, she says, and saw it happen. Not very clearly. She was a hundred yards or so into the field. Saw the girl falling and her husband jumping his horse back over the wall."

"So," Wallis said, "it went down as accidental death? Your men—I mean the State Police men—were satisfied?"

"Our men," Heimrich said. "The coroner. They have coroners in Putnam County. Yes, Mr. Wallis. Accidental death."

"Why," Wallis said, "would anybody want to bring it up? A meaningless, tragic thing?"

Heimrich did not know. A crackpot—the world was full of crackpots. Conceivably, someone who was fanatically against hunting. People are fanatically against a great many things. More probably, somebody who wanted to hurt Paul and Florence Wainright.

"There is evil under a good many surfaces," Heimrich said. "A kind of evil the law can't touch. Until, unless, it becomes evil in action."

"This is," Wallis said, in his grating, angry voice.

"Not to the law," Heimrich said. "Wainright is right about that, Mr. Wallis. It's nothing the law can reach. If the *Citizen* gets any more advertisements that look phony—and, naturally, appear to involve Wainright—let me see them before you print them. I doubt if you'll get any. The bolt's been shot."

"And gone home," Lyle Mercer said. "The poor troubled woman. It's all—all so cruel. So—needless."

"This kid who was going to marry the girl," Wallis said, and stood up. "I'd like to talk to the kid. You said his name is Pointer?"

"Andrew Pointer," Heimrich said.

"And that he writes television scripts?"

"Yes," Heimrich said. "Yes, he does come to mind, doesn't he? A year ago he was living in the city, Mr. Wallis. In the East Forties." Heimrich closed his eyes for a moment. "East Forty-sixth," Heimrich said. And gave an address.

5

As he drove her back to the country club to pick up her car, Robert Wallis was a silent man. He leaned forward over the wheel as he drove. He always, Lyle thought, seems to lean forward, to thrust at things. He drove fast and he drove well. There were a good many cars in the club's parking lot, as there usually were on Saturday evenings. He remembered where Lyle had put her Volks, which was more than she remembered, and pulled up almost beside it. He turned, abruptly, and looked at her. He said, "Make anything of it, child?"

He sounded angry, she thought. He sounded demanding.

"Something like a practical joke," Lyle said. "Played by somebody with a grudge against the Wainrights."

He continued to look at her for some seconds.

"It doesn't feel like that to me," he said, then. "The way it feels to me, somebody wants to bring the girl's death up. Without involving himself in bringing it up. Use your head, Lyle."

It was a command, brusque.

"It was an accident," Lyle said. "The horse refused. The girl wasn't set for that. Horses do, sometimes."

"I don't know a damn thing about horses," Wallis said. "Or want to. You ride them, child?"

"Since I was ten," Lyle said. "Not much recently."

"Jump them?"

"I used to. It isn't difficult. Mostly the horse knows what to do."

"The one this girl was riding sure as hell didn't," Wallis said.

46

"Somebody wonders why, maybe. Wants other people to wonder."

"It was a year ago," Lyle said. "You mean, somebody thought it wasn't an accident? And waited a year to bring it up. And then brought it up in this roundabout way. This devious way. Hoping what?"

"That people would see the advertisement about the wedding dress. Because it was—well, the more you think about it the stranger it feels. The more it sticks out. 'Size ten, never used.' There's a poignancy about it, isn't there?"

"Yes," she said. "Hoping somebody would get curious and —look into it. And bring something out. But if there's something to bring out—or somebody thinks there's something to bring out—why not be direct about it? Go to the police?"

"Somebody with nothing tangible to go on," Wallis said. "With—just call it an uneasy feeling."

"It was a cruel thing to do," Lyle said, and pulled up her door latch.

"Growing out of bitterness," Wallis said. "Who would be likely to be bitter, child?"

"Oh," she said, "the man who was going to marry the girl. The man you told the Inspector you want to talk to. What's his name?"

"Andrew Pointer," Wallis said. "As in a breed of dog."

"Pat," Lyle said. "And, apparently, a man who makes up stories for television."

She got out of the station wagon. She turned back and spoke again through the open window.

"And waits a year to do anything," she said.

"You're an argumentative kid," Wallis said. "We don't know he waited a year, do we? For all we know, he may have needled the Wainrights every hour on the hour. And got nowhere."

"Probably," Lyle said, "because there's nowhere to get."

"Go home," Wallis said. He started the motor. "And hide that pretty head of yours in your sandpile."

He's very difficult, Lyle thought, getting into the Volks. He gets fixed on things, she thought, driving the Volks home. He's a scratchy man, she thought, taking a shower. I wonder whether he was this way before his wife died. I wonder how his wife put up with him. He must all the time have made mountains out of molehills. The way he's doing—

The telephone interrupted her and she answered on the extension in her room, because her parents had gone to the Petersons' for cocktails. She was supposed to join them there, but had been doubtful about it. Reggie Peterson was a nice enough boy, but he was at the pawy stage. And, she thought, so very young about it. She said, "Hello?" into the telephone.

"Miss Mercer, please," a woman said.

"This is she."

"This is Florence Wainright," the woman said. "I wanted to tell you how thoughtful it was of you to come to us this noon. About that strange, tacky advertisement."

"Mr. Wallis was worried about it," Lyle said. "He felt we—that is, the newspaper—should have checked before the advertisement was published."

"I'm afraid I was a little vague when you came, honey," Florence Wainright said. "Headaches like I have make me sort of muzzy. After I'd had my nap I waked up and thought, I was rude to the sweet child. Really *rude*."

She didn't, Lyle thought, sound 'muzzy' now. She didn't make any special sense, but she didn't sound muzzy.

"You weren't at all," Lyle said. "I shouldn't have barged in on you like that when you weren't feeling up to things."

"Oh, but you should," Florence said. "And we do appreciate what you tried to do. You and your Mr. Wallis. It was a kindness, really. We both feel that." She paused for an instant. "Mr. Wainright and I, I mean, dear."

"It was—" Lyle began and was interrupted.

"What I really called for," Florence Wainright said, "was to see if we couldn't have dinner together. Paul—my husband, that is—has had to go into the city to see a client. And—well, I want to talk to somebody. But I suppose you're all tied up. A dear, pretty young thing like you."

"You mean this evening?"

"I surely do, honey. Because—" She paused again. "It would be so dear of you if you could possibly. Because—well, sometimes it's kind of upsetting to be alone with nobody to talk to.

48

And Paul's had this engagement for simply weeks and it's dreadfully important to him. Business."

She gave the last word deference in her tone.

"I'm not very good at being alone," Florence said, not waiting for Lyle to say anything. "Back home there was always somebody to talk to."

"I am free," Lyle said. "Should I come there, Mrs. Wainright?"

"It's just too wonderful," Florence said. "No, honey. There's nobody but Lucy today, and all she can do is frozen things. I'd say the club, but there's a do or something, isn't there?"

"The Saturday night dance," Lyle said. "Special because it's Columbus Day."

"So buzzy," Florence Wainright said. "The Inn? I'll call Mrs. Oliphant, and I'm sure she can take care of the two of us. In —what time is it, honey? My watch has stopped again. He says it's because I forget to wind it. He says I'm always forgetting things."

Lyle's watch was on the dressing table. She could just reach it.

"It's almost six," Lyle said.

"Would six-thirty be too early? Or seven, if that would be better."

"Seven," Lyle said.

"You're a dear," Florence said. "Really a dear, honey. I'll call Mrs. Oliphant."

The telephone clicked with finality, and Lyle put her own receiver back in its cradle and sat for some seconds looking absently at it. The invitation, out of the blue from a woman she had met only once, was puzzling. Her acceptance was equally puzzling. It would have been so easy to say that she was tied up for the evening; it would have been partly true, if one counted the Petersons. She had been told to put her head in her sandpile. A strange, jarring man, Robert Wallis. Put her head in her sandpile. What a thing to say. No, that wasn't precisely what he had said. Put your "pretty" head in your sandpile.

A breeze came through an open window, and the breeze, unexpectedly, was cool. It's almost like summer today, she thought, but it's really mid-October. The evening is reminding itself of that. And me, she added, shivering slightly. She got a robe and wore it while she put a face on. When she dressed, she put on a gray wool dress which had a V of yellow at the neck and yellow cuffs. It was time to think of autumn clothes.

It was not cool when she went out to the garage, but it was not warm either. As she drove down the drive she switched the car lights on. She didn't really need them yet, but she didn't quite not need them.

By the time she reached the Old Stone Inn she needed the lights. The parking lot was almost filled, but the Volks was undemanding of space. She walked in through the side door, the taproom door, of the Inn. Probably Mrs. Oliphant would have given them a table there.

There were a good many people in the taproom, which had been rearranged since the hunt breakfast. Most of the people in the long room were men, and near the bar, men were throwing darts at a target and making a good deal of noise about it. Of course—Saturday night here, as well as at the country club. On Saturday nights, as her father said, the Old Stone Inn changed into the village pub, even to the extent of a dart game. On Saturday nights even the locals ate—if they ate at the Inn at all—in the main dining room, on other nights left by locals to "off-the-roaders."

Lyle crossed the taproom to the door which let into the small lobby. Mrs. Oliphant would be stationed there, probably abetted by Tony, who would be wearing a dinner jacket in honor of Saturday night. Instead of the maroon jacket he wore as a waiter on lesser nights.

It was Mrs. Oliphant, in a black dress with a white collar. Mrs. Oliphant said, "Hello, Lyle dear. Are your parents with you? Because if they are I'm afraid I'm going to have to keep you wai—"

"No," Lyle said. "Mrs. Wainright was going to call for a table. Just for two."

"Oh," Mrs. Oliphant said. "She didn't say you were the other one. I supposed—anyway, it's all ready, dear."

Lyle followed Mrs. Oliphant across the big dining room, which was filled. Most of the men were wearing city clothes;

were off-the-roaders. It was an open room, with a good many tables in the middle of it. (Which was one reason most of the locals preferred to eat in the comparative snugness of the bar.) But the table Mrs. Oliphant led Lyle to was in a corner. Mrs. Oliphant took a "Reserved" card off the table and said, "Here you are, dear," and there Lyle Mercer was. She was still a little puzzled as to why she was.

A waiter she had never seen before, and whose maroon jacket didn't fit, said, "Cocktail before dinner, miss?" Lyle said she was meeting someone and would wait, and the imported waiter said, "Of course, miss," but not much as if he meant it, and went away.

She had got to the table at a little after seven. She waited for almost fifteen minutes.

It was noisy in the big room, and there were a good many children. Some of the men were not wearing neckties, and two of them—two in sight—were not wearing jackets, either. Standards relaxed themselves on Saturday nights, a fact over which Mrs. Oliphant gloomily shook her head. "You'd think," she had once said, bitterly, to Lytton Mercer, "that there was a Come-as-you-are sign out front."

Mrs. Oliphant, looking a little as if she were herself wearing a dinner jacket, came across the room, and Florence Wainright came after her, on very high heels. She wore a black dress which, even when it was still halfway across the room, looked to Lyle like Saks or, perhaps, Bergdorf's. She wore a black jacket over the sleek black dress, and the jacket was fringed with fur. She looked city, and as if she would not approve of tieless men, let alone men who did not wear jackets, in restaurants.

She sat down. She said, "Honey. May I call you Lyle? It was so *sweet* of you. On the spur of the moment, this way."

"It was good of you to ask me," Lyle said, for want of anything better and with the feeling that there should have been.

This was, Lyle thought, a different Florence Wainright. Earlier in the day, in a loose robe, there had been a physical looseness about the blonde woman. She was much tighter now; she also seemed appreciably younger. Early forties now;

not late forties. Of course, she had had a headache earlier in the day. A headache at the least.

"I hope your headache's gone," Lyle said.

"Headache? Oh, of course. They come and go, honey. An hour's rest and an aspirin or two. Shouldn't we have a little something to drink?"

She did not wait to be answered. She turned in her chair and said, "Oh, miss," to a waitress who was passing, leaning a little to her right under a heavy tray. The waitress nodded her head, somewhat crookedly, and continued to pass.

"They're very busy Saturday nights," Lyle said.

They waited for several minutes, and during them Mrs. Wainright turned several times in her chair, keeping watch. Finally, the imported waiter in the jacket which didn't fit too well stopped at their table and said, "Yes, ladies? A cocktail before dinner?"

"Bourbon and water," Mrs. Wainright said. "Not too much water." She turned to Lyle, hostess again. She said, "And you, dear?"

Lyle hesitated a moment; thought, transiently, of ordering a Shirley Temple. She shooed the thought away. She said, "A martini, please. Very dry, please."

The waiter went away.

"I can never drink martinis," Mrs. Wainright said. "They go right to my head. Paul drinks them, but I always say that men are different."

Lyle stopped herself from saying, "Do you?" and merely nodded her head.

"I'm so terribly sorry I had that mean headache this afternoon, dear," Mrs. Wainright said. "When you went to all that trouble to drive way out there to ask about that mean, tacky advertisement. Who could have done a dreadful thing like that?"

Lyle said she didn't know. She said, "We should have caught it. Mr. Wallis is upset about it."

"Just a typed name," Mrs. Wainright said and shook her blonde, now-shining head. "My husband's name. How could anyone?"

"I don't know," Lyle said. "Somebody's who's not quite

right, probably. What Inspector Heimrich calls a—" She stopped herself, clearly not in time.

"Inspector Heimrich?" Mrs. Wainright said, and it seemed to Lyle that the soft voice, with its Southern overlay, sharpened. "You don't mean that policeman?"

Her voice repelled the thought of a policeman.

"Yes," Lyle said. "I guess I do, Mrs. Wainright. They live in Van Brunt, you know. They're very nice people. Mrs. Heimrich has the fabric shop on the avenue. 'Susan Faye, Fabrics.'"

"A shop?" Mrs. Wainright said. "Gracious. Faye? It almost sounds Irish."

"Her first husband was named Faye," Lyle said. "He was killed in Korea." She paused for a moment. "He was an Air Force captain," she added. It seemed something Mrs. Paul Wainright would want to know.

"And she keeps a shop," Florence Wainright said, with some disbelief in her voice. But her voice had become soft again.

"Her family has lived around here for a long, long time," Lyle said. "I've known her since I was a little girl."

Florence Wainright said, "Well."

The waiter came; he took drinks off a tray and put them on the table. Lyle said, "Thank you," for hers. The waiter said, "You want to order, ladies?"

"No," Florence Wainright said. "We'll tell you when we do, boy."

The waiter looked to Lyle to be in his late fifties. Mrs. Wainright drank from her glass, and drank quite a bit from it.

"You started to tell me something," Florence Wainright said, and put her glass down on the table with a slight thump. "Something this policeman said."

"I don't—" Lyle said, and found that she did remember. "That whoever put this ad in the paper was a crackpot," she said.

"Dear," Florence Wainright said, "you didn't tell this policeman about—about the advertisement somebody put in your paper? Because my husband says he asked you not to."

"No," Lyle said. "He asked me not to print anything about it. And I said I'd tell Mr. Wallis how he felt but that it was up to Mr. Wallis."

With which she took a sip from her glass. It was a good martini. Harold made good drinks.

"Mr. Wainright said he told you it wouldn't do any good to go to the police," Florence said and shook her head and raised her glass again and drank again. "That there wasn't anything the police could do about it."

"Mr. Wallis thought we should," Lyle said. "Because he feels the *Citizen* was used. But Inspector Heimrich agrees with your husband. Says there's nothing he can do about it. Unless this —whoever this person was—does something else to hurt you and Mr. Wainright."

"Spite," Mrs. Wainright said. "It was just spite, honey. Why would anybody feel that way about us?"

"I don't know."

"On the anniversary of the dreadful accident," Florence Wainright said and lifted her glass again. But this time she put it down without drinking from it. "To—to remind us of it. Why?"

Again Lyle Mercer said she did not know. And then she saw that there were tears in Florence Wainright's rather large blue eyes.

"I'm sorry, Mrs. Wainright," Lyle said. "So terribly sorry."

"She was so young," Florence said. "So young and happy. With everything to look forward to. And to die like that. Like *that.*"

"Yes," Lyle said. Then, a little to her own surprise, she reached across the table and put a slim brown hand on Mrs. Wainright's chubby white one. She left it there a moment.

"You're sweet," Florence Wainright said. "You must be about the age she was—my child was. Boblee and I had only the one child, you know."

The "Boblee" puzzled Lyle for an instant. Then she remembered that the father of the dead girl had been Robert Lee something. Of course, Robert Lee Gant. She said. "I didn't know, Mrs. Wainright."

"From the time she was a little girl," Florence Wainright said, "she rode well. Very well. And whatever Paul thought, Alex was a good horse. Mettlesome, maybe, but not with Ginnie. I still can't believe it. I still can't."

Lyle felt there must be something she could say—something that might a little comfort. She could not think what there was to say. That there are finalities, things which must be believed even if they are not accepted? That with time grief fades a little? But there was no point in saying that. Saying that would be an impertinence.

"It had begun to dim a little," Florence said, almost as if Lyle had made the trite assurance about the healing power of time. "Then I read that—that advertisement about the wedding dress, and it all came back. Why would anybody want that?"

She finished her drink and looked around and held her glass up and beckoned with it. The waiter came. He said, "The same, ma'am?" and looked at Lyle's glass, which was still almost full, and said, "Miss?" Lyle shook her head and the waiter went away with Florence Wainright's glass.

"Mrs. Wainright," Lyle said, "you'd seen the advertisement before I showed it to you this afternoon?"

"Thursday. I'd almost forgotten when you came to the house," Florence Wainright said. "I was in the Center picking up some things and saw the paper and took it along, because Paul likes to read it. But he hadn't got home yet and I read it. Even the want ads." She shook her head slightly. "People do want to buy and sell the strangest things," she said. "And we do need a gardener. I just happened to see this advertisement about the wedding dress and it—it brought things back. It—it was as if somebody had hit me."

And again the blue eyes clouded a little with tears.

"Of course," Florence Wainright said, "I didn't know then it had anything to do with us. But—it's being the same date and everything. And Ginnie having planned to marry this nice boy and—and everything."

"Did you show it to your husband?" Lyle asked.

"No. I knew it would hurt him, too. He was so very fond of Ginnie. Almost as if she were his own daughter. Anyway, he didn't get home for a long time. He has to go to the city almost every day, you know. And the—the reminder of that awful thing—brought on one of my headaches."

The waiter returned with a filled glass and put it down in

front of Florence Wainright. He looked again at Lyle's glass, and again Lyle shook her head.

"It's almost," Florence said, "as if somebody was trying to hint that what happened to my girl wasn't an accident. Do you see what I mean, dear?"

"There's nothing in the ad to imply that," Lyle said. "Mrs. Wainright, it's bad enough for you without your imagining things."

"That's what Paul says," Mrs. Wainright said. "That I've got to get ahold of myself. Of course he says that lots of times." She drank from her refilled glass. "He's so strong," she said. "In such a lot of ways. You know, dear, before we were married he'd hardly ridden at all. And now he's almost as good as anybody. Anybody, I mean, who hasn't ridden since they were children. The way I did. And my little girl."

And again her eyes filled with tears.

She wants to talk to somebody, Lyle thought. Wants something from somebody—some sympathy spoken, some reassurance. And I am too young to know the words, if there are any words.

"You're a dear child," Florence said. "And I do know I'm blubbering, honey. But all at once everything seemed so—so empty. With Paul having to go into the city to talk to this client. About a house he wants Paul to build for him. Your drink'll get warm, child."

Obediently, Lyle sipped from her glass. The martini wasn't as cold as it had been. Lyle said, "Build a house?"

"Design," Florence said. "I didn't use the right word. Paul says I get things mixed up all the time. He's an architect, you know, dear. And does things about planning things. But mostly people tell him about homes they want and he makes plans for them. He keeps too busy, dear. And he's away so much. And he doesn't really need to work so hard."

She drank again, and emptied her glass. She was, Lyle thought briefly, going to bring on another headache. I'm flippant, she thought. But the old are so hard to understand. Even my own parents, who are dear people and sweet people, are hard to understand.

"Particularly," Florence said, "the way things are now."

56

The words jarred into Lyle's thoughts. There, they didn't mean anything. She said, "Now, Mrs. Wainright?"

"Florence, dear. It's Florence. And you're Lyle."

"Florence," Lyle said, again obedient. "I just meant I didn't know what you meant. About the way things are now."

"There's so much money now," Florence Wainright said. "There's no reason for Paul to work so hard. Have to be away so much. Because my baby wouldn't have been twenty-one for months. Waiter!"

The waiter said, "Yes, lady," and looked at the glass which had held bourbon and water—not too much water. "The same again?"

"Of course," Florence said. "Of course, waiter."

The waiter looked at Lyle Mercer's glass. Lyle shook her head again. It would have been better to go to the Petersons. Reggie didn't paw the mind.

6

By a quarter of nine the three imported waiters and Mary and Agnes, the local girls who served the Inn's dining room during the quiet between weekends, were bringing checks instead of food, and tables were emptying. The waiters from the city were hovering, with the natural anxiety of waiters, while men added and took bills out of wallets. They were going out to consult Mrs. Oliphant about signatures of locals with charge accounts. They were taking credit cards away and bringing them back and hovering. Some people tip in cash, others write in the tips. There was always the outside chance that some mildly muddled diner might do both.

Near the table at which Florence Wainright drank and Lyle Mercer waited, the man whose uniform jacket bunched at the shoulders picked up menus and put them down again.

For half an hour, Florence had said nothing. She had merely sipped, more slowly, from her glass. Lyle was not certain how many times, by then, the glass had been taken away empty and brought back full. She had finished her own martini; several times she had again shaken her head when the waiter looked at her empty glass. The evening had stalled—in boredom and in embarrassment. Also, she was getting hungry. Also, the kitchen closed at nine.

Florence Wainright had her elbows on the table and the tips of her fingers pressed against her cheeks. She looked down at her glass. There was no indication that she any longer knew that Lyle Mercer sat across the table from her.

"Mrs. Wainright," Lyle said and then, "*Florence*," the last word more loudly.

For several seconds, Florence Wainright did not speak, nor did she change her position. Then she said, "What?"

"We'd better order," Lyle said. "The kitchen closes pretty soon."

"Order?" Florence said and then, "Oh, yes, order." She finished what remained in her glass, and looked around. The waiter was very quick. Florence started to lift her empty glass once more, and Lyle said, "If we could have menus?" Florence looked at her glass and moved her head slowly from side to side.

The waiter put menus down on the table. He said, "I'm afraid we haven't any more roast beef, ladies."

As at many country inns, roast prime ribs were a specialty of Saturday evenings. They tended to be pre-empted by early diners. The waiter said, "Nice minute steaks, ladies? Broiled chicken? There's channel sole and filet of sole with a white wine sauce and—"

Florence Wainright waved a slowly impatient hand at him and held her menu rather close to her eyes and read it. She said, "What is the soup of the day?"

"Cream of spinach."

Florence shuddered, which Lyle found entirely reasonable. Florence said, "Chef's salad."

"Anything to start with? Oysters?"

"Chef's salad," Florence Wainright said. "And—"

Her plump white fingers touched her empty glass.

"A minute steak, rare," Lyle said. "If it won't take too long. I know the kitchen closes—is supposed to close—at nine."

The waiter said, "Yes'm. Chef's salad. Minute steak rare."

He went off. A bus boy in a longish, whitish apron took place plates away and put napkins and silver on the table; he brought bread in a basket with a napkin over it and a small dish of butter squares on ice. He looked at the two empty glasses. He looked at Lyle.

"Please," Lyle said. The bus boy said, "Yes, Miss Mercer," and took away the glasses. Florence Wainright put her elbows back on the table and red-tipped fingers again against her cheeks.

Lyle pulled the napkin from "assorted breads." She held the basket across the table. Florence looked at it thoughtfully and shook her head. She said, "I'm not one for bread, dear," with something like reproach in her soft voice. And with a little blur in her voice. Lyle spread butter for herself. It bobbed on ice which was turning to water; it was evasive. She broke a roll which wasn't warm, for all the shielding napkin, and put butter on it. The roll crackled between her teeth and its crackling sound seemed very loud. She thought all those left in the room would hear her chomping the crusty roll and would stare at her. She thought, They'll think, the poor thing, her mother's drunk. Or they would think, Who's that city woman Lyle Mercer is getting drunk with? She thought, It was a mistake to order steak. Steak takes too long. I want to be some place else.

But the food did not take long. The waiter served chef's salad from a wooden bowl. He put steak in front of Lyle and said, "Very hot plate, miss." Lyle's hunger, which had been overlaid, pressed down, by bored embarrassment, revived. The steak was good and almost rare, and the French fries which came with it—as, Lyle suspected, a token of the waiter's sympathy—were crisp. Put your mind on food and the taste of food, Lyle told herself. She managed it.

Florence Wainright pushed salad back and forth on her plate. Now and then, rather uncertainly, she lifted a forkful of salad to her mouth. Not all of it got there; chef's salad can be elusive food. After a time, but as Lyle was finishing her steak, Florence put her fork down on the plate and said, "Robert says I eat like a bird." She looked reproachfully at the place her glass had been. She said, "I mean Paul says that. I keep forgetting things."

Then she began to cry.

Lyle said meaningless words. She said, "There, dear. There, Mrs. Wainright." She looked around the room. The waiter was not in sight. But then Agnes was in sight. Blessedly in sight. Lyle gestured, feeling the movement of her hand and arm jerky, awkward. Agnes came and said, "Yes, Miss Mercer?" and Lyle said, "Coffee, please, Agnes." Agnes said, "Right away, Miss Mercer," with no overt sympathy in her voice. She went toward the kitchen, walking more rapidly than she usually did. She came back with cups and a metal pot and poured coffee from pot to cups.

Florence looked at the steaming cup. She said, "I drink Sanka at nights, miss."

"And if you'd get our check," Lyle said to Agnes and Agnes said, "Right away, Miss Mercer."

"Sanka," Florence said. "I don't sleep very well."

"That's Sanka," Lyle said. "Just drink some of it, dear."

"What you think is you think I'm drunk," Florence Wainright said. "That's what you think, dear."

"Of course not," Lyle said. "Drink your coffee. I mean, Sanka."

Florence lifted her cup and a little of its contents sloshed into the saucer.

"At home," she said, "they always put little paper doilies under the cups."

"Yes, dear," Lyle said. "Drink your coffee, Mrs. Wainright."

"Florence."

"Of course," Lyle said. "Drink your coffee."

She drank her own. It was hot and good. She hoped that, to Florence Wainright, it would taste like Sanka, whatever Sanka tasted like. She poured more coffee from the pot into her own cup and looked at Florence's, which was still almost full. She said, "Drink your Sanka while it's hot, dear."

Florence drank a little. She said, "I told the girl Sanka. This isn't Sanka." But she drank again. She put her cup down. She said, "There ought to be little paper doilies. It's all messy."

"Drink your coffee," Lyle said.

How did I get into this? Lyle thought. How am I going to get her home? She's not up to driving and if she drank all the coffee in the world she wouldn't be up to it. If I drive her home, how am I going to get home myself? Oh, damn, damn, damn.

Agnes brought two checks. The bar check was considerably larger than the check for food. "One martini, ex." That was right. "Five bour." Really five? It was a wonder Florence Wainright could still sit reasonably upright on her chair. Upright, steadied by elbows on the table and fingers to her cheeks; look-

61

ing down at a plate with chef's salad still on it and crying, softly now.

Lyle signed her father's name to both checks and put her own initials under the signature. She pushed her chair back and stood up and went behind Florence Wainright's chair and put her hands on the blonde woman's shoulders, pulling her back. She said, "Come on, dear. It's time to go home."

Florence said something, so softly and in so blurred a voice that Lyle had to lean down and say, "What, dear?"

"Have to pay," Florence said.

"It's all right, dear," Lyle said. "It's taken care of."

"Guest," Florence said.

"Yes, dear. You can pay me back when—when you're feeling better."

"Headache. Dreadful headache," Florence said. "Worse than this afternoon."

"Yes, dear. Time to go home."

She pulled up on the bent shoulders and, to her relief, Florence put both hands on the table and pushed herself up. Standing, she swayed a little, and Lyle kept both hands on the plump shoulders. Agnes, who had picked up the signed checks but not gone away with them, said, "Help you, Miss Mercer?"

Florence Wainright said, "Who are you, miss?" Lyle said, "She's just got a bad headache." Agnes said, "Yes, Miss Mercer. Headaches can be bad things."

Turned in the direction they must go—turned toward the impossibly long way across the big room—Florence began to walk. She walked very carefully; looked very carefully at the floor. But she walked. Lyle kept an arm about her waist and thought that all the people left in the room must be looking at them. She did not look at anybody.

They reached the door into the lobby. Mrs. Oliphant was using a little adding machine. She looked up and said, "Oh. Good night, Miss Mercer. Mrs. Wainright. I hope you en-joyed—"

She stopped and started to get up.

"She has a bad headache," Lyle said. "Good night, Mrs. Oliphant. It was a fine dinner, as always."

"Saturday nights," Mrs. Oliphant said. "And these waiters

they send up from the agency. I have to add everything over again."

Florence turned toward the main entrance door. It would be longer that way; that way one half circled the long building. Across the lobby, through the taproom, out the taproom door to the parking lot. (And then, obviously, drive Mrs. Paul Wainright home and trust there would be someone in the big hilltop house to drive her back again to the Volks.)

The taproom was not nearly so empty as the dining room had been. Most of the tables around the wall were occupied, and most of the occupants were men. And at the end near the bar the dart game was still going on.

Florence Wainright stopped halfway across the room and looked down it at the men playing darts. She said, "Darts?" and then, on a note of pleased recognition, "Darts! I'll have to tell Paul. I'm sure he doesn't know."

It was warm in the taproom. It was also smoky.

"Come on, dear," Lyle said. "It will be better outside in the air. Better for your headache."

Still with an arm around Florence Wainright's waist, Lyle took part of a step toward the door. It was only part of a step because Florence took no step at all. She did sway somewhat. And then she moved forward, impelled by another arm—an arm on the other side from Lyle's and around the blonde woman's shoulders.

"Rather got your hands full, haven't you, child?" Robert Wallis said, his voice grating down at her. "The lady's stoned."

"Head—" Lyle started to say and gave that up. "Mrs. Paul Wainright," she said. "And she sure as hell is. Five bourbons. On top of what she had earlier in the afternoon."

"Well," Wallis said. "Well, well. Mrs. Wainright. What had you planned to do with her, child? She's in no shape to drive."

"Drive her home, I suppose," Lyle said.

"And walk back?"

"Well. I—I don't really know, Mr. Wallis. There'll—I'm sure there'll be somebody at the house. Although she says her husband's in town. That's why—"

"Later," Wallis said. "Know which is her car?"

They were across the taproom, at the door which opened

63

to the parking lot. There were two stone steps down to the ground, and they took her carefully down them.

"Your car, Mrs. Wainright?" Wallis said. "Which is your car?"

"Over there," Florence Wainright said, making no gesture to indicate where "over there" might be. "It's white with a black top. It's—"

She seemed to run out of information about the car. She said, "Awful headache."

"Yes, Mrs. Wainright," Wallis said, his voice grating at her. "What kind of car? What make?"

"It's a Buick," Florence said. "Gran-something. It's white and it has a black top and—"

There were not too many cars left in the parking lot, and one of them was a black and white Buick Skylark, with the letters "GS" on its tail. They walked to it and Wallis said, "This the one you mean, Mrs. Wainright? And have you got your key?"

She swayed a black handbag toward him.

"Have a look, will you, child?" Wallis said. "I get lost in the damn things."

Lyle took the bag from Mrs. Wainright and had a look. She found a leather folder with two keys in it. She gave it to Wallis. He said, "Looks like the ones. Hold her up a minute."

Lyle held Mrs. Wainright while Wallis opened the driver's door of the black and white Buick and slid into it. He said, "Yeah," and the car's starter ground, and then the motor caught with a roar. The roar died a little but not a great deal. Wallis came back and put his arm again around Florence Wainright's shoulders. "Lot of motor for a small car," he said. "Idling rate's up. Let's get her into it."

They got her into it.

"Know how to get there?" Wallis said.

Lyle said she knew how to get there.

"O.K., I'll follow you," Wallis said. He got behind the Buick's wheel and the Buick's lights went on.

It was three miles or so from Van Brunt Center to the house above the Hudson on Long Hill Road. It seemed farther to Lyle, as she steered the Volks up the steep hills of the narrow blacktop, around its many curves. When her lights caught the house they glittered back from windows which, she thought, had no lights behind them. Then she saw lights behind windows on the second floor. And the lights of the Buick behind her were sharp, immediate, in her mirror. She swung the Volks in the graveled turnaround, so that it headed back the way it had come.

The Buick did not swing. It pulled up straight to the steps of the porch, and its lights dimmed. Lyle dimmed her own lights and swung out of her little car and crossed to the Buick, going around it to the side where they had put Florence Wainright. Robert Wallis came out of the Buick and went around it with her, and suddenly there was all the light in the world. A powerful, flooding light had come on in the porch roof. A tall, square-shouldered man came out onto the porch.

"About time," the tall man said and then looked at them and said, "Oh. Wainrights are out some place."

He came down the steps from the porch.

"Mrs. Wainright is out right here," Wallis said, his voice grating harshly. "You're not Wainright, I gather?"

The tall man looked into the Buick at Florence Wainright, who did not look at anybody; who appeared to be deeply asleep. The tall man said, "Damn!" and then, "No, of course I'm not Wainright. Bruce Gant. The lady's brother-in-law. Ex-brother-in-law, anyway. What's the matter with her?" He leaned into the Buick and said, "*Flo*," raising his voice. He got no answer.

"Mrs. Wainright's had a couple too many," Wallis said. "Lend a hand, will you?"

"Hell of a note," Gant said and lent a hand. The two men got Florence Wainright out of the car and onto her feet beside it. She walked a little, mostly was carried, to the porch steps and up them and inside the door Gant raised his voice and called, "*Lucy! You, girl!*" Lucy, still in uniform, came through a doorway at the rear of the entrance hall and said, "Yes, sir, Mr. Gant," and then, "Oh, the poor dear lady."

Lyle had followed Wallis and Bruce Gant and their burden up the porch steps and across the porch and into the house. She was not quite sure why. All in all, it was an entirely numbing evening. She stood just inside the door.

"We'd better get her upstairs, whoever you are," Gant said,

his voice still loud, as if Robert Wallis were some distance from him. "You, girl, show us where to take her."

Lucy said, "Yes sir, Mr. Gant. She's been getting these headaches recently."

She went, quickly, up a staircase at the end of the foyer. The men lifted Florence Wainright off the chair they had put her on.

"I'm all right," Florence said. "Headache."

They got her up the stairs and turned out of Lyle's sight. Lyle waited. After several minutes they came down the stairs.

"Where the hell's Paul?" Gant said, at the foot of the staircase.

"In town," Lyle said. "At least, Mrs. Wainright said he had a business appointment in town."

"I know that, Miss—" Gant said and paused for a name and was given one. He turned to the man beside him and said, "You say your name's Wallis."

"Yes," Wallis said, "I do say that. Come on, child. Our good deed's—"

"Ought to have been here an hour ago," Gant said. "Got him at their apartment in town and he said he was just leaving and for me to come on up here. What happened to Flo, you two?"

"She took Miss Mercer to dinner," Wallis said. "As you see, she got drunk. She was lucky Miss Mercer was there to take care of her."

"Look," Gant said, "I'm sorry. She'll be sorry tomorrow."

"I," Wallis said, "don't doubt it at all, Mr. Gant. Come on, Miss Mercer."

He moved toward the door. When he reached Lyle he put an arm around her shoulders. He said, again, "Come on."

"Look," Gant said, "get you both something. Way they'd want it."

"Not for me," Wallis said.

"Never saw Flo like this before," Gant said, and crossed the foyer to them. "Never got like this at home."

"She's had a bit of a jolt," Wallis said. "She'll tell you about it. Or her husband will." He paused a moment and looked at Gant, his head jutting at Gant. "Somebody brought her daughter's death up. In a strange, devious sort of way."

66

"Brought it up?"

"They'll tell you, probably," Wallis said and, once more and with more emphasis, "Come *on*, Lyle."

This time they went on. Halfway down the steep drive, Lyle had to pull almost off it as a car's lights blazed at them. She stopped the Volks, and a much bigger car went past them.

"Husband, probably," Wallis said.

Lyle drove the little Volks down the steep and winding and narrow road. She pulled it up in front of the two-story white building which housed the *Citizen* and, in an apartment on the second floor, the editor and publisher of the *Citizen*. She waited for Wallis to get out, but for some seconds he made no move to get out. Then he opened the door and put one foot out of it and stopped so and turned to her.

"Come on up for a minute," he said. "Something I want to show you." He laughed suddenly. "Not etchings, child," he said. "Come on."

She switched the Volks' lights off.

7

Robert Wallis unlocked and opened a door and reached inside. He flipped up a light switch. Two lamps responded, and Wallis stepped back and said, "Go along in." Lyle went into a square room which seemed to have more space than furniture —two low chairs and a sofa which did not match them, and, in front of the sofa, a large round low table on which books were strewn haphazardly. There were more books in shelves along two of the walls and, at an end of the room, a fireplace with logs symmetrically in it.

The lamps which had lighted when the switch was flipped were large, rather squatty, on small tables at either end of the sofa. There were tall, narrow windows, one with an air conditioner set into it, on either side of the fireplace.

"Sit down, child," Wallis said, and gestured toward the sofa and Lyle sat where she was told to sit. "Be with you in a minute," Wallis said and went through a doorway at the end of the room opposite the fireplace. He left the door open behind him, and Lyle, looking around the square room she had never seen before, heard the sound of what she took to be cupboard doors opening and closing again. Then Wallis came back with a tray with a bottle of cognac and two small glasses on it. He put the tray down on the round table, pushing books out of the way. He poured brandy into small green glasses.

"I don't—" Lyle said, and stopped because he was shaking his head at her. He also jutted his head toward her.

"Must have had quite an evening," he said. "Brandy'll be good for you."

He lifted his own glass and waited until she had lifted hers and sipped from it. Then he sipped from his own.

"Quite an evening," he repeated. "Tell me about it, Lyle."

"She called me up," Lyle said. "Wanted to take me to dinner. Wanted to talk to somebody, she said. She was all right when she came in. But afterward—"

She told him of sitting across the table from Florence Wainright and of what she could remember of what Florence had said, while she still was speaking instead of crying.

"She was—oh, shaken up. Almost shaken apart. Because of having her daughter's death brought up again the way it was. Because her husband had had to go to New York on business and had left her alone. After a time—after several drinks—she didn't make too much sense."

"Any idea why she picked on you? They've lived here a year or so. Must know people. You'd not met her before?"

"Not until I went to ask about the advertisement. No. I don't know why, Mr. Wallis. Sometimes, my father says, it's easier to talk to people you don't really know than to friends. But I don't know whether that's true."

"About her daughter's death? That's what she talked about?"

"A little. And about her husband and—oh, I don't know. It all got fuzzy. And touching. And—all right, embarrassing. One thing she said, she thought whoever put the ads in the paper was hinting her daughter's death wasn't really an accident. But the ads didn't hint at anything, did they? Just offered a wedding dress and a gun for sale."

"And a bay horse," Wallis said. "Wainright used a rifle to kill a bay horse. Here."

He took a brown envelope out of a jacket pocket.

The envelope had, "Gant, Virginia," typed on it and, in parentheses, "Wainright."

"Brewster *Sentinel* morgue," Wallis said. "Drove over this afternoon and borrowed it."

He took newspaper clippings out of the envelope. One of the clippings was long; attached to it, at right angles, was a long strip. On the strip, in large type, she read: "HEIRESS DIES IN HUNT ACCIDENT."

"Read it," Wallis said. "Not too much about the accident that Heimrich didn't tell us. But read it."

She read:

A hunting accident, unique in the annals of the Brewster Hunt Club, cost the life of one of its members early Tuesday morning. For years the hunt has ridden to the hounds, jumping the low stone fences, crossing the green fields of the open land around our community without mishap. The hunt has become a tradition, carrying on the sport pursued by the ancestors of many of our leading citizens, and reaffirming the rural character of the town.

She looked up and Wallis's smile seemed to slit his face into another face. He nodded his head.

"Goes on that way for several paragraphs," Wallis said. "Carrying on a tradition himself, Ed Wiley is. Years ago the same paper—another publisher but the same paper—ran a story which used half a column to explain the safety of a gas heater before it got around to reporting that one of them had blown up on Main Street and killed two people and set a building on fire. Quite a curio in the trade. Only takes Ed four paragraphs to get to the accident."

Lyle read:

The victim of the tragic accident Tuesday morning was Miss Virginia Gant, 20. She was the daughter of the late Robert Lee Gant, of Virginia, and the former Mrs. Gant, now the wife of the distinguished architect, Paul Bryson Wainright. According to Mr. Wainright, who was riding with his stepdaughter, her bay hunter, Rex, refused a jump. Miss Gant, although an accomplished rider, was thrown into a stone wall and suffered head injuries from which, according to Dr. William Benson, who was riding with the hunt, she died almost at once.

Lyle looked up again.

"No," Wallis said, "nothing about the accident we hadn't heard. Skim down. About the bottom of the first column."

He leaned toward her and ran a finger down the clipping.

He said, "There," and stopped the finger's movement. Lyle read:

Miss Gant was engaged to be married to Andrew Pointer, a writer, and the wedding had been tentatively set for next June, a few weeks after Miss Gant would have attained her twenty-first birthday, at which time she would have inherited a trust fund set up in her behalf by her late father, a wealthy retired corporation head. The exact amount of the trust fund has not been revealed, but is reported to be in excess of one million dollars.

Mr. Pointer was a house guest of the Wainrights at the time of the fatal accident, as was Bruce Gant, younger brother of the late Robert Lee Gant. He . . .

Lyle came to the end of the column. Another strip of newsprint was clipped to it.

. . . was riding with the hunt, but was several fields in advance of Miss Gant and her mother and stepfather. Mr. Pointer, who is the author of several television shows and at present of an afternoon TV serial entitled "In Dead of Night," was not with the hunt, but was working in a guest room in the Wainright house.

Mrs. Wainright is prostrated by her daughter's death, according to Dr. Benson, and is under sedation. Mr. Wainright, who rode back to the scene after helping to return his stepdaughter's body to the house she had left so gaily an hour or so before and destroyed the injured horse, the unwitting cause of his mistress's death, was likewise not available to the *Sentinel* reporter.

Lyle looked up again and found that Wallis was sitting very close, reading with her.

"Yes," Wallis said. "Good example of how not to write, isn't it? And everybody comes out well, including the horse named 'Rex.' Go ahead."

She went ahead:

Mr. Bruce Gant acted as spokesman from the bereaved family. It was from him the *Sentinel* learned of Miss Gant's prospective inheritance. Mr. Gant, together with Mrs. Wainright and a Warrenton, Virginia, bank, had served as trustee for the fund set up in Miss Gant's behalf. According to Mr. Gant, his niece would have received the principal sum, which he declined to estimate, on her twenty-first birthday. It is his understanding that the principal now reverts to Virginia's mother and, in smaller part, to himself.

"Not that I want it," Mr. Gant told the *Sentinel*. "Not this way —not through dear Ginnie's death, God knows."

From other sources, the *Sentinel* learned that Bruce Gant inherited the several hundred acres of the Gant estate at the time of his brother's death. The estate, in the rolling country of Virginia, has been in the Gant family since before the Civil War. Mr. Bruce Gant is a well-known breeder of hunters and operates the hereditary estate as a highly successful horse farm. He also breeds thoroughbreds, one of which finished third in the Kentucky Derby three years ago. One of his hunters, ridden by Mr. Gant himself, was the winner of a recent jumping contest held in northern Connecticut.

Funeral services for Miss Gant were to have been held today (Thursday) at St. Stephen's Episcopal Church. The body will be taken to Virginia for burial in the Gant private cemetery.

Lyle put the clip down in her lap and Wallis looked at her and waited. When she did not speak for several seconds he said, "Make you think of something?"

She still was silent for several seconds.

"While she was still making some sort of sense," Lyle said, "Mrs. Wainright said something about her husband's not having to work so hard. She said, 'Particularly now, the way things are now.' And she said the same thing—pretty much the same thing—a moment later. Something like, 'There's so much money now.'"

Wallis jutted his aggressive head again, this time away from Lyle Mercer. Then he nodded.

*　　*　　*

When they went in from the terrace to the big living room of the house which once had been a barn, Merton Heimrich lighted the fire. They did not really need a fire, although the temperature had gone down with the sun's going. But a fire is a pleasant thing to sit in front of and have dinner in front of. After dinner, Michael said, "Mother. Dad. There's a folk-song program I'd rather—"

"Channel Thirteen?" Susan said.

He looked at her through grave gray eyes and said, "Well— yes, Mother." Then he said, "I beat Tom Wilson today, Dad. The first time I ever have. Seven-five."

"That's fine," Merton Heimrich said.

72

"Only," Michael said, "we played another and he won it. Six-three." He paused again. "The leaves are getting all over the courts," he said. "You get funny bounces. It's the ash trees, mostly."

"Ash leaves fall early," Heimrich said.

"I guess they do," Michael said. He pushed his chair back from the table and looked at the watch on his wrist.

"Yes," Susan said. "Don't miss it, Michael."

Michael stood up and Colonel, with evidently more difficulty, heaved up from in front of the fire. Michael said, "No, Colonel. You know you don't like folk songs."

Colonel looked at god from reproachful brown eyes.

"No," Michael said, "all you do is whimper at them. Why don't you go find your cat?"

Colonel gave a very small woof and thumped down again. He put his head on his outstretched forepaws and looked up sadly, a rejected dog.

"Quit acting," Michael Faye told the dog. He said, "Good night, Mother. Good night, Dad," and went down the big room toward the room of his own, and the portable TV, also of his own. After a minute or two they could hear, muted and distant, music from the television set. It was folk music, all right. It sounded as if the folk were very sad.

"Can you ride a horse?" Merton Heimrich asked his wife, who said, reasonably enough, "What on earth, Merton?"

"Just, can you ride a horse?"

"If you mean jump one over a stone wall—"

"No," Heimrich said. "Look at a stone wall, maybe. Can you?"

"Not since I was quite a little girl," Susan said. "My father sent me to riding school. It was a long time ago. Merton. We had one horse. And a stable with six stalls. I don't know whether I still could."

"Probably," Merton said, "it's like riding a bicycle. Or skating. They say—"

"I know what they say, dear. Probably they're wrong. Anyway, I haven't got the right clothes and we haven't got a horse."

"We can rent horses," Heimrich said. "And slacks will be all right."

"Probably I'll fall off," Susan said. "When? And, I suppose, over near Brewster?"

"You can hold on tight," Heimrich said. "Tomorrow morning, I think. Yes, over near Brewster."

"You said," Susan told him, "that there wasn't anything you could do. That it wasn't a matter for police action. You've changed your mind?"

"It began to bother me a little after they'd gone," Heimrich said. "That is, something began to puzzle me. Why a telescopic sight?"

She raised eyebrows above gray eyes so like her son's. She shook her head.

"In the want ad," Merton said. "A gun with a telescopic sight."

"And," Susan said, "in the other one a wedding dress they say never existed. And a bay stallion."

"Yes," Heimrich said. "And a bay stallion. Who's dead, I think. Dead and long buried. Who was shot in the head a little more than a year ago because he had a broken leg."

Susan said, "I was listening too, darling. I still don't—"

"If you're going to kill an injured horse," Heimrich said, "you walk up to him and put a gun against his head and pull the trigger. You don't need a telescopic sight for that. You don't need any sight at all."

"I don't know anything about guns," Susan said. "I don't want ever to know anything about guns. I don't think there ought to be any."

"They come into your husband's trade, dear," Heimrich told her. "As long as we let other people have them."

"What they could do," Susan said, "is to make it illegal to sell ammunition. Except to policemen and, I suppose, armies. Then they could keep their guns. Or they could fight wars, if they insist on fighting wars, with bows and arrows."

"Yes, dear. And people die of arrow wounds. And it's not too difficult to make gunpowder. You'd go some place and knock on some door and say, 'Nick sent me.' They'd run ammunition in from Canada."

"You make it sound hopeless."

"Oh," Heimrich said, "it would probably be very inferior gunpowder, dear. Half the time it wouldn't go off. Will you ride horseback with me tomorrow?"

"I could just—oh, go to church or something."

"A canter in the cool of the morning," Heimrich said. "And if your horse bolts, I'll gallop after you and pluck you from the saddle."

"All right," Susan said. "Maybe it will rain. Can you ride, darling?"

"When I was a very young trooper," Heimrich said. "In the western part of the state. They made us learn. Maintain a tradition."

"You!" Susan said. "Before the invention of the internal-combustion motor, I suppose."

"Well," Heimrich said, "there were a few cars wheezing around the roads. And we rode motorcycles a bit. Yes, I think I can still ride a horse. If they can find one big enough."

She laughed at that. Then, gravely, she said, "Yes, m'lord, I will ride with you tomorrow."

They had left the front door open to moderate the heat from the fire they didn't need but liked to look at. The screen of the door rattled loudly. The big black cat named Mite banged halfway up and clung and yowled. Colonel got up and went to the door and looked up at the cat and woofed at him. Then Colonel turned and woofed at Merton and Susan Heimrich. There was reproach in his woof, and a little urgency.

"Yes, Colonel," Susan said. "I know he's stuck. He'll never learn." Then she said, "All right, Mite. I'm coming."

Mite said, "Wow-ow!" He shook the screen.

When cats jump against a screen door, to indicate that they have come home and would like to get in at once, their claws get stuck in the screening. It is quite true that they are slow to learn this and are disconcerted by it.

Susan opened the screen door, with Mite on it, and Mite made sounds indicating agony. Slowly, a claw at a time, Susan disengaged the big black cat. He wriggled for a moment in her arms and then began to purr. She carried him into the big room and put him down beside Colonel, who put his tongue in a licking position for his cat who had been in peril. Mite, who

75

prefers to lick himself, said, "Yah," and went off at a trot toward the kitchen to see if he had left himself any dinner. There was a distant crunching sound as he ate his "bullets," which, after finishing his junior beef, he left for emergencies.

Susan closed the front door and went back to the fire and said, "I suppose at the crack of dawn?"

"In the cool of the morning," Merton told her.

"I ought to have jodhpurs," Susan said. "When I was a little girl, when I was the Upton brat, I had jodhpurs. My father thought they went with horses. But some of the girls wore overalls."

Heimrich said, "Yes, dear. You're fine in slacks. The horses won't mind."

"Be disdainful, probably," Susan said. "When does dawn crack?"

"An hour or so to Brewster," Heimrich said. "Say leave about eight?"

"It'll be Sunday," Susan said. "But all right."

"Set it up," Merton said, and crossed the room to the telephone. He dialed. He said, "Heimrich. Put me on to the Brewster substation, will you?" He was put on to the Brewster substation, New York State Police, and got, "State Police, Trooper Henderson," and, when Heimrich identified himself, "Sir!" An inspector, Heimrich was learning, gets a more intense "Sir!" than a captain.

"Some place around there my wife and I can rent horses tomorrow morning?" Heimrich said.

"Jeff Brent's," Trooper Henderson said. "Shall I set it up, Inspector?"

"Appreciate it," Heimrich said. "Nine-thirty or thereabouts. Tell them to make mine a big one."

Henderson said, "Sir." Then he said, "You come by the station, Inspector, and I'll guide you over. It's a little complicated. Up toward Carmel, but there are a couple of turnoffs."

"A little after nine," Heimrich said, and put the telephone in its cradle.

Susan wasn't in the room. She had pulled the screen in front of the dying fire and her heels were clicking from the bedroom.

Heimrich turned off the lights and went toward their bedroom, hoping that Jeff Brent would have a big horse—a horse big enough for a hippopotamus. He also hoped that he had not forgotten how to ride a horse. . . .

*   *   *

Trooper Henderson, who was tall and in his twenties and immaculate in his uniform, stood at attention in the station-house and said, "Ma'am. Sir. Trooper Henderson." He looked as if he were about to salute the big man in a turtle-neck sweater and gray slacks and the slender, gray-eyed woman in a yellow pull-over and dark green slacks. He did not salute, but his eyes flickered briefly when he looked at Susan. Most men's eyes flicker slightly when they look at Susan Heimrich, who is built for the wearing of slacks.

Henderson went ahead of them on a motorcycle—went along the Brewster Main Street, which ended in a railroad station, turned right there and, after a few blocks, left where a sign pointed to Carmel, New York. The Buick followed the motor-cycle around several turns and on roads which grew more and more narrow. They stopped at a long building with a sign, "Brent's Boarding Stable," beside it, and a horse neighed in-side the stable and a thick-set, gray-haired man came out of it and said, "Hiyah, Frank boy. All set."

The Heimrichs, with the car pulled into parking space, got out of it. Henderson said, "Inspector Heimrich, Jeff. Mrs. Heim-rich." Brent said, "Hiyah, folks. I'll bring 'em out."

"I hope they're gentle," Susan said, and Jeff Brent said, "Like lambs, lady," and went into the stable. He was gone several minutes. He came out leading a big black horse with a white blaze on his forehead. Behind him, a boy of about fifteen led a brown mare. Both horses were saddled.

Susan stroked the mare's nose and the mare made a small gurgling sound, evidently of approval. The big black gelding looked at Heimrich, Heimrich thought with reproach.

Brent looked at the mare and at Susan and said, "Shorten the stirrups for you a little, Mrs. Heimrich. We call her Lady."

Susan said, "Good morning, Lady." Brent shortened stirrups. The gelding continued to look thoughtfully at Merton Heimrich. "We call him Achilles," Brent said, over his shoulder, shortening a stirrup. "Man I bought him of called him that." He straightened up. He said, "Don't make any difference to him, I've noticed. How long will you be wanting them, Inspector?"

"A few hours," Heimrich said, and watched Susan swing up on the mare. She leaned down and stroked the mare's neck. The mare went part way up on her hind legs and came down again and turned her head and looked at Susan, who sat lightly and with assurance as the horse moved. "Good girl, Lady," Susan said to the horse.

I ought to have brought a stepladder, Merton thought and said, "Good boy, Achilles," and put a foot in a stirrup, and it all came back to him and he swung up lithely. Achilles, Heimrich thought, shrugged his shoulders—probably as part of a sigh —but made no other comment.

"All I say is, don't get them lathered up too much," Brent said up to Heimrich.

"No," Heimrich said. "You board horses for people around here, Mr. Brent."

"What it says," Brent said and pointed to his sign.

"Man named Wainright ever board a horse here?" Heimrich asked. "Bay stallion? Named Alex, I think."

"Nope. Not that I don't know the horse you're talking about. One who balked a jump and threw that Miss Gant into a stone wall. That the one you mean?"

"Yes," Heimrich said.

"House Wainright had has got its own stable," Brent said. "People named Stirling own the place now. Don't ride as I know of, the Stirlings don't."

"So you don't know anything about the stallion Miss Gant was riding."

"Nope. Sure, after it happened, people said he was a bad actor. Bad-tempered. Nervous sort of horse. Could be he was. Can't say there was any talk about him before it happened."

"Did you know Miss Gant at all?"

"Met her. Pretty kid. Damn shame about it."

"Yes," Heimrich said. "Could she ride well, do you know?"

"Like she was part of the horse," Brent said. "Like she was glued to the horse."

78

"Where the accident happened," Heimrich said. "Far from here?"

"Two-three miles," Brent said. He looked up at Heimrich and his eyes narrowed slightly. He said, "Frank calls you 'Inspector.' What kind? Police?"

"Yes."

"I'll be damned," Brent said. "I'll sure as hell be damned."

Heimrich didn't say anything to that, not knowing Brent well enough to predict his future.

"Up the road half a mile or so," Brent said, "there's a gap. On your right. You turn in there and it was two-three fields on across."

Trooper Henderson, who had been sitting on his motorcycle with one foot on the ground, said, "Four fields, more like it, Jeff. I'll show them. Probably get the bike through most of the way. Did before when we were checking things out."

He started his motor. Achilles twitched slightly, disapproving the noise. He was, Heimrich thought, a rather disapproving horse.

Henderson went up the road slowly, keeping just off the narrow shoulder. They hacked after him, Susan ahead on the brown mare. Damn it, Heimrich thought, she rides beautifully. Glad she's not watching me.

She did, then turning in the saddle. He rides as if he were part of the horse, Susan thought. And probably goes on thinking of himself as a hippopotamus.

After what Heimrich guessed to be a little less than half a mile, Henderson gestured and turned his motorcycle into a path which led to a gap in the stone wall. The path showed the marks of horses' hooves. Susan's mare followed the motorcycle, not needing to be guided. The mare had, Susan thought, been this way many times before. The big gelding followed the mare through the gap in the dry stone wall and into a wide, almost level, field which had once, Heimrich thought, been a pasture.

The field had not, he thought, been plowed for a century or so. The undulations a plow makes in soil remain long after the last furrow has been made. This stretching field was level—level enough for a motorcycle to cross it without jouncing much.

Henderson went ahead across the field, toward a distant low stone wall. On either side of the field, which was almost square, stone fences marked its boundaries.

In the field, the mare named Lady began to trot, with softness under her hooves. The gelding trotted; caught up and trotted beside Lady. The sun was bright on them as they rode side by side across the field, and Susan turned in her saddle and said, "I'd forgotten how good it can be. Let's join the hunt, Merton."

"I'd have to get a pink coat," Merton Heimrich said. "I'd look like hell in a pink coat."

And they both laughed, about nothing in particular.

Fifty yards from the boundary fence, Henderson signaled and veered toward the right—veered, Heimrich could see, toward a gap. Heimrich pulled lightly on the right rein, and the black gelding slowed to a walk and then turned his head and looked back at Heimrich. Heimrich said, "Get along, Achilles. The way I tell you."

The mare saw the fence and changed from trot to gallop. Heimrich yelled, "Hey!" to Susan and nothing came of it— nothing except that the gelding went into a trot after the mare and then, like her, into a gallop. He moved like a horse who was going to take no nonsense from anybody. Fences, Achilles thought—too evidently thought—are to jump. Gaps are for motorcycles.

Heimrich thought for an instant of reining the big horse in and realized, in the same instant, that it was too late for that. It was no time to change the big gelding's mind, assuming the big gelding had a mind to change. It was a time to tighten human knees.

The mare soared up, clearing the fence by several feet. She sits the horse as if the horse were a rocking chair, Heimrich thought, and felt the gelding rise under him. Then he and horse, still together, were galloping in another level field, Susan on her mare a hundred feet or so ahead.

Susan reined her horse down to a trot, and, beside Lady, Achilles, also was content to trot.

"It's like flying," Susan said and Heimrich said, "Hmmm," and then, "There was a gap."

"Gaps are for motorcycles," Susan said and he had never, Heimrich thought, seen her more gay. He also saw that across the field, two hundred yards or so away, there was another stone wall. This field, Heimrich thought, had been hayed, as had the other. Probably, since there had been enough rainfall during the summer, hayed twice.

Henderson came across the field diagonally on his motorcycle, bouncing a little.

"There was a gap," Henderson called to them, his voice raised above the racket of his motor, strangely loud in the open field—strangely alien to the open field.

"Our horses don't like gaps," Susan called to him and patted the mare's neck. "They think gaps are dull."

They went on across the field. Ahead of them Henderson swerved off again, this time to the left. It had been a little like flying, Heimrich thought, and let the big gelding have his head. Presumably, the horses had been this way before; been this way many times before. Presumably they knew that there was safe landing beyond the stone fences. Presumably—

Again it was rather like flying—flying on a resolute and assured horse after his suddenly so gay wife, so erect in her saddle, so light in it.

This field was like the first two, but not as level. They slowed their horses to a walk in it and waited for Henderson to snort up to them. The motorcycle bounced a good deal this time, and he gestured to them and they slowed their horses and then reined them in. Henderson braced his motorcycle and walked over to them.

"The next wall is pretty high," he said. "And there's a ditch beyond it. Most of them jump it, they tell me. Some use the gap. And the field beyond—it happened at the far end of it— is pretty rough. You'll have to take it easy and, I guess, wait for me to catch up." He looked at Heimrich. He said, "O.K., sir?"

"You came up this way a year ago?" Heimrich asked him.

"Me and Ned Bates," Henderson said. "We made it, taking it easy. They brought the Jeep out the other way. Show you when we get there."

He went back to his motorcycle and rode ahead of them, much more slowly. This time the horses were content to trot;

this time they were content, also, to go as reins told them, through the gap the snorting motorcycle used.

The field they went into rose rather steeply and boulders heaved out of it, and there were some trees. In this field the meadow grass stood high. Mowed once, Heimrich thought. Probably early in July. Not raked for hay. There was mat under the tall grass. Mowed only, he thought, to reduce fire hazard.

They picked their way across the field, the horses willing now to walk and inclined to look where they were going.

At the top of the rise, the field leveled again, fifty yards or so from another stone fence. They stopped there and waited for Henderson, whose route was circuitous. He chugged up to them and braced his motorcycle.

"About over there," he said, and pointed ahead. He cut his motor. Heimrich swung down from the gelding and led him to a tree and looped the reins around the tree. He turned back and said, to Susan, "You can—" and stopped, because she was already off the mare and walking the horse toward the tree to which the gelding was tethered. The mare neighed, not loudly, and, tied, nuzzled Susan. The gelding merely snorted at Heimrich.

"No," Heimrich told him. "You can jump going back."

Henderson walked ahead of them through the tall grass. They walked side by side.

"About here, I think," Henderson said, and stopped in front of a stone wall and pointed.

The wall here had fallen to some extent, as dry stone walls will. Stones had rolled off the top of it into the fields on either side. At places little was left of the wall except the foundation boulders—boulders which, a century ago—perhaps two hundred years ago—had been prised out of the earth and dragged into place on ox sleds.

"Along here some place," Henderson said, and waved a hand back and forth. "They can get a run after it levels off back there and it's all right on the other side. But a good many of them go around." He waved the hand to his right, where the wall was hardly more than the remnants of a wall.

Heimrich walked up to the wall and looked at it, and there wasn't anything to look at except an ancient wall that was tumbling down. He hadn't supposed there would be. Where the wall stood as it had been built it was some three feet high. He looked over it. The field beyond was level; was pasture land again. There, just beyond the wall, the fallen stones had been gathered up and piled, loosely, against the wall. And on the other side there were scars where horses had come down.

Normally, Heimrich thought, riders jumped only from the side he stood on. On this side the horses might land on loose stones and fall. If, as they said, the Wainrights had jumped back after their daughter had been thrown, they had taken a chance.

Heimrich looked to his right. About a hundred yards away there was a fence at right angles to this one. It had been kept up. Stones which had fallen from it had been put back, flat stones on top. He walked toward this wall and Susan walked with him. Henderson came behind them.

This wall, when they reached it, stood higher than the others had; there was a kind of formality about this wall. Beyond it, a field which sloped up had been mowed, although again not for the hay.

The rough-mowed area reached for some two hundred yards up the slope. Then it became lawn, stretching up to a big house, fieldstone with clapboard above it.

"Whose house?" Heimrich asked Trooper Henderson.

"The Stirlings'," Henderson said. "Used to be the Wainrights'. They sold it last winter. Too close to where it happened, people say."

"It is quite close," Heimrich said. "A few minutes' walk down from the house to this wall."

He leaned over the wall and looked down at the ground beyond it. He looked down at it for several minutes.

"Well," he said, "I guess we've seen about all there is to see."

A stone wall against which a girl had been thrown, Susan thought. Stones against which a girl had died. Another wall at right angles to it, and, beyond, a house of fieldstone and white painted wood.

Perhaps, she thought as they walked back to their horses, he's seen more.

8

They rode back the way they had come, jumped the fences they had jumped before. But it is different going back, Susan thought. It isn't so much like flying. He's gone away; he's gone back into his mind, the way he does. But it was merely old stone fences and fields and, beyond one of the fences, a big house.

They hacked back to Jeff Brent's stable. (Boarding. Horses for hire.) They slid down from their horses. Achilles turned and looked at Heimrich, and there was something familiar in the reproach Heimrich thought he saw in the horse's sad brown eyes. He placed it. Achilles reminded him of Colonel. What, he wondered vaguely, had disappointed the big horse? Not enough fences jumped?

Jeff Brent came out of the stable and gathered reins into his hands and led the horses into the stable. He came back and said, "Didn't want them long, did you?" and told Heimrich what it would be. Heimrich paid him. He said, "We didn't lather them up." Brent said, "I didn't think you would," and started back toward the stable. Heimrich said, "Got a minute?" and Brent came back. He said, "Something wrong about the horses?" with challenge in his voice.

"Fine horses," Heimrich said. "Good jumpers, both of them."

"Wouldn't win any prizes," Brent said. "Jump all right. Hunters, both of them. What's wanted around here."

"I wondered," Heimrich said. "I haven't ridden for a long

84

time. Jumped a horse for years. What would make a horse refuse a jump?"

"God knows," Brent said. "They get notions, maybe. I sort
of like horses, but nobody can say they're very bright. Worked
at Aqueduct when I was a kid. Exercise boy. Jockey told me
there's nothing so damned dumb as a horse. Said a horse would
run smack into a stone wall if you didn't guide him."

"I tried to guide Achilles toward a gap," Heimrich said. "He
didn't guide. He wanted to jump."

"Trained for it," Brent said. "Probably thought you didn't
mean it. Supposing he thought at all."

"About a horse refusing," Heimrich said. "Suppose—oh, suppose just as a horse was gathering for a jump something stung
him. Throw him off stride? Make him refuse?"

"Shouldn't think so," Brent said. "Depends on the horse."
He looked intently at Heimrich. "Getting at something, Inspector?" he said. "About this horse threw the girl, maybe?"

"Maybe. Say somebody shot a horse just as the horse was
set to jump."

"Depends on where you shot him," Brent said. "Kill him
and he sure as hell wouldn't jump."

"No," Heimrich said. "I wasn't thinking of a horse's being
killed, Mr. Brent. Just, say, stung. In the flank, maybe. With
a small-caliber bullet. From, say, a rifle a hundred yards or so
away."

"Never thought about it," Brent said. "Depend on the horse,
wouldn't it? Horse like Achilles. Steady-going horse. Probably
just think a fly bit him. Get a nervous horse, I wouldn't know.
Bad-tempered one, I wouldn't know." He paused for some seconds. "Stallions are mostly more jumpy than geldings. Or mares
even. Get excited, sort of. What are you getting at, Inspector?"

"I don't know precisely what I'm getting at," Merton Heimrich told Brent. "Just poking around, I suppose."

He walked over to the Buick, in which Susan was sitting. He
beckoned Trooper Henderson, and Henderson walked over to
the car.

"I think we'll stop by the substation for a minute," Heimrich said. "Maybe you can rustle us up a cup of coffee."

"Sure thing," Henderson said. "Sure thing, sir."

They followed him back through the village to the Brewster substation, Troop K, New York State Police. There was a uniformed trooper behind the desk there.

"Trooper Bates," Henderson said. "Inspector Heimrich, Ned."

Ned Bates stood up and stood stiffly and said, "Sir." The telephone on the desk rang, and he sat down and said, "State Police, Trooper Bates."

"Get the coffee," Henderson said and started toward a back room.

"Fine," Heimrich said. "Got a copy of the report you and Bates made on the Gant accident?"

"Sure, Inspector," Henderson said. "Want I should—"

"Coffee first," Heimrich said. "We're not in any hurry."

Not, he thought, after a year. A year and three days. They sat on wooden chairs at a wooden table and after a few minutes Henderson came back with two cups steaming on a tin tray. He put the tray down on the table. He said, "It's instant, sir. Get the report for you."

He went back into the rear room and Susan and Merton Heimrich sipped coffee. It was very hot and very strong. It was also very instant. Henderson came back carrying papers and put them down on the table and stood, erect, beside it. Heimrich said, "Sit down, Henderson," and Trooper Henderson, rather stiffly, sat down. Heimrich read an accident report. "In response to a call from the residence of Paul Wainright, Wildwood Road, Brewster, proceeded—"

It was official; it was reasonably terse. It reported that a girl named Virginia Gant, twenty years old, had been thrown from a horse into a stone wall and had died of head injuries; that she had been riding with her stepfather and her mother; that the horse, a stallion named Alex, had refused a jump and fallen and had broken a leg and had been destroyed.

"All correct," Heimrich said. "All right, Henderson, tell me what you remember. Who you talked to. Who was around."

"The doctor," Henderson said. "Dr. William Benson. Wainright, a few minutes. He was shaken up. Kept saying something about 'That damn horse. I kept telling her.' Did tell us how it happened."

86

"Mrs. Wainright?"

"Went to pieces," Henderson said. "They took her upstairs —a colored maid they had and Dr. Benson." He paused for a moment and said, "For a while we could hear her screaming. It—it was pretty bad, Inspector. Remember the way it was, Ned?"

He asked that across the room to Trooper Bates at the desk.

"I sure do," Bates said. "I sure do, Inspector."

"Inspector," Henderson said, "you think we slipped up on this? Ned and I? Hearing before a J.P., like always. Accidental death. You think we slipped up? It all looked simple enough."

"Naturally," Heimrich said. "Probably it was, Henderson. When you and Bates went to check it. Look at the place it happened?"

"Sure, Inspector."

"Horse still there?"

"There," Henderson said. "Dead. Two bullet wounds in its head."

"Nothing else you saw?"

"Broken right foreleg. We weren't thinking much about the horse, sir."

"Naturally," Heimrich said. "You went up to the house then?"

"Yes. We'd left the car there. Came down across the field and over the wall. Went back up to the house and talked to the doctor and Mr. Wainright."

"The girl's body was still there?"

"Yes. They'd—they'd put a sheet or something over it. Ambulance came while we were there, and they took her to the hospital morgue."

"Other people around?"

"Seemed like a lot," Henderson said. "Couple of young men. One rather skinny and they called him Andy, way I remember it. He was shaky, almost crying. He kept saying, 'I told her. I begged her.' Something like that. And—they had her lying on a sofa and he knelt down by it and put his arms around her and—and his head down on her. It was—well, it was sort of tough, sir. And mixed up. The way things are when things like that happen."

87

"Yes," Heimrich said. "Two young men. One of them named Andy. Broken up. The other?"

"Kenneth something," Henderson said. "Inspector, we asked them if they'd seen it happen and none of them had, except Mr. Wainright, who was riding beside her. And Mrs. Wainright according to her husband. She was in the next field, he said. The doctor wouldn't let us talk to her. But anyway—"

He shrugged his square shoulders.

"No reason then to think it was different from the way Wainright said it was," Heimrich said. "No real reason now, Henderson. Others there?"

"The girl's uncle," Henderson said. "Man named Bruce Gant. Brother of the girl's father, way I understood it. He was a ways ahead with the hunt and didn't see anything. Says he heard the shots when Wainright killed the horse and came back to find out what had happened."

"Perceptive of him," Heimrich said. "Lots of people shoot off guns around here. All around here. Shoot at woodchucks. At targets. At God knows what."

"I don't know," Henderson said. "Only that's what he said."

"Good ears, probably," Heimrich said. "Knew the shots came from near the house. Anyone else?"

"A good-looking woman," Henderson said. "Maybe in her thirties. Blonde. In riding clothes. Turned out she and this uncle—Bruce Gant, that's his name—had been riding together and she came back when he did. They were both maybe two-three fields away when they turned back. Came back by a dirt road they use when they hay the fields."

"This other young man," Heimrich said. "The one who wasn't skinny. He'd been riding with the hunt?"

"Not as far as where it happened," Henderson said. "His horse pulled up lame and he walked him back to the stable."

"Brent's?"

"No. Stable at the Wainright house. Wainrights used to keep several horses. This Alex and maybe four others. Empty now, the stable there is. Wainrights sold off the horses when they sold the house. The Stirlings aren't horsy people. Do a lot of traveling, they do. In Europe now. Told us the house would be empty, except for a man who drops in couple of times a week to check on it. So one of us stops around now and then and has a look."

"Then we won't have to set it up with them," Heimrich said, and Henderson said, "Sir?"

"Tomorrow," Heimrich said, "I'm going to send up a couple of men with rakes. Rake on the other side of that high wall. On the Stirling property."

"Rake?"

"Just to see if they can find anything," Heimrich said. "Been a year and the field's been mowed a couple of times. Not likely they'll find anything."

Henderson shook his head.

"Oh," Heimrich said, "like a cartridge case, naturally." He raised his voice slightly and spoke across the room. He said, "Anything to add to it, Bates?"

Bates stood up, stiffly. He said, "No, Inspector. It was like he says."

"Probably just the way it looked," Heimrich said. "An accident."

He stood up and Susan stood, and Susan said, "Thank you for the coffee, Mr. Henderson."

At the door, Heimrich stopped and turned back. He said, "The local newspaper make a lot of this?"

"Long story," Henderson said. "Ed Wiley let himself go."

"Yes," Heimrich said. "I supposed that. Man named Wiley edits the paper?"

"Editor and publisher," Henderson said.

Heimrich closed his eyes for a moment. Then he walked back and said, "Got a telephone book handy?"

They had a telephone book handy. Edwin Francis Wiley answered his telephone. Sure he'd be glad to drive in and meet them at the *Sentinel* office. About what, Inspector? Heimrich told him about what.

"Lot of interest in that all at once," Wiley said. "I could look up back issues, I guess. Thing is, I lent the morgue envelope to Bob Wallis, who gets out the *Citizen* over in Van Brunt. And last year's file copies are down in the basement and—"

"No need to bother," Heimrich told him. "I know Mr. Wallis. Happens I live in Van Brunt, Mr. Wiley."

They drove back to Van Brunt. There was nobody at the office of the *Citizen*. They drove home. There was nobody there, either, except Colonel, disconsolate on the terrace. He made disconsolate sounds.

"Michael was going to be picked up and taken to the club," Susan said. "For tennis. And Mite's gone off somewhere and poor Colonel's deserted."

Colonel whimpered at being named in tones of sympathy.

"Waffles all right for lunch?" Susan said. "The frozen ones you pop in a toaster? And sausage?"

"You've had a hard morning with strange horses," Heimrich said. "We can have lunch at the club."

"It'll mean changing," Susan said.

"Yes," Merton Heimrich said, "I guess it'll mean changing, dear."

They changed to clothes suitable for a terrace lunch at the Van Brunt Country Club. They drove the winding, downhill, way to The Corners and turned right and drove, again on a winding road, uphill to the club. The club's golf course, in the opinion of elder members, had been laid out by a mountaineer. Most of the shady tables on the terrace were occupied, and some people sat in the sun. The Heimrichs walked the path from parking lot to terrace, walking around carts for golf bags and carts (electrical) for people.

Most of the people on the terrace looked as if they had stopped off for sustenance between the first nine and the second. The sustenance seemed to be largely liquid. At the edge of the terrace the Heimrichs stopped and looked for a shady table. "Summer's staying late this year," Susan said up to her tall husband. And Robert Wallis stood up from a table—a shady table—on the far side of the terrace and motioned to two shaded, empty chairs. He beckoned and they went between tables, exchanging "Hiyahs?" as they went.

"Hello, Susan. Inspector," Lyle Mercer said. Susan said, "Hi," and thought that Lyle, who was always a pretty child, had never looked prettier than she looked then, in a sleeveless white dress, in the chair next to the one Wallis stood behind. Merton Heimrich said, "Morning, Miss Mercer. Wallis."

"Been trying—" Wallis said as the Heimrichs sat in the vacant chairs at the table for four, and as he himself sat. A boy in a white jacket who looked somewhat harried said, "Get you something, Inspector? Mrs. Heimrich?" Heimrich said, "Gin and tonic, Joe," to the boy, who was a senior at Van Brunt High School on weekdays and a club waiter on weekends. Heimrich looked at Susan and said, "Make it two gin and tonics, Joe."

"—to get you on the phone," Wallis said.

"We've been horseback riding," Susan said.

"I didn't know—" Lyle said and let it hang.

"We don't much," Heimrich said. "Neither of us has for years. Turned out we remembered how. Anyway, Susan did. Floated her horse over stone walls." He paused for a moment. "Over near Brewster, Mr. Wallis," Inspector Heimrich said.

To that, Wallis said, "Oh." Then he said, "I thought you felt there wasn't anything—" and broke it there.

"Second thought," Heimrich said. "What did you call us about, Mr. Wallis?"

"All right," Wallis said. "I still don't like to be had, Inspector. To have the paper had. I telephoned this Pointer—man who was going to marry the girl. He—say he came to mind."

"We agreed on that yesterday," Heimrich said. "Get him, Mr. Wallis?"

"Around midnight," Wallis said. "Earlier there wasn't any answer. He'd been out on a party, I gathered."

"That kind of party?"

"From his voice, yes. But he was coherent enough. And didn't have any idea what I was talking about. Want ads? What want ads? I told him what want ads. He said, 'Why the hell should I?' and then, 'Think it's something I want to be reminded of, whoever you are?' I'd told him who I was. He said, 'What the hell makes you think I'd plant ads like those?" Only thing is, Inspector, he was practically yelling at me. As if—well, as if he'd been caught up with. Put in a corner."

"You tell him why you thought he might have sent in the ads?" Heimrich asked him and said, "Thanks, Joe," for two tall glasses.

"That I understood he was going to marry Miss Gant," Wallis said. "That having her die the way she did must have upset him a lot. And that there seemed to be a chance that the ads had been put in by somebody who wanted to bring it all up again. Who wanted to upset the Wainrights. Somebody who suspected that there was something more than an accident in the girl's death and wanted the Wainrights to start suspecting too."

"And he?"

"Said, 'You're crazy, man,' and hung up. I tried to call him back and didn't get any answer."

"He said 'plant' the ads?"

"Yes."

"Say flatly he hadn't sent them in?"

"Not flat out. No. What I tried to call back to get him to do."

"You think he felt cornered," Heimrich said. "Because he had planted the ads, naturally. And that being asked about them excited him?"

"I thought it might be that way. Inspector—" He stopped. He said, "I'm horning in, I suppose. What made you change your mind about it, Inspector?"

"Now, Mr. Wallis," Heimrich said, "I'm not sure I have. Just thought of something that made me curious."

Lyle sipped her drink. She looked from one man to the other as they spoke.

"It started with my newspaper," Wallis said. "Miss Mercer and I told you about the ads."

"Yes," Heimrich said. "And got Susan and me up at seven this morning to ride on horses. No, there's no story, Mr. Wallis. I doubt if there ever will be."

"I'm not trying to dig up a story," Wallis said. He took a swallow from his glass. He said, "Oh, maybe I am. It's my trade. Mostly it's I don't want to be used. And—that I feel I slipped up. Anyway, that my paper did."

Heimrich said, "Naturally." He also closed his eyes. He drank without opening them. Then he said, "Did you happen to know any of these people, Mr. Wallis? You knew of Gant. The girl's father. Ever, say, interview him about anything?"

"What the hell?" Wallis said. He looked at Heimrich and Heimrich opened his eyes. "No," Wallis said. "I never did. Why'd you ask that, Inspector?"

"Curiosity," Heimrich said. "That's part of my trade, Mr. Wallis. As it is of yours."

"All right," Wallis said. He jutted his head toward Heimrich. "You didn't find out anything this morning? Or if you did you're sitting on it. Is that right?"

"I looked at a stone wall the girl died against," Heimrich said. "And, beyond another wall, at the house she'd lived in. I talked to the troopers who checked it out and found nothing to indicate it wasn't an accident. I asked a man named Wiley to look at the clipping of a story he wrote about it."

"Which I—" Wallis said and stopped as Heimrich nodded his head.

"Which you borrowed from Wiley," Heimrich said. "In the course of playing detective, Mr. Wallis."

"He isn't," Lyle said. "We aren't doing that. We aren't doing that at all."

"Now, Miss Mercer," Heimrich said, "perhaps I used the wrong words. You say 'we,' Miss Mercer?"

"Lyle had dinner with Mrs. Wainright last night," Wallis said. His voice grated. "We were going to tell you about that. This 'playing detective' business."

"Skip it," Heimrich said. "I used the wrong words. Tell me about it, Miss Mercer."

She hesitated.

"Tell him, child," Wallis said. His voice didn't grate. Well, Susan thought. Well, well.

Lyle told about the murky and embarrassing dinner she had had the night before with Florence Wainright. Merton Heimrich listened with his eyes closed. When she had finished it was some seconds before he opened his eyes again.

"You hadn't known her before you went there to ask about the advertisements?" he asked her then. "Her or her husband?"

"No. I did meet Mr. Wainright at the hunt-club breakfast. But no, I hadn't known them before. Oh, that they had bought the Kynes place last—when was it, Mr. Wallis?"

"Late last fall some time," Wallis said. "Perhaps early winter. Henry Peterson passed the word along, I remember. Made an item. With 'through Henry Peterson, a local real-estate agent.' He wanted it 'realtor' but there are limits."

Heimrich said, "Hmmm." He said, "Just wanted somebody to talk to, you say, Miss Mercer?"

"It seemed that way."

"But you did tell her you and Mr. Wallis had come to me about the advertisements?"

"It slipped out," Lyle said. "I hadn't planned to."

"She seemed sober when she joined you at the Inn? Got intoxicated later?"

"When she came in there was nothing to make me think she wasn't sober," Lyle said. "I thought that she had snapped back pretty fast. Earlier, at her house, she was—well, pretty wobbly, Inspector. But maybe it was a headache. She said it was. Maybe she had taken something for the headache that made her—made her droopy."

"When we took her home from the Inn she was stoned," Wallis said. "She passed out in the car. Her brother-in-law—man named Gant—and I had to pretty much carry her into the house and upstairs. Her maid, I guess, had to put her to bed."

"Gant?" Heimrich said. "Man named Bruce Gant?"

"Yes. Brother of her late husband. Makes him the uncle of the girl who got killed, doesn't it? And—wait a minute—he was staying at the Wainright house in Brewster when the girl was killed, wasn't he? It's in Ed Wiley's piece."

He reached into the inner pocket of his sports jacket. He tried other pockets. He said, "No. Must have left it at my place."

"I want to look at it," Heimrich said. "Pick it up after lunch. Anything special in it? I know Bruce Gant was at the house, Mr. Wallis. And several other people, apparently. Pointer, for one. Another man about Pointer's age. A 'Kenneth something,' according to the trooper who checked it out. A 'good-looking blonde, maybe in her thirties.' Who, according to the story the troopers got, was riding with Gant. They rode back when they heard shots. Anything about them in the *Sentinel's* story?"

"That they were house guests," Wallis said. He jutted his

94

head, not at any of the others. He made a light fist with his right hand and tapped his head with it. He turned and jutted his head at Heimrich. "Kenneth Gaitbridge," he said. "I'm pretty sure of that. The son of old friends of the Gant family. The woman I don't—wait a minute."

They waited a minute.

"Elizabeth something," he said. "Far as I can get. A cousin of Mrs. Wainright. Didn't describe her, but I suppose she could have been the good-looking blonde."

He put both hands on the table and started to push himself up from it. He said, "Take me fifteen minutes to drive down and pick up the morgue envelope. O.K.?"

"Finish your drink, Mr. Wallis," Heimrich said. "After lunch will be plenty of time. You're both sure that Mrs. Wainright was really, as you say, stoned when she left the Inn?"

"Inspector," Lyle said, "I watched her get that way. She had five bourbons. I signed the check for them. She—while we were at the table—she just gradually fell apart. It—it was awful to watch. She was—" Lyle stopped for a moment. "I was sorry and embarrassed for her and there wasn't any way to get her to stop. She—she just wasn't there, Inspector. I doubt if she'll remember any of it."

"Perhaps not," Heimrich said. He motioned to the waiter, and when Joe, still harried, came, Heimrich gestured toward his own empty glass. But Susan shook her head and Lyle Mercer pushed her half-full glass away from her. Wallis looked at his own glass, which was almost empty, and shook his head.

"Then skip it, Joe," Heimrich said. "Let's have a look at the menus."

Joe said, "Sure thing, Inspector," and went off. He came back with menus. He said, "Mike's getting to be quite a tennis player, Inspector. He said to tell you he's here and that he's had a sandwich and that he signed your name and is it all right."

"Tell him it's all right," Heimrich said. "And that if he'll wait till we've eaten we'll drive him home," Susan said. "If he wants to go home," Heimrich said.

They ordered. Lunches at the Van Brunt Country Club are sandwiches and salads. Lyle Mercer had a tuna-fish salad; the others had hamburgers. Heimrich said, "Riding horses works up an appetite," and had two hamburgers.

"Think what it must do to the horses," Susan said. "They get all the exercise."

They went in two cars back to the Center, and the Heimrichs waited in the Buick while Robert Wallis went into the *Citizen* building and came out of it with an envelope. He gave it to Heimrich, who said, "I'll get it back to you." Wallis went over to his car, in which Lyle still sat, clearly waiting.

"We're going out to look at leaves," Lyle said. "Mr. Wallis lives right here and never looks at leaves."

When they turned into Van Brunt Pass, which is one of the ways to their white house above the Hudson, Susan said, "The child's about twenty, Merton. How old do you suppose Mr. Wallis is?"

"Middle thirties," Heimrich said. "At a guess." He said nothing further until he had turned the car into High Road and off it up a steep driveway. Then he said, "Come to that, dear, I'm a lot older than you are."

"Not fifteen years," Susan said. "Anyway, we're different. Didn't you know that, darling?"

9

Sunday night a low-pressure area which had been lurking for days over New England and pulling up almost summer air from the south moved off the coast. There was a brief thunderstorm, which only momentarily cut off power. "It used to stay off for hours," Susan said. Colonel, who is antagonistic to thunderstorms, went to the door and barked at this one. "We're getting almost urban," Susan said, when the power came on again. Merton Heimrich closed windows, and the air that blustered at him was autumn air.

It was a bright and cool Monday morning, which was a break for two troopers with rakes. Trooper Henderson had showed them the place and Inspector M. L. Heimrich had told them where to rake—a strip at least ten feet in width and at least a hundred in length along a wall that marked the boundary of the land owned now by one James P. Stirling and formerly by Mr. and Mrs. Paul Wainright.

"A twenty-five cartridge case," Trooper Latham said. "They're not very big, sir. Be easy to miss."

"Try not to," Heimrich said. "Take your time, both of you. We're a year late already. A few more hours don't matter, naturally."

The air was reasonably cool in the field which sloped down from the fieldstone-and-white-clapboard house a few miles northeast of Brewster, New York. But the sun was hot on the two men with rakes. Latham took off his shirt. Trooper Jenkins kept his on. He'd never been able to tan decently.

The sun did not reach into Inspector Heimrich's office—a corner office now that he was no longer a captain—at Hawthorne Barracks, Troop K, New York State Police. With windows open, air flowed pleasantly through the office. It was suitable, and on the whole pleasant, to have fall come back again. There may be frost tonight, he thought, as he piled papers from the IN basket on the desk in front of him and, for the most part, put "M.L.H." on them and put them in the OUT basket. There were a good many more papers to initial than there had been when he was a captain. For the most part, then as now, the initials indicated that reports had been through channels and were ready for files.

Nothing over Saturday and Sunday of special interest to the B.C.I. A man had walked into a tavern in Peekskill with an automatic and begun shooting at everybody in sight. Two dead, one in critical condition. All of it the concern of the Peekskill police, not of the State Police, who intervene in cities only on request. A man shooting at a woodchuck had hit a neighbor instead. The neighbor was expected to recover. A couple in a Mercedes had missed a curve on Route 123 in Lewisboro and gone, at an estimated seventy, into a stone wall. It had happened at about two o'clock Sunday morning. The car clock, judging by what remained of it, had stopped at 1:59. Nothing living remained of the two in the car, who had been in their late teens. The boy's blood showed a high concentration of alcohol.

Nothing in the reports he read to concern M. L. Heimrich, as Inspector, New York State Police. Much to concern him as Merton Heimrich, a man concerned by many things—by guns and knives and kids who drove fast cars on narrow roads and counted on reflexes which alcohol had dulled to substitute for skill and experience they didn't have. And now never would have. Kids even younger than a young woman who had been thrown from a horse into a stone wall.

She, on horses, had been experienced. That, at least, was what people had said of her, told a reporter—probably Edwin Wiley himself—of the Brewster *Sentinel.* People get thrown from horses often and do not die of it. Arms go up by reflex to break falls, to protect the vulnerability of heads. Anyone wanting a girl dead would, surely, have thought of some more certain way to kill her. I'm wasting time, Heimrich thought. Because somebody put an advertisement in a weekly newspaper offering a wedding dress for sale and put it in to run on the anniversary of a girl's violent death. Because, if the girl had lived some months longer, she would have inherited the capital of a trust fund which apparently was large. Not germane to anything, Heimrich thought. If they find a cartridge case, which they will not, it will prove nothing.

He sent for the most recent edition of *Who's Who in America* and looked under the "G's" for Gant. Two Gants, neither named either Robert Lee or Bruce. Apparently Robert Lee Gant had not been as important as Wallis had thought him to be. Still—head of a corporation which had made a spectacular merger with another, permitting affluent retirement to some place in Virginia.

Of course, Heimrich thought. Wrong reference book. He sent for *Who Was Who in America*. It had to be rummaged for, but it was found.

GANT, Robert Lee, industrialist; b. Warrenton, Va., Jan. 7, 1895; s. Leland and Ruth (Albemarle) G.; ed. Warrenton public schools; grad. Choate; A.B. Princeton; grad. Harvard Business School, 1918; m. Florence Tracy, Feb. 17, 1945; 1 dau., Virginia. Emp. salesman General Products Corp. 1912; exec. v.p. 1936; pres. 1940; chmn. bd. 1953–58; bd. dir. Tootle Nat. Bank, Warrenton, since 1932. Served as ens. USNR, World War I. Mem. Warrenton Country Club, Warrenton Hunt Club, Princeton Club (Richmond), Standard Horse Breeders' Assn. Address: Gant's Courthouse, Warrenton, Va. Died Sept. 20, 1963; buried Gant's Courthouse.

Heimrich pushed *Who Was* back on his desk and returned to *Who's Who*. Wainright. Several. None with first name of Paul.

For some minutes Heimrich looked across his desk at an uninteresting wall. "Wedding dress. Size 10. Never used." "Winchester rifle. Telescopic sight." "Bay stallion."

They added to nothing. Paul Bryson Wainright, termed "distinguished architect" by the Brewster *Sentinel*. Not in *Who's*

Who. Who's Who is somewhat haphazard in the selection of its biographees. Conceivably, of course, the Brewster *Sentinel* was even more haphazard in its use of the word "distinguished." Heimrich sent for the Manhattan telephone directory. There were a good many Wainrights. Yes, "Wainright Paul B archt" with an address in West Forty-sixth Street; "res" with an address in the East Sixties. The East Sixties address was, Heimrich thought, in an area where apartments cost money. Which the Wainrights obviously had. The house in Van Brunt had cost money. So had the one near Brewster.

Adding to nothing, Heimrich told himself. Drop it, Heimrich told himself and looked at the uninteresting wall across his desk. Heimrich picked up his telephone and said, "Ask Lieutenant Forniss to come in when he's free, will you?"

Lieutenants are free when desired by an inspector.

Forniss is a large and muscular man; he is even taller, by an inch or two, than Heimrich. He came in and closed the door behind him and said, "Morning, M.L."

Heimrich's first name displeases him. Its use, by others than Susan, is not encouraged.

Heimrich said, "Morning, Charlie. Know somebody who'd know about architects?"

"Could be," Forniss said, not surprising Heimrich in the least. Charles Forniss, in their long association, had almost never failed to say "Could be," to similar questions. Regardless of the alley they needed to go up, Forniss always seemed to know somebody who lived on it. Or, anyway, at the end of it.

"In general, Inspector?" Forniss said.

"Specific," Heimrich said. "A man named Wainright."

"Nope," Forniss said. "No Wainright. Man named Fulton, though. He's an architect. Major in the Corps when I was."

For Forniss, there is only one "Corps," the United States Marine Corps. Forniss was a captain in it before he was a sergeant, and longer before he was a lieutenant, New York State Police.

"Haven't seen Major Fulton in a couple of years," Forniss said. "Gather he's a big-shot architect now."

"See if you can get hold of him, Charlie," Heimrich said.

"Ask him what he knows about an architect named Wainright —Paul Bryson Wainright. What his standing is in the profession. Anything your friend Fulton knows about him."

Forniss said, "Wainright, Paul Bryson. O.K., M.L." He turned toward the door and turned back. He said, "Because why, Inspector?"

Briefly, Heimrich filled him in on the "why." Lieutenant Forniss said, "O.K.," again and went out of the corner office.

Wasting my time, Heimrich thought. Wasting Charlie's time. Wasting the time of a couple of troopers who ought to be on patrol instead of in a hayfield. Nobody kills a girl by getting her thrown from a horse. Too chancy, for one thing. She had been young; the young are flexible and have dexterity. So—

Heimrich looked at his telephone and after some seconds picked it up. He got the squad room. Yes, Raymond Crowley was on duty. Sure, he would be told the Inspector wanted to see him, sir. Heimrich lighted a cigarette and got two drags from it and his door was knocked on. "Come in, Crowley," Heimrich said.

Detective Raymond Crowley was in his late twenties and tall and lean. He wore gray slacks and a tweed jacket which fitted so well that there was nothing to show he also wore a gun under it. Crowley stopped just inside the door and said, "Sir?"

Heimrich said, "Sit down, Ray," and motioned to the chair across the desk from his own. Crowley sat on it.

"Want you to do something for me, Ray," Heimrich said. "Down in a place called Warrenton, Virginia, there's a bank called the Tootle National Bank. I want to talk to the president of it, or to the senior vice president or somebody of that size. I'd like you to get him on the phone and say that Inspector Heimrich, and so forth and so forth, wants to talk to him about a matter of importance. Lay it on a bit. See what I mean?"

"Yes," Ray Crowley said. "I guess I do, sir."

"Pull what rank you can," Heimrich said. "Come to think of it, you're 'Lieutenant' Crowley. Maybe the president or whoever isn't the stuffy sort, but maybe he is. Impress him, Ray. Talk Harvard or something like that, Ray."

"Princeton would be better," Ray said. "To a man in Virginia. Also, Princeton is where I went, Inspector. There isn't any special way of talking Princeton."

"All right," Heimrich said. "Standard eastern American. We're very high-toned up here."

"O.K.," Ray said. "Suppose he'll be named Tootle, Inspector?"

"Anything's possible, I guess," Heimrich said. "Switch him on here when you get him."

"If," Ray Crowley said. "Stuffy ones sometimes just hang up, sir. Talk to him about, Inspector?"

"Just a matter of importance, Ray. Official importance. Just spread it on."

Ray Crowley said, "O.K., sir," and went. A trooper came in and partly filled Heimrich's IN basket and removed what was in the OUT basket. Heimrich put a handful of "in"s on the desk and read and initialed. It had been much more interesting to be a captain. When he was a captain, somebody else had read most of the "in"s. I'll get fat as two hippos, just sitting here, Merton Heimrich thought. Just sitting here, initialing and delegating.

It was ten minutes before the telephone rang. He picked it up and said, "Inspector Heimrich." It was not the way he commonly answered the telephone. He'd feel damn silly if it was, say, Charlie Forniss using the telephone to report on Wainright.

"Mr. Warren is on the line, Inspector," Ray Crowley said. "Mr. Howard Warren, executive vice president of the Tootle National Bank. Will you go ahead please, Mr. Warren?" Heimrich said, "Good morning, Mr. Warren." A man—a man with a light and pleasant voice, with only a touch of Virginia in it —said, "What may this be all about, Inspector?"

"A point has come up, Mr. Warren," Heimrich said. "About the trust fund established for his daughter by the late Mr. Gant. Mr. Robert Lee Gant."

"Point? What kind of point?"

"Mr. Gant was a director of your bank, I understand. A bank is mentioned as cotrustee with Mrs. Wainright, the former Mrs. Gant. I thought it might be yours."

"It was," Warren said. "All settled months ago. Reverted to Mrs. Wainright and Mr. Gant's younger brother. All legal and court-approved. What's your interest, Inspector?"

"I'd rather not go into that, Mr. Warren," Heimrich said. "Just that it's official. Mrs. Wainright was a resident of New York State at the time the trust was transferred to her. And to Mr. Gant, of course."

"My God," Warren said. "Don't tell me the State Police up there are tax collectors. Anyway, Mrs. Wainright has a lawyer up there somewhere. Hold it a minute." He spoke off the phone. He said, "Molly, get me the Wainright file, will you, honey?" Then, again to Heimrich, "I still don't get what you're after, Inspector."

"Entirely routine," Heimrich said. "Has to do with the manner of Miss Gant's death."

"Ginnie Gant was thrown off her horse," Warren said. "More than a year ago. Hadn't you heard about it?"

"Yes, Mr. Warren. We'd heard about it. Tragic accident. You speak as if you'd known Miss Gant."

"When she was a kid," Warren said. "Very pretty kid, Inspector. The Gant women always were. So were the Tracy women, come to that. Mrs. Gant—I mean Mrs. Wainright as of now—was a Tracy before she married Boblee."

The last sounded something, but not a great deal, like a word to Merton Heimrich. He repeated it.

"Called Robert Lee Gant that, if they knew him well enough," Warren said. "Ones who didn't call him 'the Squire.' Whoever owns Gant's Courthouse is called the Squire. Bruce Gant's that now, of course."

"Gant's Courthouse?"

"Just a name now," Warren said. "Was a courthouse before the War Between the States. On Gant land. This is costing your state money, Inspector."

"It'll pass a bond issue," Heimrich said. "The Gant place? Near Warrenton?"

"Ten miles or so. Three-four hundred acres, Inspector. Very pretty country. The Gants breed horses there. Always have since anybody can remember. Hobby with Boblee, mostly. Business with Bruce and Beth."

"Successful?"

"Listen, Inspector," Warren said. "Bruce Gant's a depositor with us. We don't discuss our depositors. You ought to know that."

"All right," Heimrich said. "Mr. Gant did, I gather, come into part of his niece's trust fund. When it reverted."

"Yes," Warren said. "That's a matter of court record now. Got a fifth of it. Mrs. Wainright got the rest."

"Since it's a matter of court record," Heimrich said. "How big was the trust fund?"

"Inspector, what is all this? Doesn't sound like a tax inquiry. Never did, you know."

Heimrich thought for a moment, closing his eyes to make it easier. This bank executive was forthcoming beyond most. He might also be outgiving.

"All right, Mr. Warren," Heimrich said. "Something has come up about the manner of Miss Gant's death. Nothing conclusive. Just—call it a doubt. So we're going through certain formalities."

"For God's sake, Inspector. She got thrown from a horse. In the papers. A good deal in the papers here, she being a Gant." It was his turn to pause. "She'd ridden since she was a child," he said, and spoke slowly, like a man thinking things over as he spoke. "All the Gants always had. The Tracys too, come to that. Most people around here do. Oh, get thrown now and then, like everybody else. Still—"

"Nothing really to show Miss Gant's death wasn't an accident," Heimrich told Warren. "The trust fund, Mr. Warren?"

"Not an exact figure—it involved various bonds and blocks of stock—but something over a million," Warren said. "Part of the income to the widow, while Ginnie was still a minor. The rest went back into the trust fund, to build it up."

"So—if Miss Gant had lived to inherit?"

"Up to Ginnie, far's I know. There'd be enough to go around, I'd say. And Ginnie always was a sweet kid."

"You said, Bruce and Beth," Heimrich said. "Beth, I take it, is Mrs. Bruce Gant?"

"Yes," Warren said. "For the last six months or so. Beth Tracy before that. Cousin of Flo Gant's. Flo Wainright's, as it is now. Should have happened years ago, people say. Only Bruce married somebody else. It didn't take, but the lady hung on. Didn't live at Gant's Courthouse, but hung on wherever she was." He paused again. "She didn't come from these parts," he said. "Up North somewhere." There was pity in his tone, not condemnation.

"I gather," Heimrich said, "the first Mrs. Bruce Gant did, as you put it, finally let go."

"In Reno," Warren said.

"Recently?"

"Last winter."

"Which would," Heimrich said, "have been after Miss Gant's death, naturally. After Gant knew he was going to get a fifth of —you said more than a million?"

"Substantially more. In four years, it had built up. Before that, Bruce probably couldn't—" He stopped himself abruptly. He said, "Nosir," making it one word. The word had finality. It occurred to Heimrich that Howard Warren had suddenly, perhaps a little belatedly, realized that he was a banker as well as a Virginian willing to talk of old Virginia families.

"You've been very patient, Mr. Warren. Very patient. We appreciate—"

But Warren spoke off-phone again and said, "Thanks, honey," and there was the faint sound of rustling papers.

"Here it is," Warren said. "Gilligan, Steinberg and Forsythe." He added an address in the East Forties. Heimrich wrote the names down and the address down. "The lawyers," Warren said.

"Yes," Heimrich said. "Thanks, Mr. Warren."

"Heimrich," Warren said. "Some Heimrichs down in North Carolina. Von Heimrichs, they were in the old days. Dropped the Von."

"No," Heimrich said. "I'm a New York Stater, Mr. Warren. For some—"

Forniss opened the office door and Heimrich motioned toward a chair.

"—generations," Heimrich said. "Not a Von in any of them, far's I know. Thanks again, Mr. Warren."

He put the telephone in its cradle.

"*Cui bono?*" Heimrich said. "Several did, apparently. Directly and indirectly. Any luck, Charlie?"

"Not too much," Forniss said. "The Major knew his name. That was about all. Inquired around a little and called me back. With not too much more. Wainright isn't one of the big names in the profession. No high-rises on tops of railroad stations. No houses cantilevered over precipices. Way the Major put it. Seems—"

It seemed, from Major Fulton's inquiries, that Paul Bryson Wainright, duly licensed architect, had come to New York some eight years before from, one man thought, Indiana. Another man thought Iowa. Mostly domestic architecture, one man thought. A few taxpayers, according to another. No professional associates, as far as any of those Fulton had talked to knew. "Sounds like a desk and maybe a couple of draftsmen operation," Fulton, former Major, USMC, told Forniss, former Captain. "Claude Langley's got a feeling he's hooked up with one of the prefab outfits."

"Happens," Charlie Forniss said to Heimrich, "I know a guy's in the prefab racket. So—"

So Charles Forniss, who knows guys in almost all rackets, called the guy he knew in the prefab industry. He struck pay dirt—rather shallow pay dirt, but that for what it might be worth.

Wainright was employed, apparently on a consultive basis, by one of the manufacturers of prefabricated houses. Mostly such houses were put together from standard plans. Now and then a customer wanted a special job—a customer with enough money to pay for one and, usually, not enough time to wait for on-the-site building. Enter Wainright, or another like him, to consult with customer and make drawings for a special house. Not too special; plans which would utilize, as far as possible, standard components already in the company's warehouse. But plans which would, to some degree at least, result in a house built to a client's special requirements.

Sides of houses still were trucked to building lots; roofs trucked to put over them. Kitchens came in units to fit spaces allotted. But the houses looked like houses and could be so lived in.

"Good sound dwellings," Forniss's friend, who was in the trade of supplying them, told Forniss. "We put them together in maybe a tenth of the time it would take to build them from scratch."

Was Wainright employed by the company for which he did designs?

The guy Forniss knew didn't think so. If Forniss meant on a fixed salary. Wainright had his own office; probably had clients of his own. He was available to the prefab manufacturer when needed.

"Sort of piecework," Forniss told Heimrich.

The guy Forniss knew wouldn't even try to guess what the prefab company—it wasn't the one he was associated with—would pay an architect for these semispecial plans. It would, presumably, depend on the complexity and, to a degree, at least, on the price the customer paid. There wouldn't, for Wainright, be any fortune in it. There wouldn't be the architect's standard ten-per-cent fee. Probably, if enough customers wanted nonstandard prefabs, there would, for Wainright, be a living in it.

"Could be," Forniss said, "it's just a side line for Wainright."

"Yes," Heimrich said, "naturally, Charlie."

The morning slumped back into routine—into IN baskets and OUT baskets. A man was found dead of a bullet wound in a motel near Yorktown Heights. Probably suicide, but not a contact head wound. And the man's car, which should have been in the numbered slot in front of his motel room, was not there. Heimrich sent Ray Crowley in a cruise car. The District Attorney of Westchester County wanted, on the telephone, a report on progress in the shooting—apparently by sniper—of an insurance salesman in front of his house on the outskirts of White Plains. He was told that there was work on it, but no conclusive progress. The next-door neighbor of the dead man had a target fastened to a tree, and he sometimes shot at it with a rifle. He damn well hadn't been shooting when good old Jimmy had been killed. He'd been in his office in White Plains. Well, perhaps he had just left his office. He sure as hell hadn't been shooting.

Reading and initialing papers. Telling Charles Forniss that

the mysterious disappearance of one Ruth Anderson, reported by her husband, was his case and to use whoever he needed on it; agreeing with Forniss that the blood stains found in the Anderson car needed more explanation than Anderson could offer. Anderson said his wife was all the time cutting herself, mostly when she was opening cans. Heimrich agreed that an automobile in its own garage was an odd place in which to open cans.

The District Attorney of Putnam County said that the arraignment of Arthur Jenkins, charge of murder one, had been set for Thursday morning in Carmel, and Heimrich would be needed as the State's first witness to establish the fact, and probable time, of the death by stabbing of Francis Lennos, who had shared a summer cabin with Jenkins. There was a three-car smashup, with one fatality, on Route 22 near Bedford Village. A trailer truck had jackknifed in Cross River, tying up traffic on Routes 35 and 124. Nobody hurt but a good many considerably annoyed. Not in the province of the B.C.I. The irrelevant flows across the desk of an inspector. It submerges wisps of curiosity.

Heimrich had a ham-and-cheese sandwich and coffee at his desk. He was smoking a cigarette with the coffee when the desk sergeant called to report that a Miss Mercer wanted to see him. "Says she has something to show you, sir."

10

She was pretty standing in the doorway to Heimrich's office. She wore a dark green dress with a white sweater over her shoulders. She had, among other things, very good legs. She was also, Heimrich thought, very young. Miraculously young. He stood behind his desk, feeling clumsy and enormous and said, "Good afternoon, Miss Mercer."

"I'm interrupting your lunch," Lyle Mercer said. "But I'm supposed to interview a man who's writing a book about the Hudson Valley, and there's a German restaurant around here he likes."

She spoke rapidly and she was, Heimrich thought, excited. Perhaps about interviewing a man who was writing a book. Heimrich said, "Come and sit down, Miss Mercer. They say you've something to show me."

"We found something," Lyle said. "That is, Bob—I mean Mr. Wallis—found it."

She came into the room and sat on the chair across the desk from Heimrich. She opened a handbag, which was of a green which matched her dress. She took a legal-size envelope out of the handbag and laid it on the desk in front of Heimrich. It was somewhat crumpled; it was also somewhat dirty.

"Sometimes, when the refuse men collect, things fall out," Lyle said. "Lose things. Pieces of paper and things like that."

"Yes," Heimrich said, and picked the envelope up. He stretched it between his hands to flatten it. He read, typed on the face of the envelope, "Advertising Department, The Van Brunt Citizen, Van Brunt, New York."

There was no return address on the envelope. It was post-marked "New York, N.Y. Grand Central Station. P.M." The date was blurred.

"Mrs. Allsmith is almost sure it's one of the envelopes the ads came in," Lyle said. "She remembers because it says 'Advertising Department' instead of the usual way, which is 'Want Ads.' And Bob—that is, Mr. Wallis—says if there's a sample of the typing, the typewriter can be identified."

"Usually," Heimrich said. "Particularly if the typewriter has been used for some time. If letters get a little out of line." He turned on his desk light and put the envelope under it and moved it this way and that; lifted it so the light was brightest on it. "The 'n' is a little out of line," he said. "I'm not a technician, but probably the lab boys could identify the typewriter that was used."

"Not all the letters," Lyle said. " 'The quick brown fox jumped over the lazy dog' would be better, wouldn't it?"

Heimrich, who also had learned typing in a high-school class —probably, he thought morosely, before this pretty child was born—agreed that "The quick brown fox jumped over the lazy dog" would provide a better sample, make things easier for the technicians. Supposing they found a typewriter that was suspect.

"Whatever this Mr. Pointer says," Lyle said, "Mr. Wallis thinks he—"

Heimrich smiled at her. He said, "Yes, Miss Mercer, I gathered he does."

Color came up into the young face across his desk. The young are easily embarrassed; many of the young blush quickly when they feel they have been gauche.

"I'm sorry, Inspector," Lyle Mercer said. She was told there was nothing to be sorry for. "We thought you'd want to see it," Lyle said. "Because he's so very proud of the newspaper and thinks it's been made party to a trick. To an unpleasant trick."

"Yes," Heimrich said, "I understand how he feels, Miss Mercer."

She stood up then. She said, "I'll be late."

Heimrich stood behind his desk. He said, "I imagine he'll wait for you, Miss Mercer."

"Yes," Lyle said. "Maybe he'll be cross. A good many writers are cross. But he'll wait." She went to the door and turned, with her hand on the knob. She smiled suddenly. "I wish I liked German food," she said and opened the door and went. Heimrich lighted another cigarette and poured more coffee into his cup from the glass jug it had come in. A trooper came and took papers from the OUT basket. He did not bring papers for the IN basket. Heimrich flattened the somewhat crumpled, rather dirty envelope on his desk and looked at it. It had not changed. The letter "n" was still a little out of line. Each of the six times it appeared it was out of line. It wasn't, probably, so because the key to which it responded had been pressed in a peculiar, perhaps halfhearted, fashion. And if whoever had typed the address was a touch typist, he had pressed the "n" key with his right index finger, which for most people is strong and sure.

A wisp, Heimrich thought. A wisp of the intangible, almost certainly leading to nothing. Brush away the wisp, which has no place in the mind of an inspector, who should direct and delegate and not get notions. I've wasted enough time on this, Heimrich thought. Paid out my own money to hire horses. Susan rides a horse as if she had ridden every day since she was a little girl. And it's been years since she was on a horse. If I were still a captain I'd have gone myself to check out this suicide, with no contact wound and a bullet in the head. And his car missing from where it should have been. Not that Ray Crowley isn't a bright young man; won't find out what there is to find out.

If there were a big one in the works, I wouldn't sit here frittering mind and time away, Heimrich thought. I wouldn't be chasing wisps of nothing. A girl died in an accident a year ago and somebody played a cruel practical joke and a middle-aged woman is upset and drinks too much. The troopers didn't find anything out of the way a year ago. And the county coroner didn't find anything out of the way. There isn't anything out of the way.

Heimrich got up and flicked a Manhattan telephone directory. "Pointer Andrew" with a number and an address in the East Thirties. He went back to his desk and got an outside line and dialed the number. After four rings he got, "'Lo?" in what amounted to a growl.

"Mr. Pointer?"

"Yeah?"

"This is Inspector Heimrich, State Police. I'd like to see you for a few minutes this afternoon."

"Look," Pointer said, "I'm working. And I've got a deadline. And what the hell do you want to see me about? I can't take an afternoon traipsing up to wherever you are. What's it about, anyway?"

"Want ads in the Van Brunt *Citizen.*"

"God damn it to hell," Pointer said. "Somebody said he was a newspaper man called in the middle of the night about those damn things. I don't know a damn thing about them. I told this guy I didn't. One of you people pretending to be a newspaper editor?"

"No, Mr. Pointer. A newspaper editor who thinks his paper has been involved in a nasty trick. Upset about it, he is. And I'm not asking you to come to the barracks. I'll come around and see you." Heimrich looked at his watch. "About two-thirty," he said.

"How many times do I have to tell you I work for a living? And've got a deadline."

"Shouldn't take more than a few minutes," Heimrich said. "After all, I work for a living, too. Two-thirty?"

"I'm damned if I see—"

"Two-thirty," Heimrich said, in a tone suitable to an inspector, New York State Police. He put the receiver back in its cradle.

It would, he thought, be interesting to see whether Andrew Pointer let him in or, however busy he was, however immediate his deadline, went out at about two-thirty and had a drink. Or didn't answer his doorbell. If he had not sent the want ads in, he might well do either. If he had sent them in, he'd probably let a police inspector in at two-thirty to insist he hadn't.

Heimrich walked down a corridor to Charles Forniss's smaller office. Forniss was saying, "Yep," into his telephone. He said it several times. He said, "All right, go ask him, then," and put the receiver back and looked up at Heimrich.

"I'm going into town for a couple of hours, Charlie," Heimrich said. "Like you to sort of sit in for me."

Forniss said, "O.K., M.L."

"I'll tell them at the desk," Heimrich said. "If all hell breaks loose, you can probably reach me at—" and gave Forniss Pointer's telephone number. Forniss wrote it down.

If he lets me in, Heimrich thought, backing his car out of its marked slot. He probably knows he doesn't have to.

He drove his own car—his wisp-chasing had already cost the State of New York enough in telephone tolls—around Hawthorne Circle and down the Saw Mill River Parkway. Traffic thickened on the Henry Hudson and thickened more on the West Side Highway, and it was slow going crosstown. He had to park a block away from the street number he wanted and walk back. But it was a fine, crisp day; a northwest wind was making the city hard-edged and bright. October can be the best of the city's months.

The house he wanted was a four-story "brownstone." It was built of brick, as "brownstones" so often were. In the entry hall Heimrich found a button and pushed on it. Floor-through apartments, he gathered from the spacing of the buttons. Andrew Pointer on the top floor. He waited and pushed the button in again. He held it there, his hope diminishing. But then the inner door lock clattered at him. He climbed three flights of stairs and pressed another button.

The man who opened the door was slight. He wore a yellow sports shirt and blue slacks and canvas shoes. He had thick brown hair and he wore it rather long. He did not, however, wear a beard. He had a clean-lined face; a broad forehead and widely spaced brown eyes. Heimrich guessed he was in his mid-twenties. Heimrich said, "Mr. Pointer? Heimrich."

"You've sure as hell loused up my afternoon," Pointer said. "I don't know a damn thing about these want ads you people are making so much over. But come on in."

Heimrich followed Pointer down a short corridor and into a long room with floor-to-ceiling windows at the end of it. Between the tall windows, set on a stand so that the light would fall on the keyboard, was a portable typewriter. There

113

was paper in the typewriter and loose sheets on the stand beside it.

After he had gone halfway down the room, Pointer turned suddenly and faced Heimrich. He said, abruptly, "What's all this fuss about a couple of want ads?"

"Apparently," Heimrich said, "they were meant to stir up a fuss. Mr. Wallis—he was the one who called you last night—told you about the ads?"

"I guess so," Pointer said. "It wasn't very clear. Something about a wedding dress for sale. And a horse and a gun."

"Yes," Heimrich said. "Signed by Paul Wainright. On the typewriter. He says he didn't mail them in." He paused for a moment. "Whoever sent them in stipulated that they be printed on the anniversary of Miss Gant's death."

For a moment, Andrew Pointer's face worked. He said, "God damn it to hell. Oh, God damn it."

There was strain in his voice. It was, Heimrich thought, strain of memory—of bitter memory.

Pointer turned away from Heimrich abruptly and walked over to a chair and sat down in it. He dropped in it. He put his hands up to his face, covering his eyes. Without taking his hands down he said, "Oh, sit down somewhere."

Heimrich sat in a chair, facing Pointer. After a few seconds, Pointer took his hands down.

"All right," Pointer said. "Is that what you want? To break me up? So, all right, I loved Ginnie and she loved me and we were going to get married. Anything you understand, Inspector whatever-it-is?"

"Heimrich. Yes, I understand, Mr. Pointer. It was a shock, naturally. A bad shock. To you. To her mother and stepfather. To a good many people."

"Shock, hell," Pointer said. "It was horrible. She was gay and young and—" He broke off. "To hell with it," he said. "Maybe you're used to people getting killed."

"No," Heimrich said. "I'm not used to it, Mr. Pointer."

Pointer looked at him as if he were waiting.

"That's all," Heimrich said. "It's nothing one gets used to, Mr. Pointer. In the sense that violent death gets to be acceptable. You didn't send those want ads in?"

"I told this editor who was so worked up about it."

"Yes," Heimrich said. "Suppose you tell me. Just, flatly, that you didn't send in the want ads. Because Mr. Wallis, after he'd talked to you, felt you hadn't been definite. He called back to check with you and you didn't answer. Way you remember it, Mr. Pointer?"

"I guess so. All right, I'd been to a party and maybe I was a little fuzzy. Why the hell should I send in want ads like those? What would be the point?"

"To hurt Mr. and Mrs. Wainright. To—say, take your own bitterness about what happened out on them. Conceivably—" Heimrich closed his eyes and for some seconds did not go on. Then he said, "You weren't satisfied that Miss Gant's death was an accident? Wanted the questions in your own mind raised in other people's minds? Specifically, of course, in the minds of the Wainrights? And—went roundabout to it?"

Pointer merely shook his head, as if he did not understand. But then he said, "Is it a crime to send want ads to a newspaper? Weren't they paid for, or something? You say the instructions sent along with the ads were signed on a typewriter. Is that forgery or something?"

"No," Heimrich said. "Misrepresentation, of course. A rather unpleasant kind of practical joke. Speaking of typewriters, Mr. Pointer. Mind if I use yours for a moment?"

"What the hell?" Pointer said. "Now what the hell? Forget your notebook?"

Heimrich merely shook his head. But he got up out of his chair.

"Go ahead," Pointer said. "Play your games."

Heimrich went to the typewriter and sat in front of it. He reeled out the paper already in it. A television script, he guessed it to be. The last line stopped in midsentence. He wound fresh sheets in and typed "Advertising Department, Van Brunt Citizen, Van Brunt, N.Y." He pulled the sheet out of the typewriter and took the envelope out of his pocket and leaned back in the typist's chair and held paper and envelope up so that the light fell strongly on them. Pointer watched him.

Heimrich put the paper back into the typewriter. He typed, "The quick brown fox jumped over the lazy dog." He took the paper out of the typewriter and looked at it, holding it up to the light as he had before.

"The letter 'n' on your typewriter is a little out of line, Mr. Pointer," Heimrich said down the room. "So are several other letters."

"So what?"

"So this morning somebody found an envelope which had fallen on the ground when they were collecting refuse at the *Citizen* last Friday. And a woman who opens letters addressed to the advertising department is sure it's one of the envelopes the want ad came in. Typed address on the envelope. And, the 'n's are out of line, Mr. Pointer. Want to look?"

He left the typewriter and walked to Pointer and held out to him the envelope and the sheet on which he had copied the address. Pointer looked at them, but Heimrich thought he did not look at them intently. Then he looked up at Heimrich.

"O.K.," he said. "So O.K., Inspector. What are you going to do about it?"

Heimrich went back to his chair and sat in it and closed his eyes.

"What made you suspect your fiancée's death wasn't an accident, Mr. Pointer?" Heimrich said. His voice was low, not insistent. "Because that was what these ads were about, wasn't it? To open it up again. Make a case of it. Because you thought it wasn't really an accident."

"All right, Inspector. It didn't feel right. It still doesn't feel right."

"Why?"

"She'd ridden all her life. Since she was a little girl. Jumped hundreds of fences on a lot of horses. I didn't like that. Tried to talk her out of it. Riding, I mean. But she just laughed at me. So did her mother. People said this stallion she was riding was a nervous beast and I argued with her about riding him and she laughed again." He stopped and raised his hands part way to his face, but this time he did not cover his face. "Her laughter rippled," he said. "Like water over rocks. And what the hell difference does it make now?"

"About the horse," Heimrich said, and opened his eyes again. "She thought he was safe?"

"As a rocking horse, she said. She said if I knew anything about horses I wouldn't worry. So, I don't know anything about horses. So I thought maybe she was right. Only, she wasn't right, was she? This rocking horse killed her, didn't he?" He paused and his young face became intent and his eyes demanding, "Or," he said, "*did* he, Inspector?"

"Refused a jump," Heimrich said. "She went over his head. Into a stone wall. What makes you think it wasn't that way, Mr. Pointer? You see something which made it look another way?"

"I didn't see anything. Oh, I was at the house. I suppose you know that? There were quite a few people there. Mrs. Wainright's brother-in-law. A cousin of hers. Some kid from down their way who'd gone to school with Ginnie. Most of them were out riding horses. Following the hounds, for God's sake."

"You?"

"I've never been on a horse in my life. A burro once when I was a small kid. My parents took me out to Arizona or somewhere and I rode a burro. I think I rode a burro."

"When Miss Gant was killed?" Heimrich said.

"In my room. Working. The room I was in was on the other side of the house, so I couldn't have seen it happen."

"So there wasn't any definite basis for this suspicion of yours? Just that it didn't feel right?"

"I guess that's it."

"So that you had nothing to take to anybody. To us. But you just—say you just wanted to stir it up. After a year."

"Yes. I suppose so. Listen, Inspector—" But he paused and for some seconds gave Heimrich nothing to listen to. Then he said, "Suppose I had come to somebody like you. With this vague talk about a 'feeling.' You'd have found out that I make up stories for a living. Soap operas that go on and on and on, with bad things happening to people five afternoons a week. That I make my living by make-believe. Wouldn't you have thought, here's a nut who doesn't know what's real and what's not?"

117

"Possibly. With nothing concrete to back up this feeling of yours. This hunch of yours. You thought that if you made Mr. and Mrs. Wainright suspicious—brought it back into their minds and made them think about it—they might do something? And if they asked us to dig back into it their request would have more weight than yours?"

"I guess that was it. Did they come to you about it?"

"No. Nobody's officially come to us about it. It was Mr. Wallis who came to me. Because the ads were in his paper and he seems to be a stickler about what goes into his paper."

"All right," Pointer said. "There's still nothing tangible. Except that I put the ads in. Or is there?"

"No, Mr. Pointer."

"Then why are you, as you say, digging back into it?"

"On the outside chance that we did miss something. On a hunch, if you want to put it that way. You advertised a horse for sale, knowing the horse was dead. And a wedding dress. Did you think there really was a wedding dress?"

"No. Oh, I didn't know, actually. But we—" He stopped and took a deep breath. "We weren't to have been married for months. I don't know how far ahead girls—but no, I didn't think there was actually a wedding dress. I just dramatized it, I guess. It—well, it gets to be sort of automatic in my trade."

"Needling," Heimrich said. "It was rather cruel of you, wasn't it?"

"It didn't feel cruel," Pointer said. "I suppose I didn't think about it that way. My girl died in a cruel way, Inspector."

"Mr. Pointer," Heimrich said, "in the ad about the gun you said 'telescopic sight.' Why? Had you seen a gun like that?"

"I knew Wainright had a rifle. He had a shotgun, too. And another rifle. And heavier guns. He kept them in a closet off what he called the game room."

"Telescopic sight, Mr. Pointer. Was there such a sight on one of the rifles? The twenty-five."

"Not on it. He had one. He showed me the guns a few times. And the sight. It wasn't on the gun, but he showed me how it went on. What difference does it make?"

"The twenty-five. Was that the gun he used to kill the horse?"

"I think so. I think he went out carrying it after—" He stopped again and put his hands over his face. Heimrich waited. Pointer took his hands down. "After they brought Ginnie home," he said. "With her head—"

He did not finish that. He shook his own head.

"I'm sorry, Mr. Pointer," Heimrich said. "Sorry to bring up such bad memories. But—you wanted it brought up again. Was the telescopic sight on the rifle when he took it out to kill the horse?"

"For God's sake, man. You think I was looking at the rifle then? I was—I don't know what I was doing. Except, they told me afterward, I was shouting at her. Shouting her name at her. Over and over, they say. And she was dead. She was *dead.*"

"Yes," Heimrich said. "You wouldn't have been looking at the gun. I realize that, naturally. But—you did specify a telescopic sight in the ad. Why, Mr. Pointer? Try to think why."

"Just because I knew there was one, I guess," Pointer said. "I—" Again he paused, but this time he looked intently at Heimrich and nodded his head as if he were agreeing to something Heimrich had said. "All right," Pointer said, "I was a little fuzzy, maybe, when I got the idea of sending the ads in. I'd been—I've been going through a bad year, Inspector. Sometimes—oh, sometimes I see a girl who looks a little like Ginnie looked. Hear a girl laughing the way she used to laugh. So I have a few drinks. Just makes it worse, actually, but I always think it won't. I'd had a few when I got the idea of sending in the ads. When I typed them out, I guess." He paused again. "I still don't get it," he said. "What's so important about a telescopic sight?"

"You don't need one if you're going to walk up to a hurt horse and put a bullet in its head," Heimrich said. "I want you to think back, Mr. Pointer. To the day Miss Gant was killed. You were working in your room, you say, and it was on the far side of the house and you couldn't see anything."

"It was that way. I—I said it was just a feeling. A feeling things weren't right."

"Yes," Heimrich said. "I'm trying to find out what caused that feeling. Just shock and grief? It would have been that way, naturally. Things eat into the mind and the mind gets distorted ideas. And you're an imaginative man, Mr. Pointer. Have to be, I'd think, in what you call your 'trade.'"

"I suppose so. All right. Probably I wrote it up in my mind to something more than it was. That's what you're saying, isn't it?"

"Now, Mr. Pointer. Just wondering about it. You didn't see anything. Couldn't have. Did you hear anything, Mr. Pointer? Like a shot, say. Like somebody firing a gun nearby?"

"I don't—" Pointer said, and broke off and looked hard at Heimrich. "Up around there," he said, "most people have guns. Put targets up on trees and shoot at them. Shoot at rats. Woodchucks, I guess. Every now and then you hear guns going off."

"Yes," Heimrich said. "I live up that way. Same kind of country. You do hear people firing guns. That morning? Think back, Mr. Pointer. I know it was a year ago. Try to think back. You're in your room working. Concentrating, I'd guess. Shutting out everything but what you were doing?"

"Trying to. Usually I'm pretty good at that. Have to be if I'm going to get any work done. I suppose I was that morning. I—"

Again he interrupted himself and put his hands over his face. But this time, Heimrich thought, it was not to hide from memory. It was to concentrate on memory. When he spoke he did not take his hands down and his voice was a little muffled.

"Yes," he said. "I think I remember somebody firing a gun. It sounded rather close. It was—I think it was—ten minutes or so before somebody came running into the house and began to talk on the telephone. Almost shout into the telephone. I learned later that it was Bruce Gant, trying to get hold of a doctor. It was before that. Before I went out into the hall to find out what had happened."

"The shot? Rifle? Shotgun?"

"I don't know much about guns. Not much more than I do about horses. It—I think it cracked. Like a rifle. A shotgun makes a sort of hollow sound, doesn't it?"

"Yes," Heimrich said. "The sound's different, Mr. Pointer. You felt it was nearby?"

"That's the way I remember it felt. But listen, Inspector. It couldn't have had anything to do with what happened to Ginnie. She wasn't shot. She—she was thrown into a stone wall. Unless—there'd have been an autopsy, wouldn't there?"

"There was," Heimrich said. "No, she wasn't shot, Mr. Pointer. She died of head injuries, consonant with her having been thrown against a stone wall. Did you go down and look at the place it happened, Mr. Pointer? It's only a five-minute or so walk from the house."

"My God no! You think—you think I'd want to go and stare at the place she was killed?"

"No. This shot you heard that morning, Mr. Pointer. Any idea which direction the sound came from?"

"I had a window open. It came—seemed to come—from that direction. But it's all pretty vague. I'd forgotten it entirely—I guess I had—until you asked me about it."

"This window you had open. It was on the far side of the house. I mean, the side farthest from the field the accident happened in?"

"Yes. At the front of the house."

"And the sound of the shot, which you think was a rifle shot, came, as you remembered it, from that direction? From somewhere in front of the house?"

"I think so."

"You're quite sure you didn't walk down and look at the area Miss Gant was killed in?"

"I didn't go out of the house until the next day. Then I—I drove into New York. Drove here. To—to get a dark suit, Inspector. I didn't have anything there but slacks and a couple of sports jackets. You have to have a dark suit for—"

"Yes," Heimrich said. "Times you have to have a dark suit."

"I still don't see what a shot could have had to do with it, Inspector. Ginnie wasn't shot. The autopsy proved that. You say so yourself."

"No," Heimrich said. "Miss Gant wasn't shot. The autopsy showed that. But—there wasn't any autopsy on her horse, Mr. Pointer."

He stood up. Andrew Pointer stood too. Pointer said, "I don't get it. I don't get it at all."

"Now, Mr. Pointer," Heimrich said. "I'm not sure I do, really. Just a wisp of an idea. Might have come to you, too, if you'd seen the place where it happened. But you didn't, did you?"

Pointer shook his head, slowly, in resignation.

"Under certain circumstances," Heimrich said, "a telescopic sight might have been useful. But I've no idea those circumstances ever existed. I'll let you get back to work now, Mr. Pointer."

"Hell," Pointer said, "you think I can now?"

"I don't know," Heimrich said. "I suppose you'll try." He turned and walked up the long room and Pointer walked after him. As he was opening the door, Heimrich turned to face the slender, handsome younger man.

"If I were you," Heimrich said, "I wouldn't send any more want ads, Mr. Pointer. I wouldn't do anything more to try to stir things up."

He walked down three flights of stairs and a little over a block to his car, his theory getting wispier with each step. A rifle report. Yes. But sounding, if Pointer's memory was at all accurate, from the wrong direction. Somebody on the other side of the road, the Wainright house fronted, probably. Somebody shooting at a target or a woodchuck or, of course, a rat.

His car was wedged in against the curb. Somebody had, since he put it there, parked in front of it and backed until his rear bumper was against Heimrich's front bumper. Behind, Heimrich had a little more than two feet of clearance. He could, with time enough and wrenching enough, get the Buick out. He got out of the Buick and went to the car ahead. If it wasn't locked, he could release the brake and push it up for clearance. Most people do not lock car doors when they leave cars at curbs. Whoever had backed his car into the Buick had been cautious. He had locked up his car.

A cab came through the narrow channel parked cars had left open. Its roof light was on and Heimrich held a hand up to it. It stopped for him, and he got into it and gave an address in the East Forties. It took a time to reach it. It was the address of a tall office building. He looked at the directory until he found, "Wainright Associates, Architects. 1810." He found an elevator in the bank marked "12 to 20" and pressed a button marked "18." The button stayed in and turned green. The elevator, after waiting some seconds, presumably for other passengers to make the trip worthwhile, closed its door and went up.

Heimrich found a door with "1810, Wainright Associates," lettered on it and went into a largish room with several leather sofas along its walls and nobody sitting on them. There was a desk with a telephone on it and a typewriter beside it. Nobody was at the desk. There was a nameplate on the desk—"Miss Ruth Calvert." Heimrich sat on one of the sofas and lighted a cigarette. There was an ashtray on a stand in front of the sofa. The ashtray was empty.

He had smoked half a cigarette when a door in the far wall opened and a very pretty girl in a white dress came through it, heels clicking sharply on tile flooring. She stopped after a few steps into the room and said, "Oh, I'm sorry. I didn't know there was anybody here." She had a low voice with a kind of purr in it, a carefully planned purr. She went over and sat at the desk. She said, "Can I help you?"

Heimrich snubbed his cigarette out in the clean ashtray and went over to the desk. He said, "I'd like to see Mr. Wainright, if he's free."

She shook her head.

"I'm sorry," she said. "Mr. Wainright isn't in today. He often isn't on Mondays."

Did she have any idea where Mr. Wainright might be reached?

"Is it about a house or something like that?"

"No," Heimrich said. "It's not a professional matter. Not important at all, really."

"He might be at home," the girl said. "He lives up in Putnam County."

"Yes," Heimrich said. "I know where Mr. Wainright lives."

"I'm so sorry," the girl said. "He'll probably be in tomorrow. If you care to call and fix a time?"

"Perhaps I'll do that," Heimrich said. The girl said she was *so* sorry.

Heimrich went back to the elevator bank and pushed a "down" button. There were six elevators in the bank and all of them seemed to be going up. He waited for what seemed a considerable time, thinking numbly, Whatever goes up. After another minute or so he was proved right. He wedged himself into a car already wedged with people. It stopped at the seventeenth and sixteenth and fifteenth floors. By that time there was no more room in it. It nevertheless stopped at the fourteenth floor and at the twelfth. There was, apparently, no thirteenth. Then it dropped.

On Fifth Avenue cars streaked south. There was plenty of cabs with top lights on. And all the top lights spelled "Off Duty." Heimrich looked at his watch and found it was three-thirty. The day cabs were homing. Heimrich walked. It was a good day for walking. It hadn't been, so far as he could see, a good day for anything else. Not, certainly, for wisp-chasing.

He came to a sidewalk telephone booth and went into it and laid change out on a ledge. He put his dime in and gave a number to the operator and put more coins in. He said, "Heimrich. Lieutenant Forniss, please," to the operator at Hawthorne Barracks. He got Forniss.

"Nope," Forniss said. "Nothing hot, M.L. Latham called in. You had him and Jenkins out raking for something?"

"Yes," Heimrich said. "A cartridge case."

"Well," Forniss said, "they haven't found a cartridge case. They found a lot of oyster shells a couple of layers down. Latham says it's matted maybe a foot and that they went maybe a hundred feet along the wall and maybe fifteen feet back from it. Nothing but matted hay and oyster shells. And Latham's pretty sure they didn't miss anything."

"They're still at it?"

"Yep. I told them to be."

"Can you reach them?"

"Got their car parked close enough," Forniss said. "Got the radio on."

"Tell them to knock it off," Heimrich said. "I'm in town, Charlie. And I'm going home. Be there in maybe a couple of hours."

He had a dime left for the bridge across the Harlem River. But at the Parkway toll booth he had to change a five to get a quarter. The man in the booth counted the change out slowly, to show he didn't like fives.

It was somewhat more than two hours before he turned the Buick between boulders and drove it up a steep drive.

Susan was on the terrace with Michael and Colonel. Mite was not present. Michael was dressed for going somewhere. He even had a necktie on. And Susan wore a gray wool dress, with red accents.

"We've got low voltage," Susan said, after she had stood tiptoe to kiss her tall man. "They say men working on a highway knocked the top off a pole. The light company was very polite about it. The man said the highway men had knocked the top off the pole 'unintentionally.' And that it would be about an hour."

She looked up at him.

"Not so good?" she said.

"Low voltage all day," Heimrich said and pulled her to him and then released her. He said, "Hi, Michael," who said, "Good evening, Dad." He said, "Where's your cat, Colonel?" Colonel moved his inadequate tail a quarter of an inch. Heimrich said, "Suppose we've got any ice?" and Susan said, "The thing doesn't like low voltage but it's still got ice."

It was cool on the terrace. But not too cool. They sat side by side on chaises and Michael went to get them ice and bottles on a tray.

11

October is not summer, however much on sunny days it may pretend to be. They were halfway through their drinks on the terrace when the sun went down behind the hills beyond the Hudson. The temperature went down with it and went down abruptly. Susan shivered and Colonel stood up, part of a dog at a time, and Mite came out of nowhere to show them the way. The way was to the house.

Heimrich flipped light switches and not much came of it—dim yellowish light came of it. "It's been more than an hour," Susan said. "A good deal more than an hour. I turned things off."

The things one turns off when voltage drops are the things with big motors—in the Heimrich house the oil burner, which heats water for faucets as well as for radiators; the pump which pulls water up from a deep well. Big motors can burn themselves out when the voltage is low.

Heimrich went into the kitchen and turned a faucet on. Water came out of it, but with little enthusiasm. There was not much water left in the pressure tank, and there would not be more until power came back to normal. Heimrich went to a telephone and dialed a familiar number. The telephone numbers of local electric companies become second nature to people who live in the country. He got a busy signal. Half the town, probably, was calling to find out what the hell gave and how long it was going to. He hung up, waited thirty seconds, and dialed again. He got, "Light Company," in a male voice which sounded tired.

"Crew's working on it," the man said. "Seems like they've maybe run into a little trouble."

"How long?" Heimrich asked the tired voice.

"Now that's hard to say," the man said. "Maybe an hour or two. Hard to say. You turn off your motors, mister?"

"Yes," Heimrich said. "We turned off the motors." He put the telephone back in its cradle.

"We've got some cold meat loaf," Susan said.

Electric ranges like low voltage even less than refrigerators. A country house dangles at the end of copper wires.

A car's horn sounded outside.

"That's them now," Michael said, and went to the door and opened it and said, "Right along," into the gathering darkness. He turned and said, "I won't be late, Mother. Dad." He went out into the darkness.

"Something at the high school," Susan said. "Meeting of the student council, I gather. Hamburgers and hot dogs to follow. The cafeteria has gas stoves. Cold meat loaf? And I'll try to find a Sterno for coffee."

"The Inn has its own generator," Heimrich said. "It's open Mondays. I'll change my shirt."

"Yes," Susan said. "There won't be enough water for your shower, dear."

"I'll put a dash of after-shave lotion behind my ears," Heimrich said, and went to change his shirt.

There were more people in the taproom of the Old Stone Inn than there usually were on Monday evenings. Most of the people were locals. Many Van Brunt families rely on electric ranges. Gas comes in tanks, not by pipes.

It was bright in the taproom. There was a slight thudding sound from somewhere below it, which meant that the gasoline motor of the generator was doing its work. "I don't know whether," Mrs. Oliphant said, worry in her voice. "We don't open the main dining room on Mondays, you know. And—"

But a couple got up from a corner table. "I'll get it cleaned off right away," Mrs. Oliphant told them. "If you want to sit at the bar a—Mary!"

The bar at the end of the taproom was a busy bar. In front of it there was a group of men throwing darts at a dart board. Darts thudded into the board and thudding sounds came out of the group. Susan and Merton went to the corner table and sat at it while Mary took coffee cups and used silver from it and whisked a checkered tablecloth off and whisked another on. She said, "A cocktail, Mrs. Heimrich? Inspector? Seems like we're sort of busy tonight. They say there's a power failure or something."

They ordered drinks. Heimrich looked morosely at the checkered tablecloth.

"A bad day, darling?" Susan said. "I'm sorry if it was a bad day."

Heimrich turned and smiled at her. He nodded his head.

"A wasted one," he said. "I owe the state money. I've been chasing wisps. Probably there aren't any. Except in my mind."

"If they're there," Susan said, "they'll be good wisps, Merton. They'll congeal out of being wisps."

"Things are all right now," Merton Heimrich said, and Mary brought them drinks. She also brought them menus. She said, "There isn't any more lobster," and went away.

"The thing Lyle and Mr. Wallis told you about," Susan said. "At first you felt there wasn't anything—that it wasn't a police matter."

"I got a notion," Merton told her. "Policemen shouldn't get notions and waste time on them. I had two men raking and they ought to have been patrolling. I drove into New York and somebody jammed me into a parking place. I had a long cozy chat with a man in Virginia, at the expense of the State of New York. I found out that Mr. Paul Wainright doesn't go to his office on Mondays. I got a notion that nobody goes to his office much."

"And nothing came of any of it?"

"Oh, I found out who sent those damn want ads in. Not that it didn't stick out a mile. The man who was going to marry the girl. Only, all he had was notions, too. Nothing tangible. You see—"

Ordinarily, Merton Heimrich does not talk to Susan about his cases. But it had been a dim day, and talking to her brightened it. He told her, briefly, about Andrew Pointer and, even more briefly, about his talk with a banker in a place called Warrenton, in Virginia.

"A lot of money," Susan said. "What was your notion, dear?"

"That somebody hid behind a stone wall and shot a horse," Heimrich said. "Shot a horse to kill a girl. Because the wall was a hundred yards or so from the place the horse refused the jump and a telescopic sight would have been useful."

She waited.

"That's all, dear," Merton said. He looked at his cocktail glass, which was empty. "I think," he said, "that this is an evening for another drink. What with the low voltage and everything."

"I think," Susan said, "that another drink would be very good for both of us, darling."

When the drinks came they clicked glasses.

"To the materialization of wisps," Susan said.

Susan was halfway through sweetbreads and Merton through Dover sole when a tall man walked up to their table. The man had a long brown face and blue eyes and gray hair. He looked down at them. He said, "They tell me you're Inspector Heimrich. And that you've been told about this nasty practical joke that somebody played on my wife and me. I'm Paul Wainright."

Heimrich stood part way up behind the table and held his hand out. Wainright took it. Wainright had a hard, strong hand. Heimrich said, "This is my wife, Mr. Wainright," and Wainright said something like "Meetcha." Heimrich sat down again, and Wainright continued to lean toward them.

"I suppose these newspaper people told you," Wainright said. "Asked them not to. Nothing to drag the police into."

"Yes," Heimrich said. "Miss Mercer and Mr. Wallis did come to see me, Mr. Wainright. Wallis feels quite strongly about his newspaper. Feels it's been made part of something unpleasant."

"None of his business, is it?"

"Now, Mr. Wainright, he thinks it is. Have you got any answers to the ads?"

"Couple of people asking about the gun. One about the

horse. How much did I want for it. Only there isn't any rifle, and the only bay stallion I ever owned is dead."

"Yes," Heimrich said. "I assumed he was. About the wedding dress?"

"Some nutty woman," Wainright said. "Rambled on for a couple of pages about the sanctity of marriage. Seems only a very callous person would want to sell a wedding dress, used or not used. There wasn't—isn't—any wedding dress."

Abruptly, Wainright pulled a chair up and sat on it.

"The girl at my office," he said, "says a big man was there looking for me today. Didn't give his name. Said he didn't seem to be a client. Knew where we live. Was that you, Inspector?"

"Yes, Mr. Wainright. That was me."

"Anybody could have told you I don't often go in to the office on Mondays. Unless I have an appointment there. The girl could have told you on the telephone."

"I happened to be in town on another matter," Heimrich said.

"What it comes to, you are nosing into this business. Why the hell? Somebody with a grudge puts a couple of crazy want ads in a small-town newspaper. Just to upset my wife and me. So. Did I make a complaint about it? Go to the police about it?"

"No. Perhaps somebody thought you would, Mr. Wainright. Wanted you to."

"Somebody like that young squirt Pointer?"

Heimrich repeated the word "squirt." He made the word a question.

"Wanted to marry my stepdaughter," Wainright said. "For her money. I tried to talk her out of it, and she told him I had. Blew his top, Pointer did. Did this nasty trick to get his own back. That's all there was to it. Sticks out a mile."

"Probably the way it was," Heimrich said.

"Listen," Wainright said, but did not immediately go on. Heimrich waited. "The whole thing," Wainright said, "has been very tough on my wife. She hasn't been herself since Virginia was killed. Can't pull herself together. Now this—this bringing it all up again. She's been going around in a daze. Forgetting things. Like—like a zombie sometimes. But there's nothing you can do about that, is there?"

"No," Heimrich said.

"Then why are you nosing into it? Was it a crime to put those ads in, using my name?"

"No," Heimrich said. "Cruel. Not a crime."

"Then what business is it of yours?"

"Probably none, Mr. Wainright."

Wainright pushed his chair back and stood up.

"It seems to me," he said, "that you're acting as if it were. Prying into my business—my wife's business and mine. Trying to find me in my office. What was that, Inspector? Sightseeing tour or something?"

"No," Heimrich said. "I just wanted to ask you a question, Mr. Wainright."

Wainright jerked the chair back to the table and sat down again. He said, "All right. Ask your question." He paused for a moment and smiled in the pause. He said, "Sorry, I sort of blew up, I guess. Worried about Flo. Worried about the whole damn thing. Sorry I yelled at you."

"You didn't yell," Heimrich said. "Natural you're upset, Mr. Wainright. That your wife is."

"All right," Wainright said. "What's the big question?"

"Not a big question," Heimrich said. "Just whether you heard something."

Wainright shook his head and said he didn't get it.

"At the time of Miss Gant's accident," Heimrich said, "you were riding beside her. That's the way I understand it. Both heading for this jump."

"Yes. I was riding beside her. And that damn chancy horse of hers refused and—she went over its head. Into the stone wall."

"Yes," Heimrich said. "That's the way I understood it. Just before the horse refused and threw Miss Gant, did you hear anything?"

"What sort of thing? The hounds were baying up ahead. Couple of fields ahead, from the way it sounded. That what you mean?"

"No. A second or two before the horse refused. Or at about the same time. Did you hear a shot?"

"What the hell? People don't shoot foxes. I don't get the point of any of this, Inspector."

"I'm not entirely sure I do, Mr. Wainright. Probably there isn't any. Did you hear a shot? It would have been rather close. Off to your right. The crack of a rifle."

"No. Anyway, not that I remember. Certainly not close by. A good many people fire rifles in the country, Inspector. You ought to know that, living around here."

"Yes," Heimrich said. "I do know that. You don't remember hearing a shot?"

"No. Is that all you wanted to ask me?"

He moved his chair to stand up again.

"About all," Heimrich said. "You did have a rifle at the Brewster house?"

"Two. And a shotgun."

"And used one of the rifles—a twenty-five—to kill the horse which had thrown your stepdaughter?"

"He broke his right foreleg. There wasn't anything else to do."

"No. I don't suppose there was. You had a telescopic sight for the rifle?"

"Yes." Instead of standing, Paul Wainright put his elbows on the table and leaned forward. "You're getting back to these damn ads, aren't you? Yes, I had a telescopic sight."

"When you got the rifle," Heimrich said. "Took it down to kill the horse. Did it have the sight on it?"

"My God," Wainright said. "This all happened a year ago. I'd—I'd just seen my daughter killed. Could be the sight was on the rifle. Could be it wasn't. What the hell difference does it make?"

"Probably none," Heimrich said.

"I don't get any part of it," Wainright said. "My God, man, you're making it sound as if you think somebody shot Virginia. You must be crazy."

"No," Heimrich said, "I don't think anybody shot Miss Gant, Mr. Wainright. And I'm sorry the accident—the bad times for you and your wife—were brought up again this way. Any way."

Wainright pushed his chair back and stood up. He said, "That's all you wanted to ask me about."

"Yes," Heimrich said. "That's all, Mr. Wainright."

They watched as Wainright went up the long taproom. He went to a table for four, with two women and a man at it. He sat down there.

"One of the women," Susan said, "is Mrs. Wainright. She looks all right now. From here."

"Yes," Heimrich said. "I didn't know you knew her."

"Not until this morning," Susan said. "She came into the shop. With the other woman at the table now. She's a cousin, Mrs. Wainright said. Mrs. Gant."

"Came to the shop?"

"To look at fabrics. She wants new curtains for her living room. She calls them 'drapes.' I'm to take some swatches out tomorrow to see about colors. I'm afraid she's going to want something pinkish."

Susan does not like things which are pinkish. There are no pinks in any of her own designs, which are dominant in *susan faye, fabrics* on Van Brunt Avenue. If customers are insistent enough, Susan will, regretfully, get them curtain materials and upholstery fabrics in which pink shilly-shallys.

"It will be good for her to redecorate," Susan said, absently, to her empty plate. "It is always good for women to redecorate."

Mary said. "Finished, folks? There aren't any more pastries."

"Coffee," Heimrich said, and Mary carried used plates away.

"And to switch furniture around," Susan said. "That's good for women, too. What's the line from that song—one of the old songs that doesn't die?"

"'A lady needs a change,'" Heimrich told her.

They sipped coffee. Heimrich looked now and then at the table up the room where the Wainrights and Mrs. Gant—and, presumably, Bruce Gant—had finished food and returned to drinks.

Soon the two men at the table up the room got up from it and walked, side by side, across to the dart board. The group which had been thudding darts into it had finished; four of them were standing against the bar. Wainright and Gant pulled darts out of the board and moved away and began to throw darts at the board.

Heimrich watched briefly and turned to Susan. He said, "Do we want brandies? On account of low voltage?"

"No," Susan said. "I don't think we want brandies, dear. Let's go home," she said. "Let's go home and have a fire."

There had been half a moon in sight when they went into Old Stone Inn. The moon had been shining bright. It was still there, if one looked for it. But now it was a hazy luminance behind clouds.

They had turned dim yellow lights off when they left the house above the Hudson. Heimrich flicked the switch by the front door, and the lights came brightly on. He flicked up another switch, and the furnace coughed and began to thump. The pump did nothing at all when its switch was flicked. Heimrich laid a fire and lighted it, and they sat in front of it.

Colonel, who had been lying in a corner with Mite between his outstretched paws, got up in sections and Mite, disturbed, said "Ow-uh," as two words. Colonel went in front of the fire and collapsed; Mite went to the door and said he wanted to go out.

"All right," Susan said. "It's probably going to rain, but all right."

She let Mite out and went back to her chair. Flames licked up around the logs and Susan said, "Maybe after all."

"I was thinking the same thing," Heimrich said, and got them cognacs in very small glasses. They clicked the glasses.

"To the materialization of wisps," Merton Heimrich said.

There was, Susan thought, a difference in his voice and she looked at him and raised her eyebrows.

"Perhaps," Merton said. "Perhaps a new light on things, with the voltage back."

Car lights flashed in a window and swerved, and Merton Heimrich went to the door to let his stepson in. Michael said, "Thank you, Dad." At first, Heimrich thought, he always called me "Sir." As if he were speaking from far off, across a chasm.

"Was it a good meeting, Michael?" Susan said.

"It was all right," Michael said. "Tony Caspiri and Mike

134

Rayburn want us to draw up a petition against Mr. Larrimore, because he's oppressive. But nobody else wanted to."

"Did you have anything to eat, Michael?"

"Hamburgers," Michael said. "Is there any cake left, Mother?"

"Yes, dear," Susan said. "And there's Coke on ice. Or sort of on ice, because of the electricity."

"At the school," Michael said, "it's been all right for more than an hour."

He went to the kitchen for cake and Coke. He did not come back to sit with them in front of the fire. He said, "Good night, Mother. Dad," and carried a plate and a glass and a bottle of Coke into his room.

Mite rattled the screen door and was urgent about it. Merton Heimrich let him in and Mite had a good many things to say about the delay. He went over in front of the fire and began to lick himself. Merton leaned down and touched the sleek black coat. It was damp, even where Mite had not licked.

"We told you it was going to rain," Merton Heimrich told their cat. "You ought to listen to people."

Mite said "Yah" and went back to licking.

The rainfall started modestly, like a gentle, almost summer shower. It rapidly outgrew modesty and the wind rose. By a little after eleven rain slashed at the windows of the hilltop house and wind and rain plastered red and yellow leaves against the panes. Heimrich dialed WE6-1212 and a voice which was cheerfully dulcet said "Good evening. United States Weather Bureau forecast for New York City. Eleven P.M. Central Park readings: Temperature fifty-seven degrees, barometric pressure twenty-nine and ninety-one one hundredths and falling. Rain moderate to heavy tonight, continuing through tomorrow, with increasing northeast winds becoming thirty to thirty-five miles per hour with stronger gusts. Temperatures remaining in the fifties except in the forties in normally cooler interior sections. Partial clearing and colder tomorrow night; Wednesday, partly cloudy, windy and unseasonably cool."

October had charged out of summer. It had ended up in late November. October can be a fickle month.

All night long rain poured on the house and the wind raged

135

at it; the partly opened bedroom window on the lee side shook and rattled and a big ash tree on the windward side rasped and squeaked against the roof. Things were worse when morning came dimly and they turned on lights. The school bus, due at a quarter of eight, was almost ten minutes late, and Michael waited for it, braced against the wind, in a slicker which reached to his ankles. Colonel, who is faithful in his fashion, and who was wearing nothing at all, stood beside him and shivered and made small moaning sounds. When the bus finally came and god got into it, Colonel did not wait to watch it safely around the bend. Colonel went home in bounds, revived.

Mite sat on a window sill and looked out into the violent world. He said "Yah" at it and went to his rainy-day corner of a sofa and curled tightly and put a paw over his eyes.

Heimrich put on a winter suit. At breakfast he said to Susan, "The Wainright place is at the end of nowhere. The wind will blow the squab off the road." The "squab" is Susan's tiny SAAB. "The road will be covered with wet leaves. Slippery wet leaves."

"I know," Susan said. "As bad as ice, almost. I'll be careful, darling."

Heimrich was careful in the Buick and crept on slippery, leaf-plastered roads to Hawthorne Barracks. From his slot in the parking lot—a slot with his name and rank painted on it—he ran to shelter. His topcoat was supposed to be water-repellent. The driven rain taught it better. A good day to sit at a desk and delegate, Heimrich thought, hanging up his damp coat. The bottoms of his trousers were wet on his ankles. A very good day to sit at a desk and delegate.

He was reaching toward his IN basket, full already at nine-thirty in the morning, when his telephone rang. He said his name into it.

"Morning, M.L.," Lieutenant Charles Forniss said. "A hell of a nasty one, isn't it? Mrs. Wainright died in the night. In her sleep, apparently. Overdose of sleeping pills, the doctor thinks. And he can't sign the certificate because he's never treated Mrs. Wainright. Patrick Kelly, the doctor is. Says there ought to be an autopsy. So he called in. I've got a trooper from the Brewster station on his way over. Seems—"

It seemed that Florence Wainright usually awakened early—seven-thirty or eight—and rang for coffee. That morning she had not rung. At a little before nine, Claire Prender—half the couple which served the house—had gone up to Mrs. Wainright's bedroom and knocked at a closed door and, when there was no response from behind it, opened the door. Mrs. Wainright was lying on her back in the bed, and Mrs. Prender pulled curtains open, thinking that the light, what little there was of it, would awaken the sleeping woman. It did not. Neither did Mrs. Prender's voice. And neither, when it came to that, did Mrs. Prender's hand.

"What they told the doctor," Forniss said. "Lives just down the road, the doctor does."

"Yes," Heimrich said. "I know Pat Kelly. Know where he lives. Mrs. Prender call him?"

Paul Wainright had called the doctor; had caught him just as he was about to leave for his office in the Center. It had taken Kelly five minutes to reach the Wainright house. It was his estimate that Florence Wainright had been dead at least three hours.

"And," Forniss said, "the doc says there was an empty bottle on the table by her bed. Empty bottle and a water glass with a little water in it. Prescription number on the bottle. And 'Nembutal' typed on the label. And 'One at bedtime for sleep.' He'd never prescribed Nembutal for her, Doc Kelly says. Never prescribed anything for her. And—Hold it a minute, will you, M.L.? Other phone's ringing. Could be—"

Heimrich could hear the other telephone ringing in Forniss's small office. He could hear Forniss speak into it, saying his name. He could hear Forniss say, "Hold it a minute, Trooper." Forniss came back on Heimrich's phone. "Trooper named Henderson," Forniss said. "At the Wainright house. Pretty much a kid, sounds like. Sounds like he thinks he's come on something. Want I—"

Delegate, Heimrich told himself. "Switch him over to me, Charlie," he said to Forniss.

He hung up. Almost at once the telephone rang and he said, "Heimrich," into it. Then he said, "Go ahead, Henderson. The Lieutenant thinks you've come on something."

What Henderson had come on was an absence—the absence of one Lucy Fowler, Mrs. Wainright's personal maid.

"Seems—" Henderson said.

It seemed that Lucy Fowler, colored, age about nineteen, sometimes slept in the dressing room off Mrs. Wainright's bedroom. She had a room of her own in another part of the house —"One hell of a big house, this one is"—but slept in the dressing room when Mrs. Wainright wanted her there. The bed in the dressing room had been slept in that night. "Last night," Henderson said, "because I thought maybe they just hadn't got around to making it up. But Mrs. Prender says she changes all the beds every Monday, because the laundry truck comes Tuesday, and that she made all the beds up fresh yesterday."

"The girl's own room? This Lucy Fowler's own room?"

"They looked when they couldn't find her," Henderson said. "Bed wasn't slept in. Or, of course, was slept in and made up afterward. But this Mrs. Prender says it wasn't. Says she makes up a tight bed and Lucy, when she does her own, doesn't make it tight. This one's tight."

"Clothes?"

"Most of them still in her closet, this Mrs. Prender thinks. Can't be sure, because she doesn't know what clothes Lucy had. But a couple of fresh uniforms, and a wool dress and two pairs of shoes. Underclothes and things like that in the drawers of the bureau. And a suitcase under the bed where, Mrs. Prender says, it's always been since she's been here. Says Lucy was here when she and Sam—Sam's her husband; does outdoor work and drives the cars when he's wanted—when she and her husband first went to work for the Wainrights. Lucy'd been Mrs. Wainright's maid when the Wainrights lived over Brewster way. Brought her over to Van Brunt with them."

"Description of the girl?"

"About five-four, Mrs. Prender says. No idea what she weighs, but it can't be much. Pretty little things, as nigras go, Mrs. Prender said."

"'Nigras?' Like that, Henderson?"

"Way it sounded to me."

"It's a Southern variant," Heimrich said. "Between 'nigger,' which they're beginning—some of them are beginning—not to use so much and 'Negro,' which a lot of them can't get used to. Mrs. Prender have a Southern accent otherwise?"

"I didn't notice it, sir. Sounded just like anybody else."

Henderson himself had, in moderation, a New England accent. Heimrich assumed Mrs. Prender had picked up "nigra" by association. He told Henderson to stick around. He put his telephone back on its cradle; then he put his hand on it and looked at the wall. He picked up the telephone and got an outside line and dialed a familiar number. After two rings he got, "Susan Faye Fabrics, good morning." That was from Stella Barnes, who assisted in the shop. He got, "Of course, Inspector." He waited half a minute and got, "I'm all covered with paint, darling," from Susan, who does her fabric designs in the back room of the shop on Van Brunt Avenue.

"You won't have to take samples to Mrs. Wainright," Merton told his wife. "Mrs. Wainright's dead, dear. Took too many sleeping pills and died in her sleep."

"How dreadful," Susan said. "How very *dreadful*. She meant to?"

"I don't know," Heimrich said. "She had made a date with you for this morning. Doesn't look as if she planned to kill herself, but it's hard to be sure, naturally. I'm going up and look around."

"Remember," Susan said, "that wet leaves make the roads slippery."

12

Heimrich drove the Buick north through slashing rain with which the wipers almost kept up. Forniss followed him in a car from the pool. In Van Brunt Center, Heimrich slowed and made his stoplights flash on and off. He ran the window on the far side down and reached across the car and pointed and got a honk for an answer. In the mirror, he saw Forniss turn the police car into a driveway by a sign which said, "Patrick Kelly, M.D." Heimrich drove on and turned off Van Brunt Avenue and climbed on a slippery blacktop. Now and then he lost traction on the soaked leaf cover, and wheels spun. Near the top of the last rise to the Wainright house he pulled far right onto a narrow shoulder to let an ambulance from the Cold Harbor Hospital creep past him.

Forniss stopped behind the big white house on Van Brunt Avenue and went to a door which had DOCTOR'S OFFICE on a plaque beside it.

There were six people in Dr. Patrick Kelly's reception room, which was all the people there were chairs for. But two of the people were very small ones and were crawling on the floor. One of them pushed a toy dump truck violently at Forniss. He managed not to step on it. He went to a door across the room and knocked on it. A woman in a white uniform, but without a nurse's cap, opened the door and said, "Come in; have you an appointment?"

Forniss went into a small room, largely occupied by a desk,

140

and admitted he did not have an appointment and told the woman in white who he was and that he'd like to see the doctor for a minute or two.

"Doctor's with a patient," the woman told him. "I can't bother him. And there are a lot waiting. Is it important, Lieutenant?"

"I saw the people waiting," Forniss said. "Yes, it's important. It shouldn't take more than a few minutes."

"Well," the woman said, "just sit down and I'll see. Doctor's so *very* busy."

Forniss sat down on the only chair there was. Dr. Kelly's secretary went to the desk and typed for some seconds. Then she pulled paper out of the typewriter and put an envelope in it and typed again, briefly. She folded the paper and put it in the envelope. Then she lifted the telephone and pushed a button in its base and there was a buzzing sound from somewhere.

"There's a policeman wants to see you, Doctor," the secretary said. "He didn't say—"

"Tell him it's about Mrs. Wainright," Forniss said.

She was dutiful. She said, "He says about Mrs. Wainright," into the telephone. She said, "Yes, Doctor. I'll tell him," and put the telephone back in its cradle. "He says in the back room," she told Forniss. "When he can make it. It's through there." She pointed, and Forniss went through a door into a corridor. "Turn right," she said after him. He turned right. He went into a room with a desk and an examining table in it and sat down and waited. He waited about ten minutes.

Dr. Kelly was a lean man in his forties, with thick white hair. He sat down at the desk and lighted a cigarette and drew on it deeply. He looked at Forniss and said, "Molly tells me you're a policeman."

"Yes," Forniss said, and added to it.

"Well, Lieutenant," Kelly said. "There's nothing much I can tell you about Mrs. Wainright. Except that she's dead, which I take it you know already. Probably from an overdose of a barbiturate. Probably Nembutal. The bottle by her bed was labeled 'Nembutal.' The doctor's name was Benson. The pre-

141

scription was filled by a pharmacist in Brewster. On October second."

"This Dr. Benson?"

"Good man. General practice."

"She used to live near Brewster," Forniss said. "You'd gather Dr. Benson was still her physician?"

"Yes."

"And she went over to Brewster on the second and saw him? And he prescribed Nembutal?"

"Not necessarily," Kelly said. "If he'd prescribed Nembutal before. She could have called him when she ran out and he could have called the drugstore and authorized a refill. Not supposed to, actually. But we all do."

Dr. Kelly put out his cigarette and lighted another. Forniss watched him, and suddenly Kelly took the cigarette out of his mouth and grinned. He had a wide grin.

"All right," he said, "I'm one of those who didn't quit." He held the cigarette pack toward Forniss, a cigarette protruding. Forniss took the cigarette out and used his lighter. "It may," Dr. Kelly said, "be hazardous to your health. Says so on the package."

"A good many things are," Forniss said. "You say the bottle by Mrs. Wainright's bed was labeled 'Nembutal'?"

"Yes."

"Most prescriptions I get just have a number," Forniss said.

"Nowadays," Kelly said, "a good many of us have the name of the medication typed on. Keeps people from taking the wrong thing. That's the idea, anyway."

He drew deeply on his cigarette, to the hazard of his health. "The bottle was empty?"

"Yes, Lieutenant. No, I don't know how many capsules Dr. Benson specified. Perhaps fifty. Perhaps a hundred. Yes, I know that October second wasn't too long ago."

"How many would she have had to take to cause her death?"

"Now," Kelly said, "that would vary, Lieutenant. Some people are more susceptible than others. And more susceptible at some times than at other times. The capsules were a grain and a half, probably. Which comes to one tenth of a gram, roughly.

142

One capsule is the standard medicinal dosage. Or two if they're three-quarter grain, of course. A gram of any of the barbiturates can be lethal."

"Ten of these capsules, then. A good many to take accidentally, wouldn't it be?"

"Yes," Dr. Kelly said. "Oh, sometimes people forget they've taken sleeping medicine and take it again. Sometimes they forget again and take it again. Maybe she was unusually sensitive to barbiturates. But, yes. Taking ten or so accidentally isn't very likely. Only—"

He got up from his desk and went to a bookshelf, which was solid with thick books. He fingered a book out of the shelf and brought it back to his desk. It was a heavy green book. Forniss looked at the title—"*Legal Medicine, Pathology and Toxicology*. Gonzales, Vance, Halpern, Umberger."

A slip of paper marked a place in the book. Kelly opened it there and ran a finger down a page. "If she'd been drinking a lot," Kelly said. "And the other night at the Inn she was drinking a lot. A good many people noticed it, unfortunately. Made things difficult for that nice Mercer girl. Here, read it yourself."

He reached the book to Forniss, his finger still marking a spot on a page.

Forniss read, "Toxic action of the barbiturates is enhanced by the synergistic action of the alcohol, both poisons having a depressant action on the central nervous system." Forniss looked up from the book and raised his eyebrows.

"Been known to happen," Kelly said. "Normal amount of barbiturate; normal amount of alcohol. Oh, maybe a little more than the usual amount of both. But not enough of either, taken separately, to do any special damage. Together—" He shrugged his shoulders. He put his cigarette out and lighted another. "While back," he said, "there was a case like that. Woman who was pretty well known. A good deal of publicity about it. A doctor told the reporters that alcohol and sleeping medicine make a risky combination. They printed that."

"Doctor, do you know if Mrs. Wainright had been drinking a good deal last night?"

"No way of telling from looking at her," Kelly said. "She was dead, Lieutenant."

143

"With this in mind," Forniss said, "and I see you marked the place in this legal medicine book—did you ask anybody at the Wainright house?"

"Yes," Kelly said. "Man named Gant, who seems to be visiting there. Brother of her first husband or something. I didn't see Wainright himself. Knocked out by it, Gant said. As to her drinking last night—they'd been out to dinner and they'd all had a few. No way of telling what he meant by 'a few,' of course."

Forniss closed the book and handed it back to Dr. Patrick Kelly and said, "Thanks. Appreciate your sparing the time."

"It's O.K.," Kelly said. "I don't smoke when I'm examining patients. Kids, particularly. Call it a cigarette break, Lieutenant." He looked at his watch. He said, "Damn it," and stood up.

"If I telephoned this Dr. Benson," Forniss said, "would he tell me anything about Mrs. Wainright? Whether he examined her recently? And how many capsules he stipulated in this last prescription?"

"Shouldn't think so," Kelly said. "Rule is, we don't talk about patients." He looked thoughtfully at Forniss. He said, "Oh, all right. I'm running late anyway," and sat down at his desk and picked up the telephone. He said, "Outside line, dear," into it. Then he dialed. He waited, apparently, for a good many rings. Then he said, "Dr. Benson, please. Dr. Kelly calling." He waited a minute or more. He said, "Morning, Bill. Good day for pneumonia. Pat Kelly. Seems a Mrs. Wainright—Mrs. Paul Wainright—was a patient of yours. She died last night. Overdose, probably. They're doing a post. You prescribed Nembutal for her. Filled last time early this month. She go over there to see you?"

Forniss heard the scratch of a responding voice. He could not hear the words.

"Do it pretty often myself," Kelly said. "How many?"

He listened again. He said, "Fifty?" and was answered. He said, "Thanks, Bill. Got called in on it. Dead when I got there. Never consulted me, so you know the routine." He listened again. He said, "Probably the way it was, Doctor. Breaks them

144

up sometimes, of course. You got the virus going around, too?" He listened again. He said, "Yes, mine expect miracles, too." He hung up.

"Mrs. Wainright called him up and asked him to O.K. a refill," Kelly said. "He called the pharmacist. He specified fifty, grain and a half. She was his patient for several years when they lived in Brewster. She'd never had a bad reaction to Nembutal. She was in reasonably good physical condition, making allowance for the fact she was going through menopause." He looked at his watch again and again stood up. Forniss, who had sat while Kelly telephoned, stood up too. He said, "Thanks again, Doctor."

"Not much help, I'm afraid," Kelly said. "They'll know more when they finish the p.m. Pretty close to how much she took. And how much she'd had to drink." He started toward the door and stopped and turned back. "Menopause hits some women hard," he said. "Now and then they go off their rockers. You know that, Lieutenant?"

"Yes," Forniss said. "I've heard that."

"Now and then," Kelly said. "Not often, but now and then, they go into depressions. Usually come out of them in a year or so. Unless they decide they can't take it."

Forniss said, "Yep. I've heard that, Doctor," and followed the lean, white-haired physician out of the little examining room.

A police car was parked in front of the Wainright house. Heimrich pulled the Buick in behind it and went fifty feet through slashing rain, his not very water-resistant coat flapping about him. He pushed a button and could hear chimes from inside the house. After a little time, a squarely built woman, gray-haired, in her fifties, opened the door. She wore a black dress with a yellow sweater over it.

She looked up at Heimrich and shook her head and said, "No, mister. Whatever it is. We've got trouble here."

"I know you have," Heimrich said, and told her who he was. He said, "Mrs. Prender?" and the square woman said, "That's right, mister. You said 'Inspector'?"

He said, "Yes, Mrs. Prender."

"There's a policeman here already," she said. "He's out in the kitchen drinking coffee. He's a nice boy. He asked a lot of questions. Mostly about this Lucy. How many of you there's going to be?"

"Not too many," Heimrich said. "Mr. Wainright up to talking to me, would you say?"

"I'd say not," she said. "The poor man. What would you think? And the poor lady, too." Heimrich started to unbutton his top coat. "Oh, all right," Mrs. Prender said. "Come on in if you've got to. No point in standing here with the door open."

She pulled the door farther open, and Heimrich went into the house. There was a wide, carpeted area beyond the door. At the end of it a staircase went up to a landing and there split into two curving staircases. "He's back there," Mrs. Prender said, and pointed to one of the passages which ran back on either side of the stairway. "Drinking coffee."

"Presently," Heimrich said. "Sit down, Mrs. Prender. Tell me about Miss Fowler."

"Nothing to tell about Lucy," Mrs. Prender said. "Except she's just lit out. They're afraid of dead people. Everybody knows that."

"Not taking her clothes," Heimrich said. "Or her suitcase. That's what you told the trooper, isn't it?"

"Her grip's under the bed," Mrs. Prender said. "There was room in the closet but she just pushed it under the bed. I don't know about her clothes. Some are still in the closet. I told the other policeman about that."

"Yes," Heimrich said. "Did she take a handbag, Mrs. Prender?"

"I guess so. It's not in her room, far's I could see."

"What does she look like, Mrs. Prender?"

"She's a colored girl," the square woman said. "Not very big. Maybe some would think she's pretty, for all she's a nigra."

"Very dark? Her complexion, I mean?"

"Medium," Mrs. Prender said. "Just brown I'd call it. Though now, from what I hear, they've all started calling themselves 'blacks.' "

"Yes," Heimrich said. "Black hair, I suppose? Straight or curly?"

146

"Straight," Mrs. Prender said. "Not black, really. Sort of brown like. She'd had something done to it, I shouldn't wonder."

Mrs. Prender's hair was straight, too—straight and a rather streaky gray. She hadn't had anything done to it. She wouldn't—Heimrich scanned his mind for the phrase—she wouldn't hold with having something done to her hair.

"A small girl, you told the trooper."

"Shorter than I am," Mrs. Prender, who was, at a guess, five feet five. "Doesn't weigh much of anything. Nice little figure, I'll say that for her. The poor lady set a store by her, seemed like."

"She is—was—Mrs. Wainright's personal maid, I gather?"

"Lot of people in, she'd help wait on people. And mostly she did her own room. Except when I make all the beds up fresh for the laundry."

"Which you did yesterday, you told the trooper. And you told him you were pretty sure she hadn't slept in hers last night."

"Lots of times she didn't. Lots of times the poor lady had her sleep upstairs, in that dressing room of hers. Guess she did last night. But she was gone when I went in to wake the poor lady up. When—when I found what had happened I looked in the dressing room and the girl wasn't there. Slept in the bed, all right, but wasn't there then. I was going to tell her to go get Mr. Wainright. She wasn't there."

"I take it," Heimrich said, "that Mr. and Mrs. Wainright had separate bedrooms?"

"Adjoining," Mrs. Prender said. "But mostly the door between them was closed. When I did the rooms, anyway."

"Separate bathrooms, I suppose?"

"Sure. This house's got more bathrooms than you can shake a stick at. I told the other policeman all that."

"I'm sure you did, Mrs. Prender. We do go over and over things. You see, we want to find Miss Fowler. Bad day to be wandering around in."

"I can't," Mrs. Prender said, "see what where Mr. and Mrs. Wainright slept has got to do with this girl. She just got scared and took off, the way they do. Maybe she found the poor lady

147

before I did and—and just got scared and ran. They don't like dead people."

"None of us does," Heimrich said, but without hope of modifying the square woman's encompassing "they." "Were you and your husband up when Mr. and Mrs. Wainright and their guests came home last night?"

"Not us," Mrs. Prender said. "Sam and I work hard. We keep decent hours."

"They got in late?"

"Mister, I just said I don't know when they got in. Because Sam and I'd been asleep from about ten o'clock. Working the way we do, we've got to get our rest."

"Of course," Heimrich said. "If Mr. Wainright isn't up to talking to me—and I can see why he wouldn't be; see what a bad time it is for him—I wonder if you'd ask Mr. and Mrs. Gant if I can see them?"

"What would they know about this girl you're so set on finding?"

"I don't know," Heimrich said. "Tell them I'd like to talk to them, will you?"

"Well—"

"Yes," Heimrich said. "Go tell them, Mrs. Prender. Either of them or both of them."

She looked up at him and he nodded his head firmly, like an inspector of police. She went up the stairs, and where the staircase divided she turned to the right. Heimrich could hear her walking, heavily, along a corridor above him. He could hear her knock at a door somewhere. He heard other footfalls and a tall, square-shouldered man came down the stairs. He came quickly down the stairs. He was a trim man. He wore a blue turtle-neck shirt and gray slacks. When he was at the bottom of the stairs he said, "Bruce Gant. Mrs. Prender says you want to talk to me. About poor Flo, I suppose. An awful thing, Inspector."

"Yes," Heimrich said. "A very sad thing, Mr. Gant. Unexpected death, the way hers was, is a hard thing to take. And something we have to check up on, naturally. Have to whenever a doctor can't sign a death certificate, you know."

"Clear enough, I'd think," Gant said. "She took too many

sleeping pills. Ought to be a law against the damn things, way I see it."

"Oh," Heimrich said, "there are certain laws, Mr. Gant. Not against their use, of course. Covering their distribution." He had sat while he talked to Mrs. Prender. He stood up.

"Yes," Gant said, "you're right, Inspector. Drafty in here. It's a hell of a day out. Hell of a day all around, come to that. Beth's pretty much knocked out by the whole thing. Fond of Flo, she was. We all were. Doesn't want to talk about it. So, unless you have to see her, she'd—"

"Probably won't need to," Heimrich said, and Gant said, "Come along, then," and went through a doorway off the entry hall. Heimrich followed him into a big room with deep windows at the end of it. Through them there was an excellent view of driving rain and swaying trees and wet leaves blowing.

A small fire burned in a fireplace. Gant put a log on it and said, "Gets cold as hell all of a sudden up here, doesn't it? Milder where I come from." He motioned toward a chair, but he himself went across the room and looked out one of the windows. "Keeps up like this," he said, "it'll rain us out. Rain the whole damn show out."

Heimrich stood in front of the chair Gant had gestured toward until Gant turned and shrugged his shoulders and came, lithely, back across the room.

"Got two hunters entered in the Ridgewood show," Gant said. "One of them doesn't like wet going. This keeps up too long and I probably won't jump him. After shipping him all the way up there. Figuring him to be pretty much a shoo-in for the green working hunter championship. With Beth riding him."

Heimrich's interest in the green working hunter championship, whatever it might be, was minuscule. But there was no need to hurry things. He asked when the show was to be held. He was told it was to be Friday and Saturday. He said that it probably would dry up by then. He did not add that nor'easters thereabouts sometimes went on for days. There was no reason to discourage Bruce Gant or, for that matter, himself.

"All right," Gant said. "There's nothing I can tell you about poor Flo. Except, this doctor said, she'd probably taken an

149

overdose of sleeping pills. She did forget things, especially when she'd been—" He stopped. "Probably took a couple of pills and forgot she had and took a couple more. And maybe waked up and took some more. Best way of looking at it, isn't it? Best for Paul. Best for everybody."

"Yes," Heimrich said. "Probably the way it was. Usually, when it's intentional, they leave a note. Not always, but usually. Also, she had an appointment to look at some fabrics." He looked at his watch. "About now," he said. "Doesn't prove anything, of course. People change their plans."

Gant said, "Fabrics?"

"My wife designs them," Heimrich said. "She was to have brought what they call swatches here today to show Mrs. Wainright. Tell me about last night, Mr. Gant. You had dinner at the Inn. Mr. Wainright came over to our table for a minute. You four were still there when we left. Then?"

"Can't say I see what difference it makes," Gant said. "However—"

They had, he told Heimrich, got home about eleven. Thereabouts, anyway. They had had nightcaps. About eleven-fifteen, Mrs. Wainright had said she was sleepy and that she was going up to bed. "Paul helped—Paul went along with her." Wainright had come back down in about ten minutes and said that Lucy was "taking care of everything." The three of them had had another drink. At about midnight, the Gants had gone up to their room, leaving Wainright sitting—"Where you're sitting now, Inspector"—finishing his drink.

"All I know about it," Gant said. "All Beth knows about it. Until this Mrs. Prender banged on our door this morning and said an awful thing had happened. Doesn't help you much, does it? Just an ordinary evening."

"Yes," Heimrich said. "Mrs. Wainright seemed normal? Not upset? Or depressed or anything like that?"

"She seemed all right."

"Mr. Gant," Heimrich said, "had Mrs. Wainright been drinking a lot?"

"We'd all been drinking."

"She particularly? Because, you see, if she'd been drinking a good deal it might—oh, might make her forget things."

"All right," Gant said. "She'd had a bit more than she could carry. Had been drinking a good deal since Beth and I've been here. New thing with her, far's I know. Maybe not so new at that. We hadn't seen them for about a year."

"Since your niece was killed in the accident," Heimrich said. "You and Mrs. Gant were visiting the Wainrights then, weren't you?"

"Know about that, do you?"

"Yes," Merton Heimrich said, "I know about that, Mr. Gant."

"Beth and I weren't married then," Gant said. "Maybe you know about that, too? Seems to me, Inspector, you've been nosing into a good many things."

"My job," Heimrich said. "You'd known Mrs. Wainright for some time? Before she married Mr. Wainright?"

"Years," Gant said. "All the time she was married to my brother. Lived at the place with them. Managed the farm, actually. Boblee had other things to do. What people called my brother, Boblee."

"She didn't drink then?"

"Of course she drank. Who doesn't? If you mean too much, no. Kept fit and that sort of thing. Rode a lot. All the Tracys always ride a lot. It's horse country down there. I breed horses. Hunters. Some Thoroughbreds. I suppose you know that too?"

Heimrich said he did know that. He said, "You know Miss Fowler's missing, Mr. Gant? Hasn't been seen since Mrs. Prender found Mrs. Wainright's body?"

Gant said, "Miss Fowler?" Then he said, "Oh, you mean Lucy."

"Yes," Heimrich said. "Lucy Fowler. You know she's missing?"

"Sure. Paul's sort of upset about it. God knows the poor guy's enough upset without this darky acting up."

"She's been Mrs. Wainright's maid for some time? Was when they lived over near Brewster?"

"Before that," Gant said. "Before Flo married Paul. A while after Boblee died, Flo had an apartment in New York. Wanted to get away from where she and Boblee had been together. She couldn't find a maid to suit her. What it came to, the

nigras around New York are uppity. So she had me send Lucy
up from Virginia. The girl must have been—oh, fifteen or sixteen maybe. Flo married Paul and kept the girl on. Got sort
of fond of her, the way we get fond of them."

"You sent Miss Fowler up? She'd been working for you?"

"Sure," Gant said. He paused for a moment, as if thinking
something out carefully, preparing to explain something which
Heimrich might find it difficult to understand. "Way it is," he
said, and spoke very slowly, "the Fowler people have been
working for the family for a lot of years. Three, maybe four,
generations they've worked for Gants. This Lucy's mother cooks
for us now, and old Tim, he's Lucy's father, is the butler.
House is full of Fowler folks. Fields too, come to that. Lucy's
grandmother—maybe great-grandmother; hard to keep track of
them—took care of me when I was a baby. That's what they
say, anyway. Good darkies, the Fowlers are."

"Can you describe Lucy, Mr. Gant? You see, we want to
find her. Want to find out if anything's happened to her."

"Just got scared and lit out," Gant said. "When she found
out poor Flo'd passed away. Like that, lots of them."

"Could be the way it was," Heimrich said. "What does she
look like, Mr. Gant?"

"Little thing. Not very dark. Could be she's part Gant herself, from way back. Nice little figure."

"How does she speak? I mean, has she got a noticeable
accent?"

"No, I wouldn't say that. Pretty much like anybody else
down our way. On account of, Boblee saw that she and a lot
of the rest of them—she's got umpteen brothers and sisters
and a lot of cousins and whatnot—got educated. Lot of people thought he was spoiling them. Thought they ought to go to
the nigra schools like everybody else."

"Lucy didn't? And her brothers and sisters and whatnot?"

"Boblee was funny someways. Lived up North mostly a good
many years. Got the notion that our nigra schools weren't good
enough. So you know what he did?"

Heimrich shook his head.

"Set up a school for them. Right there at the Courthouse.
What they call our place—the Courthouse. Always have, al-

though the last courthouse must have been before the War Between the States. Anyway—he hired two teachers. White teachers, for God's sake. Gave all these darky kids what one of them—one of the teachers—said was the equivalent of a high-school education. Boblee was sure as hell funny in some ways. Full of notions. Our nigra schools were all right, until a lot of you people got to messing around in things. Good as the white schools, lots of ways."

"That's fine," Heimrich said. "So Miss Fowler is educated? Talks like an educated person?"

"Just hearing her talk, you wouldn't know she was a darky. Apparently didn't make her uppity, though. Poor Flo wouldn't have had an uppity nigra around."

"You happen to know whether there's a picture of Miss Fowler around anywhere?"

"How'd I know that? I'm just visiting here, Inspector. Visiting family, on my way up to show some horses. Way it was last year when poor Ginnie got thrown off her horse. Damned strange thing that was. On a horse she was like a burr. Had been since she was a kid. Boblee taught her and Flo taught her, and when she was maybe fifteen she won a jumping prize. And was second for the horsemanship championship. Shows you, doesn't it?"

"Yes," Heimrich said. "It was strange she got thrown that way."

"Horse fell," Gant said. "Maybe he stumbled or something. Paul thinks he just refused the jump, but Paul doesn't know a lot about horses. Grew up in the North somewhere. Indiana, I think it was. Took up riding after he met Flo when she was living in New York. Hacked around in Central Park, for God's sake."

The thought caused Bruce Gant to shudder slightly.

Heimrich said he was sorry to have taken up so much of Gant's time and thanked him and went out of the big room, leaving Bruce Gant sitting by his little fire.

Mrs. Prender was waiting in the entrance hall, apparently to be sure that he left. She, with some reluctance, took him to the kitchen, where Trooper Henderson was still drinking coffee. Heimrich told Henderson to go back on patrol.

Mrs. Prender took Heimrich to Lucy Fowler's room, which was small and neat and beyond the kitchen. It took Heimrich five minutes not to find a picture of Lucy Fowler.

He went out into the rain and drove back to the center and to the Old Stone Inn, where, unless something had come up to sidetrack him, Charles Forniss would be waiting. Nothing had come up to sidetrack Lieutenant Forniss. He was at a corner table, having a drink. Heimrich joined him and had a drink and listened to what Forniss had read in a textbook on forensic medicine and been told by Dr. Patrick Kelly.

They had ordered lunch when Lyle Mercer and Robert Wallis came in through the door to the parking lot—were more or less blown into the taproom and were noticeably wet.

Lyle flicked a hand at Heimrich, and Wallis came across the room to the corner table and jutted across it. He also dripped on it. He said, "Got anything for the press, Inspector? About Mrs. Wainright. Pat Kelly clams up."

"Mrs. Wainright is dead," Heimrich said. "Which you apparently already know. She died, the doctor thinks, of an overdose of sleeping pills."

"Suicide?"

"I don't know, Mr. Wallis. There wasn't any note. Usually they leave notes. Probably her death was accidental."

"You're investigating, though."

"Now, Mr. Wallis," Heimrich said. "A formality. Required when the physician is unable to sign a death certificate. Mrs. Wainright had never been a patient of Dr. Kelly's."

"So," Wallis said, "you clam up too. Autopsy?"

Heimrich hesitated a moment before he said, "Yes. Mr. Wallis. No results as yet."

"You're a help," Wallis said, his voice grating even more than usual. "Who was it put you onto this, Inspector?"

"I don't know," Heimrich said, "that we've been put on to anything. That there's anything to be put onto."

Wallis, who seemed to be in a bad mood, used one word to answer that and jutted away from them to a table near the bar which Lyle Mercer had found for them. It was, Heimrich thought, a day to put anybody in a dark mood. The office of the Van Brunt *Citizen* was, he thought, not much more than across the street from the Old Stone Inn. Convenient enough for an editor and one of his reporters if they finished work at the same time and felt like having lunch together.

Heimrich and Forniss had lunch and sloshed to their car and drove back to the barracks. The rain wasn't letting up, nor was Heimrich's topcoat growing more resistant.

In his office, with wet feet, Inspector M.L. Heimrich took papers out of his IN basket and put his initials on them and put them in the OUT basket. An alarm was out for Lucy Fowler, about nineteen, colored, weighing perhaps a hundred and four pounds and standing about five feet four. No information on what she was last seen wearing. Reportedly pretty; features not noticeably negroid. Not much to go on. Nor were the license numbers of the Wainrights' two cars, one of which she might have taken. She had not; both cars were in the Wainrights' garage.

It was late afternoon before the autopsy report came in from Cold Harbor Hospital.

Florence Wainright had been white, female, in her late forties or early fifties. She had been well-nourished. Visceral analysis showed 11.6 mg of barbiturate in 500 gm liver tissue. Blood analysis showed 2.5 parts of alcohol per thousand in the blood. Death had resulted from congestion of the lungs.

The pathologist added information for the nonprofessional. "Probably in a coma at time of death from combination of alcohol and barbiturates. Percentage of alcohol in blood would indicate considerable state of intoxication at time barbiturate was ingested. Almost certainly a degree of physical incapacity and difficulty of articulation."

So Mrs. Florence Wainright had staggered on the way up the stairs to the room she died in, and her husband had needed to help her up. She had slurred her words, if she had had words to say.

13

For Lyle Mercer it was a dark afternoon of odds and ends. "Dig up what you can about Florence Wainright." She dug up what she could, which was not much. She telephoned a resident she knew at the Cold Harbor Hospital and asked about the results of the autopsy on the body of Florence Wainright. The resident was sorry, Lyle, nothing for the press on it. Anyway, he didn't know whether it had been completed. Anyway, it would be the pathologist who would report the findings, assuming the State cops wanted him to, which they probably wouldn't.

She telephoned the Wainright house and got "Mr. Wainright's residence" and no, Mr. Wainright wasn't talking to anybody, and neither was anybody else. She looked in the files and there was nothing about the Wainrights, except that they had bought the Kynes house on Long Hill Road and that Paul Wainright was a "distinguished architect." She looked up Paul Wainright in *"Who's Who"*—last year's, which was all the *Citizen* had—and he was not listed in it.

Rain beat against the *Citizen* building and wind shook it. And this was to have been the day of the annual Sidewalk Sale, during which the merchants along Van Brunt Avenue put out on sidewalk tables at reduced prices articles which weren't moving very well. She called the Chamber of Commerce and learned that the Sidewalk Sale had been postponed until Thursday because of "inclement weather," and the radio said it was going on raining cats and dogs at least through tomorrow. So it was to be, "The Annual Sidewalk Sale, postponed from

156

Tuesday because of the heavy rain, was scheduled to have been held today (Thursday) along the length of Van Brunt Avenue." A weekly newspaper encounters a good many "was to have beens" in regard to events scheduled for press day. She telephoned the Van Brunt police and learned that the Van Brunt area known as The Flats was flooding and that cars were still getting through if they were careful but that the village policeman—name of Asa Purvis—wouldn't want to guess how long they'd be able to. She telephoned the "Activities Director" at Van Brunt High School and learned that preparations for the Hallowe'en party to be held in the school gymnasium—with the idea of keeping the kids away from rural mailboxes—were going along swimmingly and that there was going to be an accordion. She wrote several paragraphs about the death, in Coral Gables, of Angus Ferguson, formerly a resident of Van Brunt, in his ninety-eighth year.

Behind the closed door of Robert Wallis's office a typewriter was sounding in frantic spurts and longer pauses. He certainly bangs hard when he bangs at all, Lyle thought. It was fun having lunch with him after he got over being so mad at Inspector Heimrich. Reginald Peterson's typewriter tapped slowly. There was always a kind of anxiety about the sound of Reggie's typewriter.

Lyle edited the weekly report, "Happenings in Cold Harbor," taking out exclamation points, to which Hazel Frompton was addicted. She took out little else; Hazel was paid space rates and needed the money. Besides, she almost always spelled names correctly and she used a lot of them.

At a little after five, the telephone rang on her desk. She said, "The Van Brunt *Citizen*," into it and her mother said, "Lyle darling. They say the Saw Mill's flooded and your father thinks—"

Lytton and Grace Mercer had driven into the city that morning, Mercer to the office it was his day for, and Grace with him to "do some shopping." They were not people to let a little rain stop them, and anyway, it probably wouldn't last long. Grace Mercer was one to look on the bright side of things.

But now, calling from New York, there was no bright side of things to look on.

"He thinks," Grace told her daughter, "that it would be foolish and even risky to drive home on a night like this and that we'd better stay over at the Princeton Club and drive up tomorrow, and will you be all right, dear? Because it's Katy's afternoon off, you know, and you know what the television means to her."

Katy is half the Mercers' couple. She is an admirable cook and a woman who knows her rights.

"I'll be fine, Mother," Lyle said. "Just fine. I'll get something out of the freezer."

"Not one of those terrible TV dinners," Grace said, and was firm about it. "Promise me that, dear."

"Promised," Lyle said. "Have a good time, both of you."

"There aren't any taxicabs," Grace Mercer said. "And you know how your father is about parking the car. Is it raining up there?"

"Torrents."

"You *will* be careful driving?"

"Very careful, Mother."

"You should have gone home hours ago while it was still light."

"There were things to do," Lyle said. "And Mr. Wallis hasn't given me good night."

"That man," Grace Mercer said. "Do be careful, dear."

"I'll be very careful, Mother," Lyle said. "I'll be perfectly all right."

A trouble with older people is that they worry about the simplest things. They don't understand that young people can take care of themselves.

At a quarter of six, the door of Robert Wallis's office flew open and Wallis jutted out of it. He said, "You still here? I told you to go home, child." On the first sentence his voice grated; on the second it was unexpectedly softer.

"I didn't hear you, Mr. Wallis," Lyle said.

"Unless you want to come upstairs and have a drink with me," Wallis said.

"No," she said. "Not with all this rain to drive in."

He said, "All right. Be careful, child," and went back into his office, closing the door. After a few minutes, while Lyle was putting on a coat and a rain hat, Wallis's typewriter started up again. It started up fast, and then it stopped. As she went out of the outer editorial room, Lyle could hear Robert Wallis walking in his office. He was stamping, really. When he was writing his lead editorial he always wrote in spurts and stamped between them. This week, Lyle thought—going out into the rain, running to her little Volks—it probably will be about the zoning board. He's very annoyed with the zoning board.

Wind shook the little car as she drove it a block up Van Brunt Avenue and rain beat on it. The lights groped dimly through driving rain as she climbed familiar hills toward home. To get anywhere in the town of Van Brunt it is necessary to climb hills, or creep down them.

There wasn't really anything to worry about, Lyle thought, creeping around curves. There were, to be sure, signs of warning—"Slippery When Wet." But she had no attention to pay to signs.

Most people were staying home tonight. Only once in the four slow miles from the *Citizen* to the big house she lived in did contesting lights blur at her through the rain. She slowed and pulled far right and the other car slowed too and they edged past each other. She almost missed her own drive when she got to it, but didn't miss it and went up it, wet gravel crunching under tires.

The house was not quite dark; Katy had left the hall light on. Not the porch light; Katy believes electricity is meant to be saved.

Lyle turned the Volks toward the big three-car garage and said, "Damn." All three doors of the garage were closed. She had, she was quite sure she had, left open the overhead door to the section the Volks lived in. Katy? Who thought that doors open to an empty garage enticed burglars and worse? Lyle said "Damn" again, which didn't help particularly, and got out of the Volks and ran to the garage and jerked the door up. It stuck for a moment, as it always did. It flew up and banged against its stops. She ran back to the car and drove into the garage, her lights flooding it.

And at the far end of the garage there was movement—movement quick and light and out of the car's beams. For a moment she was frightened and for that moment merely sat in the car and felt that she was shaking slightly. Then she rolled her window down and said, loudly, "Who is it?"

For a moment there was no answer. Then a very small voice came out of the semidarkness—out of a shadowy corner of the big garage. It was a woman's voice—almost a child's voice—and it trembled.

"Miss Mercer? Is it Miss Mercer?"

"Yes," Lyle said. "Who are you and what are you doing here?"

She was no longer frightened; the trembling young voice had no threat in it.

"Lucy, ma'am," the girl said, and then she came out into the brightness of the headlights. "Lucy Fowler. I thought you'd never come. Never, never come. That nobody would come to help me."

Lyle swung out of the car and went up to the girl, who stood still in the light.

"Help you, Lucy?" Lyle said. "I don't understand."

"I had to run," Lucy Fowler said, and her voice shook. "They'll blame me. They always blame us. You know they do, Miss Mercer. You *know* they do."

Lyle went up to the slight, dark girl and put her hands on the girl's shoulders. The girl was trembling; her shoulders were wet. She wore the uniform Lyle had seen her in at the Wainright house, and the thin cotton uniform clung, was plastered to, Lucy's slender body.

"You seemed nice," Lucy said. "I had to get away and hide. I don't know anybody around here, miss. And it's awfully cold." The slight, wet girl was shaking with the cold.

"Inside," Lyle said. "You can tell me inside."

She put an arm around the shaking shoulders.

"It'll be all right," Lyle said. "Nobody will blame you for anything."

"You don't know," Lucy said. "You're white, miss. You don't know. She's dead, Miss Mercer. Dead and cold."

"Yes," Lyle said. "Mrs. Wainright is dead. Come on!"

She had to tug at the girl to get her to move. But then she did and, with Lyle's arm still around the shivering shoulders, they ran together through the rain to the porch. Lyle found her fingers were shaking as she groped for the key in her handbag. Released from the holding arm, Lucy moved as if she were about to run out into the night.

"No," Lyle said, "it will be warm inside," and the slim, dark girl in a cotton uniform which dripped on flagstones went with her to the wide front door.

The key turned—sometimes it stuck—and Lyle pushed the wide door open. It was warm inside—warm and dry inside. She closed the door after them and said, "Come on, Lucy," and again put a guiding arm around wet shoulders. "Upstairs," Lyle said, and when they had crossed the big entrance hall to the staircase at the far end of it, flicked a light switch, and light went on bright at the head of the stairs.

Lucy Fowler was obedient to the guiding arm around her shoulders. She kept on shaking, shivering. They went along a corridor and Lyle pushed open the door to her room and flicked another switch and light leaped into the room.

"I had to run," Lucy said, in the same small, shaking voice. "I had to run. I didn't know where else to go."

"You're all right now," Lyle said. "Nobody'll chase you here. Get out of those things." She closed her bedroom door. "Before," Lyle said, "you catch your death." The worn words sounded strange in her own ears. "Or pneumonia, anyway," Lyle said. She reached for the zipper of the soaked uniform.

"No, miss," Lucy said. "You don't need to help me. I'll do it."

She pulled the zipper down and the uniform sopped on the floor. She stood shivering in pants and bra.

"Everything," Lyle said. "And then a hot bath."

She went into the bathroom and turned hot water on in the tub. When she went back, Lucy was still in bra and pants and white shoes. She was looking around the big, softly lighted room; at the wide, low bed.

"Get undressed," Lyle said. "The water's running." For seconds, Lucy Fowler stood without moving, except that she still

161

shook with the cold. "Do what I say," Lyle said. "Do you hear me, Lucy?"

"Yes," Lucy said. "I hear you, Miss Mercer."

She did what she had been told to do. Actually, Lyle thought, looking at her, watching her cross the room, carrying her wet clothes, toward the bath, it's good color to be. If it were only a color, only a skin's color. It's a warm, fine color.

"As hot as you can stand it," she said to the back of the delicately moving, slender girl.

Lucy said, "Yes, Miss Mercer," and went into the bathroom and closed the door after her. Lyle wished the frightened girl had left the door open, but when she went across the room and stood outside the closed door, she heard splashing sounds from beyond it and then, a girl's "Ow!" Too hot, obviously. But that was up to the girl.

Lyle Mercer went to her closet and got a winter robe out of it. She hung the robe on the knob of the bathroom door and, belatedly, took off her own coat and rain hat. The coat was wet. Lyle turned a thermostat up and a radiator began to talk about the hot water running through it. Lyle looped the wet topcoat over the radiator and sat in a low chair and lighted a cigarette. Now, she thought, I could use that drink he offered me. She waited.

After a time she heard a splashing sound as the girl got out of the tub. Then for minutes, which seemed like long minutes, she heard nothing. She crushed out her cigarette and started to get up to go to the closed door. But then the door opened and Lucy, slim and rounded and brown, stood in the doorway. She said, "I washed the tub, miss. Is it all right if I leave the wet things on the radiator?"

"Of course," Lyle said. "Put the robe on, Lucy."

Lucy looked at the white, warm winter robe. She looked at Lyle.

"Put it on," Lyle said, and Lucy put the woolly white robe on. Involuntarily, Lyle thought, she snuggled in it.

"Come and sit down," Lyle said. "Have a cigarette."

"No, miss," the girl said. "I don't smoke."

But she came to a chair and sat in it. She pulled the robe

close around her, and Lyle thought, She's hiding her darkness in the robe.

"Why were you scared, Lucy? Tell me what frightened you."

"She's dead," Lucy said. "They'll blame me somehow. I was supposed to take care of her. Mr. Wainright told me to take care of her."

Lyle shook her head.

"You don't understand," Lucy said. "Really you don't, miss. They always blame us when something bad happens. They'll say I did something to her to—to make her die that way. They'll tell the policemen I did something and the policemen will hurt me."

"Lucy," Lyle said, and spoke slowly, "nobody did anything to make Mrs. Wainright die. She took too many sleeping pills. They're almost sure of that. Maybe she forgot how many she'd taken. Maybe she meant to take too many. But nobody thinks anybody did anything to her."

"She did forget things," Lucy said. "Especially when she—" The girl stopped with that and shook her head.

"Lucy," Lyle said, "we brought her home the other night. Mr. Wallis and I. She'd—well, she'd had too much to drink. She forgot things that night. Was she that way last night?"

"Sort of," Lucy said. "She was a nice lady, miss. But sometimes she got that way. She didn't use to. When I first went to work for her she never did. That was in the city. After Mr. Gant died and before she married Mr. Wainright."

"It was after she married Mr. Wainright she started drinking too much?"

"No'm. Not right away. It was after that awful accident in the other place. You hear about that, Miss Mercer?"

"When her daughter was killed," Lyle said. "Yes, I've heard about that. Last night, Lucy. Had she had a good deal to drink last night?"

"Yes'm," Lucy said. "I guess so, miss. Mr. Wainright helped her upstairs and told me to take care of her. Sometimes she wanted me to sleep in the room with her. Not in the same room, really. There's a sort of dressing room off her bedroom and I sleep in there when she wants me to."

"Was that often?"

"The last few weeks it was almost every night," Lucy said. "I was already there last night when he—when she came upstairs. I hadn't gone to bed because—because I never did until I was sure she was all right."

She's more relaxed now, Lyle thought. It is good for her to talk about it. To tell somebody about it.

"Mr. Wainright came up with her," Lyle said. "And?"

"Told me to take care of her. So—"

So, she had helped Mrs. Wainright into bed, after Wainright had gone downstairs again. "To be with Mr. Gant and Mrs. Gant." She had got a glass of water and got out Mrs. Wainright's pills. "The yellow pills she always took." Lucy had held her up while she took one of the pills and left another on the table by the bed, because sometimes Mrs. Wainright woke up in the night and wanted another pill.

"And I put the bottle back in the table drawer," Lucy said. "The way I always did. Because Mr. Wainright was afraid she'd forget she'd had her medicine and take it again. He told me always to do that. And I did last night, miss. They'll say I didn't, but I did."

"Why would they say that, Lucy?"

"They blame us for things," Lucy said. "Because we're black they blame us for things."

You're not black, Lyle thought. You're a very warm fine brown. But "black" is the word you want now. Are, anyway, being taught that.

"The bottle," Lyle said, "was in a drawer. Could she reach it? Without getting out of bed?"

"No, miss. Anyway, she went to sleep right away."

"After taking one of the yellow pills?"

"That's all I saw her take, Miss Mercer. There was another she could reach if she wanted to. And I guess she did, because later she woke up. She was talking in her sleep, maybe, and woke herself up. Woke me up too. It was like she was talking to somebody. Kind of loud like."

"Did you hear anybody else? Anybody else talking?"

"Miss Mercer, I was still muzzy like. I thought maybe I— well, I did hear somebody else talking. Talking low, not the way she was. As if he didn't want really to wake her up."

"He, Lucy?"

"I was muzzy," Lucy said. "I thought it was Mr. Wainright maybe, come up to see if she was all right. But I was mostly still asleep."

"You heard her," Lyle said. "What did she say, Lucy? When you thought she was talking in her sleep. You remember what she said?"

"Something about having it in your hand," Lucy said. "Wait a minute. 'You had it in your hand.' That's what she said. 'I saw you. You had it in your hand.' I'm almost sure that's what she said, miss."

There needs to be a little of the detective in reporters. Lyle was learning to be a reporter.

"Lucy," Lyle said, "when you put this bottle back in the drawer. There were still these yellow pills in it?"

"Yes'm. Quite a lot of them."

Lyle had lighted another cigarette. She put it out. She went to her chest of drawers and got panties and a bra out of it. "We're pretty much the same size," she said, and took the underthings to Lucy, who took them and did nothing about them. She looked up at Lyle and her dark eyes widened.

Lyle went to her closet. She got a skirt out of it and a sweater and a heavy cloth coat.

"Get dressed, Lucy," Lyle said. "We're going somewhere. I'm going to take you somewhere."

"No," Lucy said. "No, Miss Mercer. They'll catch me. I don't want to go anywhere. Please, Miss Mercer. *Please.*"

"Get dressed," Lyle said. "Nobody'll hurt you. I won't let anybody hurt you."

She watched the girl begin, slowly, unwillingly, to dress. She went to her telephone and spun the dial.

*   *   *

The fire in the Heimrichs' living room was not, this violent night, solely for the gaiety of fire. It was gay and leaping; it also provided warmth. Old houses, however remodeled, however tightened up, are not as resistant to raging wind as young houses. In old houses windows rattle in a storm and wind comes in through cracks.

The Heimrichs had finished dinner by eight. They sat in front of their fire and listened to records—heard songs from "Jacques Brel Is Alive and Well and Living in Paris." They had heard the songs a good many times since Susan had bought the album as a present for the house.

"Sometime," Susan said in front of the fire, "I'm going to get all the lyrics. Even in the marathon one."

Merton Heimrich said, "Mmm."

Colonel was lying in front of the fire. It had been necessary for him to go out into the rain an hour or so before, and he smelled of drying dog. Mite, as a very young cat, had made several attempts to wash Colonel when Colonel smelled like wet dog, but had learned that Colonel was too much wet dog for a single cat. Nowadays, Mite merely stayed away from a wet dog. This night he was in his rainy-day corner of the sofa, which, since he had first looked out a window in the morning, he had left only for food and other needs.

It was a good night to be home in front of a fire.

The telephone rang. It was Susan who answered it after saying "Oh, damn," and turning down the volume of the record player. (The song was the one about the boredom of bulls on Sunday afternoons, and it was one she liked especially.) She stopped the telephone's ringing with a slightly resentful "Hello?" Then she said, "Oh, hello, Lyle." Then she listened for almost a minute. Then she said, "Of course, dear. It's an awful night. Be careful," and came back to the fire.

Merton Heimrich had opened his eyes.

"Lyle Mercer," Susan said. "She's found this Lucy Fowler. Mrs. Wainright's—"

"Yes," Heimrich said. "Found her?"

"Apparently," Susan said, "it was more the other way around. Anyway, Lyle's bringing the girl here. She thinks you'll want to talk to her."

"Yes," Heimrich said, "I'd very much like to talk to Miss Fowler." He closed his eyes. "Naturally," he said.

*   *   *

The heater only slightly warmed the little Volks as it crept down blacktop roads—"Slippery When Wet"—and along Van

Brunt Avenue and then up twisting blacktop roads which seemed to have narrowed in the rain, as if the rain had shrunk them, and which also were slippery when wet, although here no signs warned of that. Once Lyle slowed the car almost to a stop, as its lights groped at a fork in the road. Then she remembered and took the fork to the right and was on High Road, which immediately justified its name by going almost straight up.

She was, at a guess, a hundred yards from the Heimrich driveway—in a night of slashing rain one goes by guess on country roads—when she pushed down hard on the brake pedal. The Volks skidded slightly but stopped in time. It stopped behind a big car with no lights on. The big car was in the middle of the narrow road.

The girl beside her said, "Oh. *Oh!*" in a shaking voice.

Lyle put up her hand to touch the arm of the girl beside her. Under the thick coat she could feel the arm shaking.

"It's all right," Lyle said. "It's got nothing to do with us, Lucy. It's just—just broken down or something. The points got wet or something, probably."

It looked in the Volks' lights like a new and noticeably solid car, not like a car which would stall in a rainstorm.

There was not room on either side of the blocking car for the Volks to pass. Lyle was certain of that; the road was very narrow and almost without shoulders. But she got out of the Volks, pulling her raincoat tight around her and braced herself against the wind and sloshed to make certain.

There was no room on either side; the car, which was as big a car as it had first looked in the Volks' yellowish lights, was precisely on the crown of the blacktop. It was a wall across the road. And there was nobody in it.

The grade was steep there. All that the driver of the car would have had to do—would have had to do in the most rudimentary decency—would have been to release the brake and let the car roll back and to the side to give passage to other cars. He wouldn't have needed his engine to do that small thing.

Lyle found that she was shivering. That was because of the

raging wind and the beating rain. Enough to make anyone shiver.

She went back to the Volks, this time on Lucy Fowler's side of the little car. She opened the door.

"We can't get by," she told Lucy. "Somebody's blocked the road entirely. We'll have to run for it. It's—it's not far up the hill."

She hoped she was right; that the Heimrich house was not far up the hill.

Lucy shrank away when Lyle reached a hand toward her. She said, "No. No. I can't, Miss Mercer." There was a wailing note in her thin, small voice. "Somebody did it on purpose. Can't you see somebody did it on purpose? To—to catch me. Can't you *see?*"

"Lucy," Lyle said, "it's just a stalled car. Stalled in a bad place. It hasn't anything to do with us."

With the door open there was a little light in the car. Lyle could see the frightened girl pulling away, and shaking her head. She could hear her, again, saying, "No. No. I can't. I can't."

"You have to," Lyle said, and tried to make her voice firm, commanding, for the flinching girl—for a girl who had, all day, fled in the rain with fear fleeing beside her; had walked seven or eight miles in the storm; who, probably, had lost herself many times and climbed stone fences into tangled fields to hide when cars came along the roads she walked. "You have to," Lyle said. "It's—this stalled car—it's just bad luck. Nobody knew we were coming here."

"The one you called," Lucy said. "The one you called Susan. She knew we were coming."

Lyle had not told the frightened girl that they were going to see an inspector of the New York State Police. She had not wanted to see terror mount again in the dark eyes. She had, more prosaically, not wanted to try to use force on a lithe and frantic girl. She had doubted she had the force to use.

"She's a friend," Lyle said. "She'll help us. Come *on.*"

She had, now, to use force. She had to pull the girl from the little car. But Lucy Fowler did not try to run away. She merely stood and trembled and again Lyle put an arm firmly around slim, shaking shoulders.

"I'll leave the lights on so we can see," Lyle said. "It's only a little way."

Lucy did not say anything. She let herself be guided the few steps of darkness along the car. They came out into the beams of the headlights.

There was the sharp crack of a rifle and, it seemed at the same moment, a metallic clang against the Volks. The rifle cracked again and this time there was the whining sound of a bullet and something tugged at the sleeve of Lyle's coat.

She pulled them down into the ditch at the side of the road. Water was coursing through the ditch.

14

❦

The fourth side of the "Jacques Brel" album reached the end of its track and turned itself off with a click. Mite removed the paw which he had clamped tight over his exposed left ear. Colonel sighed deeply and slightly moved his tail. The noise of the wind and the rain seemed to increase with the music stilled. The fire had passed the crackling stage. It had subsided into a warm glow.

"It will take them a while to get here from the Mercer house," Susan said. "It's such a bad night. I hate to think of them on these roads this kind of—"

A sharp crack interrupted her. It snapped through the sound of wind and beating rain. Almost at once there was a second crack.

Heimrich was on his feet by then. Mite was on a windowsill with the second crack, staring out into the night, head and ears pointing to the left. The rifle cracks had come from that way.

Heimrich was across the room in three long strides; he yanked the coat-closet door open and grabbed a suede windbreaker from a hanger. He grabbed a .32-caliber revolver from the shelf it lived on and jammed it into a windbreaker pocket. Susan was at the door an instant before him. As he had opened the door the floodlight over the garage blazed on the driveway.

He ran down the steep drive in the lashing rain, the revolver in his pocket banging against his hip. He was halfway to the road when the rifle cracked again—cracked twice again.

On the road he turned left and ran down the hill. The sounds of shots had come from that way. And nobody on a night like this was shooting at a target or at a woodchuck.

He had run down the hill, in the center of the road, for perhaps twenty yards when a car's lights glared up in front of him. Then a car's motor roared, racing. The lights charged up the hill at him, and Heimrich, yanking the gun out of his pocket, leaped to his left.

The car missed him by inches, and he slipped and almost fell in a muddy, water-swept ditch which was all the storm had left of a narrow earth and gravel shoulder. He grabbed bushes to catch himself.

He turned when his feet were under him. The car had crested the hill. As he looked, its taillights vanished.

It had seemed a big car. Any car which charges at you through the rain seems like a big car.

Heimrich, jamming the revolver back into its pocket, ran on down the hill—ran toward the yellowish headlights of a stationary car which had been behind the one which had started up so savagely.

As he ran on, a slight figure came up out of the ditch in front of the stopped car. For a moment the figure—a girl from its movements—swayed in the car lights. Then the girl began to run away from him down the hill.

He yelled, then. He yelled, "Stop!" He took a chance on which of them was running. He yelled, "Miss Fowler. Lucy! I tell you stop!"

The girl, uncertain in what appeared to be a heavy coat, ran on, stumbled on, beside the stopped car. Again he called to her to stop and used the name which was the more likely. Lyle Mercer wouldn't run away from him. She would run uphill toward him. If she could run.

Heimrich yanked the revolver from his pocket and fired a shot into the air.

The girl was out of the lights, now. She was a moving shadow behind the car. Heimrich called again, and he thought the dim shadow beyond the car moved more slowly. He fired once more, straight up. The shadow stopped moving.

Another figure came up out of the ditch and now he was

close enough to see that it was another slight girl. This one was in a raincoat, belted around her. By the car, clutching its fender, the girl stood, her back to him.

She called out too, and the wind seemed to sweep her voice back to him. But now he was only a few feet away.

"Lucy!" Lyle Mercer called into the rain and darkness.

For a moment, the shadow beyond the car did not move. Then, very slowly, it moved toward them. It moved into the light and became a small girl in a heavy coat. Then Lucy Fowler put her hands up.

He had reached them, then. He said, "Is either of you hurt?" and Lyle said, "We're all right, Inspector."

"Then for God's sake," Heimrich said, "put your hands down, Lucy Fowler."

She said something he couldn't hear. He saw Lyle put an arm around the other girl. Lucy spoke again. Her voice was high and shaking.

"You're a policeman," Lucy said. "I didn't do anything bad."

He got them into the Volks, Lucy Fowler first into the cramped seat in the back. She did not resist; did not try to run. She did not say anything at all.

It had been some time since Heimrich had driven a gear-shift car. It came back to him on the second try. (The first try stalled the engine.) The Volks pushed itself up the steep road and up the steeper drive and into the floodlight above the garage. Lyle ran to the open door, with Susan waiting in the doorway.

The dark girl sat huddled in the back of the Volks and did not move. "Come on, Lucy," Heimrich said, and kept his voice low and gentle. She still did not move. He reached toward her and she shrank away. She said, "I didn't do anything bad. Don't hurt me."

"You didn't do anything bad," Heimrich said. "Nobody's going to hurt you."

She came out of the car, then. She walked very slowly toward the house and Heimrich walked beside her, not trying to help her walk against the wind and rain; ready only to reach out if she stumbled. She did not stumble.

Susan had built up the fire. Lyle was standing in front of it, still with her raincoat belted about her. When Lucy Fowler went into the room, with Heimrich tall behind her, Mite leaped from the sofa and went under it and looked out from under it, light reflected in his eyes so that he seemed to glare at them.

"Get over by the fire," Heimrich told Lucy. "Don't fall over the dog."

Colonel jointed his way to his feet and went across the room and tried to get under the sofa with his cat. He was too big to.

"Take that coat off, Miss Fowler," Heimrich said. "Get over by the fire. And—"

He stopped and looked at Lyle Mercer.

"Your coat sleeve's torn," he said to her. "Did he hit you?"

She looked down at the left sleeve of her raincoat. It had been ripped open. "I didn't feel anything," Lyle said. "Except a sort of tugging. I'm all right."

"By a few inches," Heimrich said. "Did you tell anybody you were coming here, Miss Mercer?"

"No," she said. "Not anybody."

"A good guesser, somebody was," Heimrich said. "Was afraid she'd come here. Because you have something to tell me, Miss Fowler?"

Lucy Fowler had come just inside the door. She did not go to stand in front of the fire.

"Merton," Susan Heimrich said in a pointedly reasonable voice. "They're both soaking wet. Before anything else, we'll have to get them dry. Come on, Lyle."

She went the length of the room toward the bedroom door. Lyle followed her. Lucy still stood where she had been standing near the door. The heavy wet coat seemed to pull her down. She stood a little stooped under its weight.

"Go with them, Miss Fowler," Heimrich said. "Nobody's going to hurt you."

She went after the others, walking very slowly, dragged down by the wet coat and by fear. Heimrich sat in front of the fire and Colonel came back and put a heavy head on the most available knee. After a few minutes, Susan came out of the bedroom carrying a raincoat and a cloth coat and other garments. She carried them into the kitchen, toward the furnace room. She came back. "They're getting dry," she said. "One of them's going to have to wear your bathrobe." She sat down beside Merton in front of the fire. Then she got up and put two more logs on the fire, which welcomed them, licked around them.

Lucy came through the doorway first, lost in a bathrobe which seemed to drag at her as the wet coat had dragged. It dragged on the floor around her feet. Lyle followed, a hand on each of the dark girl's enveloped shoulders. She wore a yellow robe of Susan's which was also too long on her, but not by a good many inches as much too long. Heimrich pulled up chairs for them in front of the fire. Lyle stretched slim legs out toward it. Lucy Fowler huddled in the robe.

"Last night," Lyle said, "Lucy was sleeping in Mrs. Wainright's dressing room. Something waked her up. Tell him, Lucy. Tell Inspector Heimrich."

"I didn't do anything bad," Lucy said, her voice small, as if the thick bathrobe smothered it. "Nobody ought to say I did anything bad."

"Now, child," Heimrich said. "Nobody has. What waked you up?"

"First I thought she was talking in her sleep," Lucy said, her voice distant and shaking a little. "But then—"

Slowly, carefully, she told him about the night before. He listened without interrupting her. She said, "That's all, sir. I didn't do anything to her."

"No," Heimrich said. "You didn't do anything to her, Miss Fowler. When was it, about, you went into her room and found her—found her dead, you thought?"

"About seven, I guess. She usually waked up about seven. I would go down and bring her tray up. She was dead, sir. When I went in she was dead. I tried to wake her up and touched her and—and she wasn't warm any more. Not the way people are warm."

"And you were frightened," Heimrich said. "And got out of the house and—walked all day in the rain? Trying to find Miss Mercer's house?"

"I don't know anybody around here," the girl said. Her voice had steadied as she told of the night before. "Miss Mercer seemed like a nice lady. I thought maybe she'd help me. I thought they'd try to blame something on me."

"Who would, Miss Fowler? Mr. Wainright? Mr. Gant?"

"I don't know," the dark girl said.

"You thought there was somebody in the room with her? Thought you heard another voice. A man's voice or a woman's voice?"

"It was low," Lucy said. "Just a whisper almost. I don't know. I thought probably it was Mr. Wainright, going to see if she was all right. But I was mostly asleep."

"It could have been Mrs. Gant?"

"I guess so. It could have been anybody. It could have been Mrs. Prender, I guess. Her voice is sort of low. Maybe I just dreamed there was somebody with her."

"Last night," Heimrich said, "after you helped her into bed, you helped her take sleeping medicine. Left a glass of water on her table and another capsule if she needed another. When you went in this morning, was the second capsule gone?"

"I don't remember," Lucy said. "Really I don't remember, sir."

"Try to, Miss Fowler."

"I don't remember seeing it."

"The glass? Was it there?"

"I don't—" the small voice stopped. "Yes," she said after a pause. "I think it was, sir. And it was empty. I think it was empty."

"'You had it in your hand,'" Heimrich said. "'I saw you. You had it in your hand.' That's what she said when you thought she was talking in her sleep?"

"I think that's what she said. I wasn't very much awake, but I think that's what she said."

"This other person you think was in the room with her—by the way, was the door between the dressing room where you were and the other room closed?"

"Not quite, Inspector. A little open so I could hear her if she called."

"Did the others in the house—Mr. Wainright, Mr. and Mrs. Gant, the Prenders—did they know you were going to sleep in the dressing room last night?"

"I don't guess they did, sir. Mr. Wainright said after I saw she was all right, and to be sure she took her sleeping pill, I was to go to bed myself. 'She'll be all right,' he said. 'You run on downstairs and get some sleep of your own.' But, I didn't . . ."

"This other person, whom you can't identify. You just heard a whisper? The murmur of a voice?"

"Yes."

"Couldn't make out any words? Think, Miss Fowler. Because somebody is afraid you did, you see. Tried to kill you—you and Miss Mercer—because he's afraid you did. Before you could get to me and tell me what you heard."

Lucy did not answer. She sat huddled in the robe and looked into the fire.

"Try to remember," Heimrich said. "Try to bring it back. Her voice wakened you—partly wakened you. You remember her words. Then you heard another voice. You assumed it was Mr. Wainright's, naturally. That he had gone into his wife's room to see if she was all right. But it might have been Mr. Gant. For the same reason. Or Mrs. Gant, who's Mrs. Wainright's cousin. Probably not Mrs. Prender. She and her husband were in bed asleep. Anyway, she says they were. Try—"

"I don't," Lucy said toward the fire leaping in the fireplace. "I just don't, sir. Only—" She paused and shook her head. "Only," she said, "it's as if I almost remember. As if there were something I almost heard. I forget what—"

She stopped speaking. But then she looked at Heimrich instead of at the fire.

"That's it," she said. "I think that's it. 'You forgot again.' Something like that. That's why I thought it was Mr. Wainright. Because he was all the time having to remind her of things. Lately she's—lately she'd been that way. Forgetting things."

"Like taking pills? There were other things she was supposed to take? Other pills and she kept forgetting to take them?"

"Four or five others," Lucy said. "I'd help her remember sometimes. Sometimes Mr. Wainright would. We both tried—tried to take care of her. She hadn't been very sure about things since her daughter was killed that way. That awful way."

"'You forgot again.' You think that was what the other person in the room said?"

"Something like that. I think it was something like that. That's all I remember. Truly that's all I remember."

"All right," Heimrich said. "Mr. Gant tells me you were Mrs. Wainright's maid when she was living in New York after her first husband died and before she married Mr. Wainright. In an apartment."

"Yes. She was all right then. She was fine and nice to me."

"Was her daughter living in the apartment when you were there?"

"Mostly Miss Virginia was away at school. Sometimes she was there for a week or two at a time."

"After her mother married Mr. Wainright. Did Miss Gant still come to the apartment?"

"Just once, I think. We didn't live there very long after they were married. Mr. Wainright bought this house up near Brewster. So his wife and Miss Virginia could have horses. They'd always had horses back home."

"Yes," Heimrich said. "In the apartment. In the Brewster house. Did Mr. Wainright and Miss Virginia get along all right?"

"He was very nice to her. He would do nice things for her. Buy her things sometimes. So she'd like him better, I thought."

"Better? She didn't like him very well?"

"I never heard her say so. Only—well, she had been very close to her real father. To the Squire, that is. He—he was a wonderful gentleman, sir. She used to talk about him a lot."

"Lucy," Heimrich said, "did you feel she resented Mr. Wainright? As if she thought he was trying to take the place of her real father?"

"Maybe," Lucy Fowler said. She was looking into the fire again, as if she saw the past there. "A watch she had her father had given her. It stopped and Mr. Wainright bought her another like it. Only she broke the one Mr. Wainright gave her. It fell off of something and she—I guess she stepped on it. Anyway, it was all broken."

"This happened up at the Brewster house?"

"Yes, sir. A few days before the accident."

Heimrich looked at the fire for some moments. He closed his eyes then, but did not turn his head. He opened his eyes and looked at Susan.

"Susan," he said, "do you suppose you can fix these young ladies up with something dry to wear? Something they can wear out?"

"Yes," Susan said. "They won't fit very well, but yes. Only— have you two had anything to eat this evening?"

The question was for Lyle, who said, "Oh! How awful of me. I meant to fix something but—but I just forgot."

"Lucy?"

"No, ma'am, I guess I haven't had anything to eat for a long time."

"I'll get you both something," Susan said. She looked at her husband. "You don't," she said, "take them anywhere until they've had something hot to eat."

"No, ma'am," Heimrich said. "Only, not too long, dear? I don't want us to have to wake people up."

Susan was not too long and the two girls ate soup and warmed meat loaf in front of the fire. Lucy Fowler ate carefully, but as if it had indeed been a long time since she had eaten at all.

Merton Heimrich, who was somewhat wet himself when he came to think about it, went to change to dry slacks and shoes. He also buckled on his shoulder holster and put the .32 in it.

He dialed WE6-1212. At nine P.M. the temperature had been fifty-two and the humidity ninety-five per cent. "Cloudy with moderate to heavy rain tonight, continuing into tomorrow. Winds northeasterly, thirty to thirty-five miles an hour. Risk of flooding in low-lying areas. Tides may run two to three feet above normal. Partial clearing and colder tomorrow night."

It was, Heimrich thought, the first time the Weather Bureau had used the word "colder" since early April. He went back into the living room.

Lyle and Lucy Fowler went into the bedroom and Susan went with them to find them clothing—dry things and warm things. Heimrich sat in front of the fire and waited. Mite came out from under the sofa and jumped to Merton Heimrich's lap, and Heimrich stroked the sleek black cat, who purred appreciation. When, after several minutes, Heimrich lifted him down and said, "Thanks for reminding me, Mite," Mite said "Ya-ah!" and went back under the sofa.

Heimrich looked up a number in the Manhattan telephone directory and dialed that number. The telephone was answered after three rings—answered by a female voice with a purr in it. The purr was gratifying.

"The Wainright apartment?" Heimrich said.

"Yes." She could get a purr even into "Yes."

"Is Mr. Wainright in?" Heimrich asked her.

"No," she said. "Oh, no. They won't be back until next month. I'm a sublet. They're up in the country. I can give you their number there. If you'll wait—"

"Doesn't matter," Heimrich said. "I'm a friend of his. From out in Indiana. But I'm only in town for a couple of hours. Sorry to have bothered you, miss."

He was told that that was perfectly all right. The voice still had a purr in it.

So, Heimrich thought, back in his chair in front of the fire —so, it held together well enough. As a mindful of wisps, with nothing to tie them together; a structure of theory with no foundation under it.

The girls came out again, wearing Susan's clothes. The skirts came down to the midcalf of each of the slender girls. Susan is a ten, too. But she is a longer ten.

Heimrich stood up when the two came in, with Susan after them.

"I don't suppose," Heimrich said, "that either of you noticed the license number of the car that blocked you?"

"Heavens," Lyle said, "we were being shot at, Inspector."

"The lights of Miss Mercer's car were shining on the other car," Lucy said. "I saw the number. I'm pretty good at remembering numbers, sir. There was a little mud on the license plate. But it was R C and then—" She gave the numbers. The numbers were familiar to Merton Heimrich, to his pleasure but not to his surprise.

"Not R C, Miss Fowler," Heimrich said. "P C. For Putnam County."

He told Susan that he hoped they wouldn't be long.

He had to move the Volks out of the way before he could get the Buick out of the garage. He got wet again.

15

No lights showed in the front windows of the Wainright house. Heimrich swung the Buick so it faced a three-car garage. He switched the lights off. He said, "Sit tight a minute," to the girls, who had shared the front seat with him.

The garage doors were closed. He went around the garage, through a breezeway which connected it with the house, and got wet again. The side door wasn't locked and Heimrich went into the garage. He took a pencil flashlight out of his pocket, and it gave him a little light.

There were three cars in the garage—a black and white Buick; a dark Continental; a Jaguar with Virginia plates. The Buick was dry. The Continental had dripped on the garage floor. Also, the windshield wipers had left crescents and there was still water on the glass the wipers had not touched. The Continental's plate had the P C number he was looking for. A block for a foundation. The Jag had been out in the rain too. But not so recently. The Jag's hood was cool to Heimrich's touch. The hood of the Continental was warm.

He went back to his own Buick and opened a door and leaned into it. "Five minutes, Miss Mercer," he said, repeating instructions he had given as they drove up through the rain. "After I'm let in. If, naturally, I am let in."

"Yes," Lyle Mercer said. "Five minutes."

Heimrich went up onto the dark porch of the Wainright house and found a button and pushed it. Chimes sounded inside the house. He waited. After a few seconds he pressed the button again and again chimes sounded. It was thirty seconds more before the light went on inside the house. Then a light went on on the porch, and Elizabeth Gant looked at him through the door glass. He reached into his windbreaker pocket to get a badge to show her, but that was not necessary. She opened the door and said, "It's Inspector Heimrich, isn't it? You want to see—?"

"Mr. Wainright," Heimrich said. "Your husband too, Mrs. Gant."

"They're both down in the game room," she said. "Come on, I'll show you. Is it—has something happened?"

"Yes," Heimrich said. And followed the slight, pretty woman through a hallway and down a flight of stairs into a big room —a room big enough for both a pool table and a ping-pong table. Bruce Gant was sitting in a leather chair with a drink; Paul Wainright was plugging darts into a target board. He stood twenty feet or so from the board. As Heimrich followed Beth Gant into the room, Wainright threw a dart which panged into the bull's-eye. Its spike went in deep.

Heimrich was sorry to bother them so late in the evening. But a point had come up.

"A point?" Wainright said. "Anything we can do. A drink?"

"No," Heimrich said. "Thanks, but no."

"A point about—?" Wainright said. He still stood, holding darts in his left hand and one, ready to throw, in his right. "Wait. Not about the poor kid? The poor Lucy kid?"

"I'm afraid so," Heimrich said.

Wainright put the darts he held on a table. He walked a few paces toward Heimrich. He said, "You've found her? We've been looking for her all day. The three of us."

"Yes," Heimrich said. "We've found her, Mr. Wainright."

"You sound," Wainright said, "like it's bad news. I hope it isn't. She was a nice—"

"Yes," Heimrich said, "I'm afraid it's bad news, Mr. Wainright. I—"

The clock in his head said five minutes.

"I'm afraid—" he said and hesitated. Four minutes would have been better, he thought.

"She's dead?" Wainright said.

182

The chimes sounded.

"One of my men's to meet me here," Heimrich said. "Probably him. I'll get it."

He went back upstairs, and let Lyle Mercer and Lucy Fowler into the big house. He went ahead of them down the stairs. Wainright had gone back to stand in front of the dart board. He snapped a dart into the target. Another bull's-eye. Bruce Gant stood up as the girls came down the stairs and Wainright turned and Beth Gant said, "Oh! You made it sound—"

"No, Mr. Wainright," Heimrich said. "Miss Fowler isn't dead. You thought she might be?"

"What you said," Wainright said. "Bad news, you said." His face had tightened when the girls came down the stairs, Heimrich thought. A policeman watches people's faces.

"Now, Mr. Wainright," Heimrich said. "It is, isn't it? For you, I mean? She's alive. And she has a good memory for numbers. For numbers and other things."

Wainright shook his head. He said, "That supposed to mean something? What do you mean, it's bad news for me the girl's alive?"

"Alive," Heimrich said. "With a good memory for the numbers on a license plate. And for voices she heard in the night. Last night, Mr. Wainright. Your wife's voice. And—it was your voice too, wasn't it? You didn't know Lucy was sleeping in the dressing room, did you? You thought she'd gone down to her own room, as you'd told her to do. That was the way it was, wasn't it?"

Wainright shook his head again. He said, "I don't get what you're driving at. If you're driving at anything."

"Yes," Heimrich said. "I think you do. What did your wife mean when she said—tell him what she said, Miss Fowler."

"She said, 'You had it in your hand,'" Lucy said. "She said, 'I saw you, you had it in your hand.' I heard her, sir. That's what she said. Loud like. It woke me up."

"You had a dream," Wainright said. "You heard things in your dream."

"Now, Mr. Wainright, how do you know that? Mrs. Wainright might have been talking in her sleep. At first, Miss Fowler thought she was. Until she heard the other voice—heard your voice, didn't she? Telling your wife she'd forgotten to take her sleeping pills. And—*seeing she took enough of them.* That was the way it was, wasn't it? And giving her something to drink with more pills dissolved in it. So as to be entirely sure."

"She was taking barbiturate," Wainright said. "Barbiturates don't dissolve in water."

"Not readily," Heimrich said. "Interesting you know that, isn't it? Looked it up, probably. But they dissolve very readily in alcohol. Hundred-proof bourbon is half alcohol, Mr. Wainright. It wasn't hard to get her to drink bourbon, was it?"

"This black kid is lying," Wainright said. "She didn't hear my voice. Not saying anything. I wasn't in my wife's room. In my own. With the door between them closed. You can't believe a damn thing they say, Inspector. You ought to know that. She's a liar like all the nig—"

"Just hold it, Paul," Bruce Gant said. "Just hold it." There was more of the South in his voice than Heimrich had heard in it before. But the accent seemed to lend slowness to his voice. "Lucy here's one of the Fowler folks. Never knew one of them to be a liar, Paul. Known Fowlers all my life and they're good darkies. Maybe the girl got things mixed up a little. But she's not the kind to tell lies." He half smiled at Paul Wainright. "You people up North," he said, "don't know about darkies. Not about our kind, anyhow."

Heimrich, who had been watching Wainright—and had seen that Wainright was twisting a dart between the fingers of his right hand—turned to Gant. He said, "You and Mrs. Gant were out looking for Miss Fowler today, Mr. Gant? In the Jaguar. Why?"

"She's one of our people, Inspector," Gant said. "We aim to look after our people."

"And you, Mr. Wainright. You were looking for her too. Until quite late, wasn't it? Until long after dark. Why?"

"Like Bruce and Beth," Wainright said. "Didn't like the idea of her wandering around in the rain. Probably scared half to death."

"No," Heimrich said, "I don't think that was your reason. I think you wanted to stop her getting to somebody. Somebody like me. Wanted to keep her from telling what she heard last night. That's the way it was, isn't it? That's why you tried to kill her and Miss Mercer. Blocked the road to my house if she came by car. Didn't know how she'd come, probably. But even if she came on foot she'd have to go out to the ditch to get around the car, wouldn't she? Bring her close to where you were waiting with that gun of yours. The one you used to kill the horse with, Mr. Wainright. After he'd failed a jump because you threw a dart into him just as he was gathering for it—failed a jump and killed your stepdaughter. Except—you had to kill her yourself, didn't you? Had to make sure, anyway, because she might have caught herself before she hit the wall. That was what you had in your hand, wasn't it? One of the loose stones that had fallen from the wall. That was what your wife saw in your hand, wasn't it?"

"She couldn't have seen anything," Wainright said. "She was in the next field. If she got some crazy notion—"

He stopped. His face showed he knew he had not stopped soon enough.

"If she got some crazy notion, you talked her out of it, didn't you?" Heimrich said. "Talked her out of it for a year. Until young Pointer stirred it all up again with those ads in the paper. She wanted to hide from herself what she remembered, didn't she? Try to believe what you told her. But when it was stirred up again she couldn't any more. So you decided you had to do something about it."

Wainright was not facing the dart board any more. He was facing Heimrich and Lyle and Lucy Fowler. He held a dart between the fingers of his right hand. He held it up a little.

"You're a hell of a cop," Wainright said. "You ought to write stories. Cock-and-bull stories."

"No," Heimrich said. "Just read them, Mr. Wainright. Just read them."

"Make them up as you go along," Wainright said. "Get girls like Lucy here to lie for you. What for, Inspector? To make yourself look like some sort of a big shot? When you can't prove a damn thing and know damn well you can't."

"Now, Mr. Wainright. The District Attorney may have different ideas about that. Up to him. After we talk to Miss Calvert. That'll help, won't it? Your sublet, as she calls herself. Very pretty girl, Miss Calvert is. You see, Mr. Wainright, things add up if you give them time. Get tied together if you give them time. Now Miss Fowler here remembered the license number of your car. Saw it while she and Miss Mercer were lying in a ditch. Being shot at."

"Nobody'll—"

"Where's the rifle you used, Mr. Wainright?"

Wainright did not move. But his eyes moved—moved to his right, moved, involuntarily, toward a narrow closet door.

He realized what he had done as he did it. It was then he raised the hand which held the dart, cocked his wrist and moved the arm back a little.

Bruce Gant was nearest, and it was he who moved. He brought the edge of his hand down hard on Paul Wainright's wrist, and the wrist gave and the dart fell on the floor. It landed point downward and bit into the floor.

"Can't have you throwing those things at people," Gant said. "Bad enough to have you throwing them at horses. Good horse, old Alex was."

Heimrich had his revolver in his hand and he held it loosely as he opened the closet door. There were three guns in the closet, including the one he wanted. He took it out, lifting it by the stock. Wood doesn't take prints as well as metal. He sniffed it. Wainright hadn't had time to clean the rifle.

"All right, Wainright," Heimrich said. "Attempted murder for now. After that we'll see."

He dangled his own gun where Wainright could see it.

"Nobody'll believe the girl," Wainright said. "About the license number. About anything else. There's not a damn thing you can prove."

"Up to your lawyer," Heimrich said. "He'll say there isn't, naturally. What lawyers are for. We know about where you were standing when you tried to kill Miss Fowler, Wainright. And Miss Mercer too, when you found there were two of them. We'll know where to look for the cartridge cases, when it quits raining. See how firing-pin impressions match up with this gun of yours. Helpful things, they can be. Come along, Wainright."

186

Paul Wainright went along, ahead of Heimrich, who did not holster his revolver. Bruce Gant said, "Could be you'll need a hand, Inspector," and went along too.

Lucy Fowler went up the stairs after them. They could hear her feet beating on the floor above. She was running. "To her room to hide," Beth said.

*　　　*　　　*

Beth Gant drove the Jag, explaining that Jags are tricky if you don't know them. It was raining as hard as ever and, with Lyle directing, they rode streaming blacktop roads until they came to, and crept up, High Road to the Heimrich house. Neither had said anything except Lyle Mercer, who said, "You turn right here. Left at the next fork," and "Here you go straight through."

The floodlight over the Heimrich garage was on. There were two cars standing under it—Lyle's Volks and another, a station wagon.

Beth swung the Jaguar so it faced out again. She said, "Run for it, Miss Mercer. I'll go back and see that Lucy's all right."

Lyle looked at her a moment.

"Oh," Beth Gant said, "we'll take care of her, Bruce and I. Probably take her back home with us when we go. If she wants to go."

Lyle ran for it through the rain. The Jag roared as it was revved up, sent abruptly down the steep drive.

The door opened as Lyle reached it, and Susan Heimrich, holding it open, said, "You're wet again, dear. Come in by the fire."

Lyle went into the living room where a fire jumped in the fireplace.

"I'm all right," she said. "Just a little damp around the edges." Then she said, "*Oh!*" because Robert Wallis was sitting in front of the fire with a black cat sitting on his lap. He put Mite down gently and Mite said, "Yah," in a plaintive voice.

Wallis jutted his way across the room and put hands firmly on Lyle's shoulders.

"You scared hell out of me, child," he said, his voice grating. He looked down at her for a moment. "You ought to have sense enough not to go out in the rain and get shot at." He held her shoulders hard. Then, gently, he shook her. "Child," Robert Wallis said, and there was no harshness in his voice. "You *are* wet. Come over by the fire."

"I don't—" Lyle said, and did not finish as she walked toward the fire.

"Simple," Wallis said. "Your mother called. She'd called the house and there'd been no answer and she got the idea I was keeping you at the office. Going to tell me off about it. 'You ought to know better on a night like this,' she said. Cross with me. I told her you'd gone home. Didn't tell her you'd been gone long enough to get home twice. Told myself that and called your house and didn't get an answer and—well, came here to tell the Inspector we'd lost ourselves another girl. Tell him we were getting damn careless here in Van Brunt."

He picked Mite up, and Mite, who was inclined to run from strangers, cuddled and purred. He had a loud purr. Of course, it had been a rainy day and one very dull for cats.

"Mrs. Heimrich filled me in," Wallis said. "So, naturally, I waited. Did you lose the Inspector?"

"He's taking a man to jail," Lyle said. "Mr. Wainright."

"High time," Wallis said.

"Because—" Lyle said, and Susan interrupted her.

"Tell us about it later," Susan said. "Go in and get out of those wet clothes. Your things are dry by now."

Lyle went into the bedroom, and Susan brought dry, if somewhat wrinkled, clothes to her. Wallis sat down again and Mite jumped onto his lap. This time, Mite dug his claws in to make sure. Wallis said, "Ouch, cat," and scratched behind black ears.

Lyle came out of the bedroom in dry clothes. "Because," she said, "he tried to kill Lucy—and me, just in passing—because she—" Lyle broke off. "There seems to be quite a lot to it," she said.

"Tomorrow you can write it," Wallis said, and put Mite down again. "I'll give you a by-line. Come on."

He went to her, jutting as much as usual, and put an arm around her shoulders.

"Got to call your mother and tell her you're all right. My place is closest. Come *on*."

Susan Heimrich watched them go. There did not seem any special point in telling them that there was a much nearer telephone—a telephone merely across a room.

16

It was sunny Friday—sunny and cool, but most of the bright leaves had gone from the trees. Heimrich had not seen much of the day. He had spent most of the day in Carmel—in the office of the Putnam County District Attorney, who was not too happy about things, and before the Putnam County Grand Jury, which brought in an indictment charging Paul Wainright with murder in the first degree for the wilful killing, by administration of poison, of his wife, Florence.

It was late afternoon when Heimrich ran the Buick up the steep drive and into the garage. He crossed the terrace, on which they would not sit much more that year, and went into the house where Susan had a fire burning. Susan got up from in front of the fire and came to him and looked up at him and raised her eyebrows.

"Murder one," Heimrich said. "The D.A.'s not happy. Wants more. Thinks it would be better if Lucy Fowler were sure it was Wainright's voice."

"His wife, then," Susan said. "Not his stepdaughter?"

"His wife," Heimrich said, and went over to the bar and started to pour. He poured bourbon for both of them, which was an admission that gin days had gone with summer. He brought the drinks back and sat with Susan in front of the fire.

"We can't tie him to the girl's death," Heimrich said. "I'm sure and the D.A.'s sure and a jury wouldn't be. A dart to throw the horse off. Not a rifle from behind a wall, as I thought at first. Neater, from his point of view. Quieter. Also, naturally, he was there to make sure with a loose stone."

He sipped and closed his eyes and shook his head.

"I almost muffed it," Heimrich said and shook his head again. "Should have realized from the start that merely getting the girl thrown wasn't enough. Too chancy a way to kill. Didn't come to me until I watched him and Gant throwing darts at the Inn."

Once more he shook his head. He also sighed.

"Could be," he told the fire. "I'm getting old for this kind of thing. Grope up blind alleys."

"You grope fine," Susan told him. "The girl because she was going to come into the trust fund, leaving her in a position to dole money out to her mother and her mother's husband. Whom she resented?"

"The shape of it," Heimrich said. "The feel of its shape. No way of proving it. His wife saw it but—oh, didn't want to accept it. But it haunted her—haunted her for a year. Grew dimmer, I suppose, until it was brought up again. Then she started to drink too much—a lot too much. Worried him, naturally. Got him afraid she'd blurt things out when she'd had too much. Blurt to the wrong people. People like me. Under her will, he inherits everything. Also, there's this Ruth Calvert of his. Very definitely of his."

"She admits it?"

"As good as, by the time Charlie'd finished with her. At first, just good friends. Oh, perhaps he did come around to the apartment, which she was subletting—was really subletting—now and then. But she'd never thought—never *dreamed*—of anything like this happening. Well, she had thought perhaps they'd get married after he got his divorce. But nothing like *this*. Well, yes, she did know he—anyway his wife and he—had a lot of money. No, he didn't come in to the office very often. Well, no, neither did anybody else."

"A wife who might tell what she'd seen," Susan said. "And who would leave him a couple of millions if she died. And a girl who would marry him. Young and pretty, this Miss Calvert?"

"Yes," Heimrich said. "Young and pretty. Oh, it's all clear

enough. Except, the District Attorney keeps pointing out, proving it. If Wainright had just sat it out—not tried to kill Lucy Fowler because of what he was afraid she'd overheard—well, he made it easier for us. They do sometimes."

"This D.A. of yours? He's satisfied about that?"

"About that," Heimrich said, "everybody's satisfied. Except Wainright's lawyer, of course. Raked up the cartridge shells yesterday. Firing-pin impressions match up. Oh, they'll dig up experts who'll say they don't. But they do. And we got a break. One of the bullets lodged in a tree across the road. Instead of hitting a rock and getting banged out of shape. It came from Wainright's rifle. And Lucy's memory of the license number and a jury'll buy it. We're pretty sure of that."

Heimrich put his feet on Colonel, who made an excellent footstool and who approved of being one with a fire going. Mite came over and sat in front of Susan and looked up at her and made a remark. "I've got to get dinner pretty soon," Susan said. "But come on up if you want to."

Mite wanted to.

"Lucy brought my clothes back yesterday," Susan said. "The Gants are going to take her to Virginia with them. She wants to go. She says it's too cold and wet up here."

They drank slowly in front of the fire. He's getting rested, Susan thought. That thing of his about getting old!

"Lyle Mercer had a by-line on her story about it," Susan said. "Don't put your claws in so deep, cat. It was quite a good story, I think. Shall I get it for you?"

"I was there," Heimrich said.

"There's that," Susan said. "Mr. Wallis was in a state when he came here the other night to tell you she'd got lost somehow. As if—as if a world were lost with her."

"He's a good deal older than she is," Merton Heimrich said.

"Men!" Susan said. "Could we do with another drink or do you want to eat?"

Heimrich took his feet off Colonel and went over to the bar. He brought drinks back.

"Be a shame to disturb Mite," he said. "Just when he's got settled."